Guilty News

Noreen A. Biehl

ISBN:9798761104419

To my family and friends who love the written word

Acknowledgements

Writing a novel was challenging for someone who has spent decades writing everything but fiction. While Ann Delaney is a fictional character, her shoes are my size, and her parents are my parents. My imagination created the rest of her family and friends, although a few of her colleagues are based on people I know. I made up names but not places and built a fake hospital on a real island.

My thanks begin with all the amazing people who shaped my careers in newsrooms and hospitals over the years and taught me to value the written and spoken word. Next, thank you to my writer friends in the Jewett Writers Group especially Brian Evan-Jones for probing questions and continuous encouragement. This novel barely resembles its first iterations thanks to readers whose patience and wit I cherish, including my first reader and trusted friend Patricia Kennedy followed by Jewett writer Susan Morse and Nancy Coltrera from the River Goddesses Book Club.

Former hospital trustee and fellow Rotarian Jerry Daley provided thoughtful comments about the beginning, and corrected passport references. Hospital colleague and dear friend Bill Irvine loved the twisted ending. Cathy Beaudoin, editor of my history book about Wentworth-Douglass Hospital, highlighted errors and, along with Donna Rinaldi and Jody Bloom, urged me to publish. Roger Evans, MD, suggested changes to medical jargon and did not mind being the inspiration for one of the key characters. My daughter Shannon Biehl and her husband Joe Zammit took notes, debated timelines, and suggested better phrases. My granddaughter Alisha Biehl was surprised I could author a novel.

I am truly grateful for Frank Biehl's love and support throughout this literary journey.

Table of Contents

CHAPTER 1

The mist rising from the depths of Niagara Falls soaked a group of tourists intent on capturing the majesty of the moment with their cell phone cameras. They maneuvered between other world travelers and slippery spaces to get as close as possible to the river's edge, daring elusive rainbows to stay in place until they got the perfect shot.

I was just as wet as the rest of them on this early Friday morning, yet, it was warm enough not to care about the drenching or a photo op; all I wanted was to resurrect the feeling—the roar of the falls, its power, and the scary possibilities of falling in. I loved this place. Just like the honeymooners and daredevils who thought they could survive its wrath, I understood Niagara's magnetism. I was born here. Memories bubbled up as I strolled along the paths and bridges over the churning river I described as "crazy water" on similar walks, hand in my dad's. Those tall, tubby binoculars, once out of my reach, were still there, ready to get a closeup of the Cave of the Winds or the Maid of the Mist swirling below us.

The ping of a text message interrupted my reverie, reminding me that crafting the outbursts of an impetuous hospital CEO into positive news stories was more than a full-time job. Were the media slithering around corners again, looking for reasons to debunk the medical center's innovative surgery or animal research? I had kept them at bay for weeks and earned their respect, I thought. This late August day off was more than warranted. I shrugged at the thought of changing plans as I slipped my phone from my pocket. It read, "Call me."

After a muffled "dammit," I turned around, crossed the bridges to the main state park, and found an old iron bench away from the mist to call. The text was from Bob McCarthy, an abrasive reporter who wore wrinkled khakis with pride. In his mid-20s, he looked years older. I had met him a few months ago wearing his Buffalo News press badge and wondered what had happened to the paper's once-strict dress code. It was The Buffalo Evening News when I had worked there as an intern, and Bob wasn't born yet.

After my internship, I chose a job in Boston as a medical reporter, followed by a career in hospital media relations. I never thought I would leave until six months ago when I accepted the offer to become vice president of public affairs for a hospital on Grand Island. I left New England and all I loved about living there—crisp autumn days, ocean breezes, and mountain hikes. It also meant leaving the loneliness of a recent empty nest and a charred marriage.

Until I visited the Milton Center for Advanced Orthopedic Medicine, I considered Grand Island a flat, unmemorable space between Niagara Falls and Buffalo. In only three years since its founding, this multi-million-dollar medical mecca had earned accolades for its innovative bone and joint repairs despite Bob McCarthy's relentless efforts to tarnish its reputation. He roamed hospital hallways and monitored ambulances on the lookout for skeletons and gore, convinced doctors and hospital administrators were charlatans. I held my breath every time the sloppy reporter appeared, avoiding whiffs of his stale cigars and unfounded accusations. He loitered in staff-only restricted areas as if he belonged. When he was on a story, he was relentless. For someone who could write lengthy diatribes, his two-word text annoyed me.

I sat back on the hard bench, took a breath, and called the inquisitor. He answered on the first ring. "Hey, Delaney. I need to talk to your boss; your hospital's hiding a few things. Infection rates are off the charts, animal blood is everywhere, and Dr. Stratton butchered one of your patients, if not more. And, don't give me that HIPAA argument. Patient confidentiality evaporates if docs are murdering people. I have solid sources, and the dead patient's wife is talking."

Could this be a cruel joke? Bob wasn't a funny guy; his glib suggestion of murder and mayhem caught me off guard. If he had slapped me in the face, I would not have been more startled.

"Hey Del, are you there?"

I found my lost voice and remembered my job was to talk to the media, including Bob. "Good morning to you too, Bob," I said, ignoring the urge to respond to his ludicrous comments. Every word I uttered could be published in the next news cycle. Instead, I chose one question. "Who's the patient?"

"We're running this story on Monday… front page. Tell Mr. Football to call me." He hung up.

"Damn you, Bob McCarthy," I shouted to a blank cell screen, already conjuring the distraught face of my boss, Scott Marino, aka Mr. Football, as I reeled off the reporter's bloody accusations. Scott was the CEO of the Milton Center. We had worked together before at a smaller hospital near Boston. A respected leader, he looked somewhat out of place in the corner office and more at ease on a football field ready to barrel into an opponent. He gave up the game years ago but continued to tackle any opponent of his policies and decisions. A tinge of grey in his thick, wavy hair gave him an air of elegance despite the shadow of a dark beard bristling below his olive skin. Scott loved attention and the battle of running a hospital. It was my job to keep him focused and away from news hounds intent on trouble.

The magnitude of Bob's call settled in as I tried to convince myself the highs and lows of this job were normal. I pocketed my phone, glanced at the rushing water while thinking about the Milton Center; a rocky plunge awaited at both.

On my walk back to my Falls Street apartment, I mentally erased plans to hunt for a bungalow with enough room for my vagabond daughter. The city of my youth had changed. Urban development had spread through the oldest neighborhoods, replacing worn homes, including that of my parents with cinder block buildings and placid parks. Niagara Falls, NY, was in transition, as I was, suffering from the harsh reminders of better days. Hopeful endeavors such as the new culinary school and the Seneca Niagara Casino & Hotel suggested a brighter future. I hoped I'd made the right move.

I entered everything Bob said, adding the football jab, into my phone's notepad and called Scott.

CHAPTER 2

After Scott left Boston to lead the Island's medical center, he built a house in the Lewiston section of the city on Mountain View Drive, overlooking Lake Ontario and only a golf cart trip away from Niagara Falls Country Club. Unless there was a blizzard, Scott spent most of his free time chasing a white ball down the fairways, chatting with board members and potential donors. His frequent golf partner was the founder of the Milton Center for Advanced Orthopedic Medicine, the very man who gave him his job and expected quality performance and unhesitating loyalty in return.

The enigmatic Benjamin "Milt" Milton, MD, was an odd partner on and off the golf course. Milt was a lean man with narrow, deep-set eyes, thin lips, and a groomed fringe of pale hair that stretched around his nearly bald head. He spoke in modulated tones and stood back while listening to conversations, clasping his long fingers behind his back, safe from uncertain interactions. He nodded whenever we passed in a hallway but never mentioned my name or uttered a greeting.

Scott blustered through his days, more obstreperous than a typical healthcare CEO, wrapping his expansive arms around the good ol' boys and gals. He filled the room the moment he entered. Beneath his bravado was a puzzle of intricate emotional pieces; he could be tender, aggressive, sullen, and mysterious. I never knew what to expect.

My call to Scott went to voicemail. A few minutes later, my phone rang. "Hi, Ann. I had to move off the course to call. Aren't you taking a vacation day?"

I muffled a laugh. "We'll both be back to the office soon. Bob McCarthy, from Buffalo News, called. He wants to talk to you about a few things—infection rates, animal blood everywhere, and he said Dr. Stratton murdered a patient. The story's running Monday."

"That's insane. Where'd he get this?"

I imagined his face getting redder by the second. "I wish I knew."

"What's his number?" he asked, spitting into the phone.

"Hold on, Scott. We need to discuss this, get Stratton in, the board chairman, the bio lab manager, legal, and Dr. Milton. This won't be a one-day story."

I could hear a few sighs and a muted voice in the background. "Ann, you're overreacting. Milt and I are on the ninth tee. We'll be done in a couple of hours. Invite everyone else to the clubhouse for drinks."

Leave it to Scott to suggest a meeting at the golf club. He'd jumped from anger to denial in a nanosecond, or maybe they'd found the drink cart early in the round. Bob's accusations had the power to crush the center's reputation. I needed Scott to grasp the reality that innocence was hard to prove in guilty news stories. "Scott, be serious; you can't blow this off. We need to meet at the hospital. Let's try for 4 p.m. I'll order sandwiches, soft drinks, and lots of coffee."

"Shit."

"I agree. See you at 4."

Scott was probably swearing in Italian by now, adding hand gestures inherited from his beloved grandfather who had once lived in my old neighborhood in Niagara Falls—a place where grape vines edged the borders between small brick houses and the smell of garlic oozed from pizza and the pores of young and old.

When I was 12, my Irish family had moved to the city's Little Italy neighborhood. My mom adapted to change with ease, but the 20-year age difference between my parents often sparked some tense moments. Our flat was on the second floor in a home owned by a man named Mario. His wife made sauce every Sunday. The aroma from stewing tomatoes and oregano crept up the back stairs to our apartment unabated, causing my anti-Italian, World War II vet father to sputter, "Jesus H. Christ" as the aroma intensified. I mouthed the expletive too, with just the right emphasis on the "H", having years of experience as an accomplished mimic. My mother shook her head and tried not to smile. I lived in that boxy brick house with wide front porches until the day I left to work in Boston. While I was ecstatic to leave, my dad was mute, and my mother just sobbed. Every time Scott talked about the joys of making grappa with his granddad, I wondered why I had left.

My childhood reverie evaporated after a quick shower and thoughts of the meeting ahead. I dug my designer suit out of my closet and my not-so-comfortable black pumps. These lofty stilettos always boosted my self-confidence when debating issues or swaying opinions. I had worn them earlier in the year during my interview with Scott; they did their best to shore up my nerves, even if my toes were numb.

Scott had welcomed me to the top floor with one of his bear hugs, wrapping his woodsy aftershave around me. He turned on his charm with a captivating smile and escorted me to one of the leather club chairs across from a glass-topped coffee table and a matching leather sofa. My spiky heels sunk into the thick, colorful rug that separated the conversation area from the rest of his office. Windowed walls overlooking the medical center's sprawling campus surrounded glossy hardwood floors. In the distance, mist floated from Niagara Falls, mixing with faint clouds on a sunny afternoon.

"Nice, isn't it?" he said, adjusting the light-diffusing blinds. I noticed his deep navy suit fit to perfection, emphasizing his wide shoulders and narrow waist. He crossed the room to join me, placing a tray of steaming coffee on the gleaming glass table between us.

"Good to see you again, Ann. You look amazing. What's it been… two, three years? How's Todd and Julie?"

I smiled at the compliment and thought the same about him. "Three years—hard to believe. Julie graduated in May. She's off to see the world, and … Todd's another story."

"What's the healthcare guru doing these days?"

"I'm not sure. We divorced last year." I withheld the bitter details about Todd's philandering and risky deals. Scott sensed my hesitation.

"Sorry. It's difficult … been there, done that, as they say. I'm glad you came."

"Scott, why do you want me to work for you?"

Scott was out of his seat, pacing as he answered. "I can get off on tangents, overreact, and ignore things 'til they get worse. Milt sensed we were in for scrutiny and hired a national PR group when we opened. They never connected. Local media rejected their efforts to get positive news coverage. I believe you can change this. You've done it before."

Dr. Milton and the board had put mounds of faith and money into recruiting Scott to head the center and make it a magnet for patients seeking state-of-the-art treatment. "We take away our patients' clothes then give them drugs that render them unconscious—it's demeaning. We need to counter that with extraordinary care, or our reputation will suffer."

Scott's reputation and million-dollar salary were on the line, too. He inserted enough compassion in his answer to influence my decision. Not all CEOs, even those with MDs after their names, referred to the people in their care. Too often, they focused on net revenue and results in the aggregate, hiring healthcare consultants like Todd Delaney to analyze the numbers and prop up their inflated egos.

"I'm glad you mentioned the patients, Scott. From what I've read so far, you could package your message by saying your approach to orthopedics is innovative, a place where patient care is exceptional—"

"Ann, you put all our work together in a simple statement. Love it," he said, leaning against his sleek black desk, dark eyes penetrating the space between us. "You're just what we need. This job may be the right choice at the right time. Please say you will consider working with me again. I've missed you ... er ... working with you."

His familiar scent still lingering in the room was as welcoming as his smile. I realized how much I had missed working with Scott, too, even though I felt he knew more about Todd and me than he let on. We reminisced about the events that shaped our careers in Boston, especially the tough times: the escaped convict who shot himself and lived for days in our ICU while AP reporters waited impatiently for his last breath; the face-disfiguring injuries inflicted on one of our ER nurses by a patient high on drugs, and then the bombing—a tragedy and turning point in Scott's career.

Scott and I had rushed to the ER after the Boston Marathon bombing, not knowing if the bombers were mixed in with the patients. We were not caregivers, but we did what we could, rustling up coffee and compassion for family and friends of the victims, some so brutally injured we had to look away. The sights and coppery smells of clotting blood mixed with bone fragments and the pure terror on so many faces gripped both of us; we ran outside for air more than once, choking back tears and disbelief. These people were just watching a race when their world blew up.

We did our best to get the names and inform the media, who were just as emotional as the rest of us. It was terrifying and exhausting. We spent days and nights supporting our team. I even fell asleep in the staff lounge, embarrassed to wake up with my head leaning on Scott's shoulder. He just grinned and never left the ER until all the patients were identified and receiving care. Soon after that emotional time, Scott and his wife Maria separated. Even though his marriage had been troubled, the tragic bombing seemed to push him to a decision. He left our community hospital to take on the challenges of running a for-profit health system and soon discovered its tight focus on costs and cutting included taking the caring out. Dr. Milton's invitation for Scott to join him in this new venture on Grand Island came at the right time.

For a moment, he was quiet, then his eyes lit up, and he smiled. "I love it here. I hope you'll join me." He gave me an overview of his team members and walked to his wall of windows to share his plans for the center's future, pointing out exterior landmarks six floors below. I was ready for a change.

"I'll give it some thought. Good to see you again, Scott."

The meeting ended with a warm handshake. I knew I would be back.

CHAPTER 3

I connected my cell phone to my car's charger and headed for the park-way, the shortest route to the North Bridge. The river churned next to me, navigating ragged rocks with ease. I envied its fierceness, hoping to find some of my own. "Dammit, Bob," I cursed the air again at the scoop-hungry reporter. His tactics were familiar: connect with everyone involved in this bizarre scenario except us, catch us off guard and confirm our guilt in a sweep of innuendo. There were no charges, lawsuits, warnings, noth-ing. It would be a trial-by-news story—no judge or jury. This was not the type of good news I planned to deliver when I accepted Scott's offer.

I spent my first months at the Milton Center snooping. An ID badge with access to the entire medical complex was one of my first requests, along with a pair of Milton scrubs. A few days into my tenure, I grabbed a pair of clogs and my pale blue scrubs, pressed my ID against the proximity reader and walked into the OR's staff lounge, the strings on my face mask dangling along my neck. A few surgical techs had just finished a case and welcomed me into their inner sanctum, grabbing crackers from a bag and scooping up gobs of peanut butter from a communal crock. The coffee reeked of stale grounds and looked thick. Word was out; they knew I planned to write a story about the OR and the famous Dr. Milton for the quarterly magazine.

A young nurse named Trish was the first to fill me in on Milton. "Milt's a genius—made lots of money in the stock market, doesn't do much sur-gery, and prefers to work in the lab. His skinny fingers kind of drip off his hands, freaky looking, but I heard he's a wiz at the piano. Milt went to the University of Buffalo with Scott Marino, got his MD, and scored a stint at the Mayo. He came back to build this place. I guess he missed the Buffalo wings."

We all laughed. Kyle spoke next. A bulky tech with arms covered in tattoos, he had concerns. "We've had rough news stories, Ann, focused on our lab. We use animal parts to fix joints, but we're not the first. It's amazing science. Some old fart ortho docs at the med school act like we are conducting secret experiments. Guess your job is to set them straight and get the good news out."

"That's the plan, Kyle." After a few more nuggets of insider info, I thanked everyone for sharing their stories and their snacks.

Six months had passed since that day in the OR lounge. A new crock of peanut butter had replaced the last, and my plan for good news was failing apart. Bob McCarthy's call had turned my offensive strategy into a defensive game that could anger staff and destroy careers, mine included. When I walked through the door to my first-floor office, my assistant Alice looked up, noticed my shoes, and stopped typing. "Hey, what's up?"

"Alice, get the team in here now. We're having an exec session at 4, and I have a lot of calls to make."

Alice wore bright colors, sang in a local choir, and often hummed as she worked. Wisps of blond curls framed her soft cheeks and bright blue eyes. Even the crankiest complainer left our office feeling better after meeting her. A wise woman, she knew when to speak and when to keep typing.

Our team was small, only three of us—Alice, my Cyber guy Matt and me. Within minutes, they assembled in my office, sitting at a round table in the corner. I read them my notes from Bob's call and reviewed my conversation with Scott. With thumbs tapping odd refrains, they each checked social media sites for leaks; nothing showed up except old complaints about artwork and on-hold music. Our Facebook page and Twitter feed had nothing out of the ordinary.

As the team left, I moved to my desk, picked up a well-used printed version of our online Milton Center directory, then kicked off my stiff shoes with a sigh of relief. Stratton was first on my call list. A disinterested staffer told me he was away and not on-call. With growing irritation, I suggested someone check his home or wherever he was. "Just find him," I said.

David Brown, board chair, was next. A financial investment advisor, he always answered. Like me, he was not an academic or a clinician. He seemed interested in making the medical center a glowing example of excellent care; it was also his gateway for future business contacts. The details of Bob's accusations irritated him.

"Damn, every time we turn around, someone is accusing us of something. I'll be there."

"Thanks, Dave."

Unlike smaller hospitals, Milton employed an in-house legal team for our extensive research contracts. Jennifer Newton, a dynamic, 40-year-old lawyer, headed the group. She had worked for 15 years at a large malpractice firm in Buffalo before taking on this new role at the center. When I called, she asked if I thought the reporter was exaggerating.

"I'm sure he is, but we still need to respond."

"Okay, I'm in. See you soon."

I asked Alice to find Laurie Mahoney from regulatory compliance and bio lab manager Lukas King when Dr. Stratton called.

"Mrs. Delaney, this is Dr. Stratton. Have we met? What's so fucking urgent?"

I wasn't sure how to begin. "Thanks for returning my call, Dr. Stratton. No, we haven't met. I've only been her about six months. I was spokesperson for a Boston hospital where Scott Marino was CEO before I moved here. He recruited me a few months ago to join him here."

"Isn't that grand. What do you want?"

"I spoke with Bob McCarthy, this morning; he's a reporter from The Buffalo News. They're running a story in Monday's paper about a patient he says you 'butchered'—and that's a quote."

"You believe that crap?"

"I didn't say I believed it. It's what Bob said, and now we need to respond."

"He's an ass. I'm not saying a word."

I should have expected his response.

"Mrs. Delaney, tell this inept fellow I'm the best god-damned surgeon in this place. I haven't butchered anyone."

He hung up. I shook my head and sighed. I needed a surgeon in the meeting, so I called the chief of surgery, Dr. Ian Rogers, who muttered and swore, then agreed to show up. What was it with surgeons?

11

CHAPTER 4

With my shoes back on, I gathered my notes, slung my laptop case over my shoulder, and headed to the sixth floor Smith Conference Room. I swiped my ID badge across the reader next to door, arriving early for the meeting. The late afternoon sun kept the room awash in soft light. Dietary had delivered trays of finger sandwiches, an urn of coffee, and assorted teas.

Scott, Milton, and Dave Brown arrived together, talking in muffled tones, suggesting they had already held a private huddle. Smiles were brief. After pouring coffee, Scott took the wide-armed chair at the head of the table. Jennifer Newton, our lawyer, sat on one side of Scott; Milt on the other next to Chairman Brown.

Lukas King, the bio lab manager, and Laurie Mahoney from compliance took seats near each other. Dr. Rogers stroked his stubby brush cut, loosened his tie, and slumped in a chair next to Jennifer. Except for the rattle of dishes, the room was still. Scott stood up, pausing until everyone turned toward him.

"Thank you for coming. Ann, please bring us up to date."

"Good afternoon. We will hold this meeting and any others related to this subject in the strictest confidence. I'm sure everyone agrees." Heads nodded, no one spoke. "I received a call this morning from Bob McCarthy, a Buffalo News reporter, accusing the Milton Center and Dr. Stratton of causing a patient's death. I expect this will be a back-and-forth news story over several days, even weeks. We'll need to respond."

Dr. Rogers sat upright in his chair. "Ann, why don't we tell him to shove off? This is a waste of our time. I talked to Stratton, and he's rip shit."

The chief's remark seemed to elicit agreement from the group, all eager to leave. In the short time since I'd known him, Dr. Rogers had impressed me with his concern for his patients, but my only encounters were in perfunctory department meetings. I took a deep breath, stood up, and moved a few inches closer to him. "How does this sound, Ian? 'Hospital chief of surgery calls accusation of murder a waste of his time.' I imagine that would make the front page; don't you think?"

He sat back, rebuffed. "I know you're this smart-ass newswoman, but I'm no slouch, either. In case you haven't noticed, I am the chief of surgery around here. So, what's your great idea?"

Scott turned to Rogers, trying to soothe his ruffled ego. "Ian, Ann's just doing her job, so let her continue."

"Scott, this is a waste of time," Rogers said, crossing his arms.

I ignored the huffy doctor and projected the context of the accusations, in bullet format, on the drop-down screen. "Dr. Rogers, Scott, please, let's look at Bob's comments. First, he wants to talk to the CEO; second, infections are rampant; third, animal blood is everywhere; and fourth, Dr. Stratton butchered a patient."

Scott squirmed in his chair, waiting for me to continue. "Regarding the first point, Scott, I'm sure you are willing to talk to this reporter and others, but I recommend I remain as the spokesperson as we sort things out."

Scott's tight lips and reddening face suggested he did not agree. "Jesus, Ann—this is my job, my responsibility. I've played golf with the editor over there. He'll kill the story if I ask him."

My transient defender, the guy who enticed me to take this job, was shoving me aside. The current editor/golfer "Big John" Rodham was my mentor years ago. Scruffier than Bob, I knew he salivated when juicy news fell in his lap—holding this story for two days was rare but only suggested the depth of their ongoing investigation. Before Scott's or my blood vessels burst, David Brown spoke up. "Scott, Ann's right. Let's examine the complaints. We don't want Stratton running off at the mouth and ruining our reputation. We've put a lot of work, not to say money, into this unique hospital, and we don't want it to go up in smoke from some angry remarks."

Scott scanned the room for fellow dissenters and found none. "All right," he spat out. "I'll stay out of it for now. So, let's get moving. Number two is easy. Laurie, compile everything we have on infection rates here and national comparisons and double-check Dr. Stratton. The third item sounds alarming, but we know our bio lab is as sterile as any lab on earth. Lukas, prepare a sentence or two to include in our spokesperson's statement." Lukas raised his bent head at an odd angle and looked at me for support.

Ignoring Scott's arrogance and hoping to keep tempers calm, I suggested we move on to Stratton. "I understand Dr. Stratton is known to intimidate, but fellow surgeons praise his expertise, and from what I know, we've never lost a patient because of his or any other doc's surgery here."

Dr. Milton nodded but kept silent. I asked Dr. Rogers to go through Stratton's peer review records. "I am his peer, and there's nothing to find. Besides, we don't know the patient's name."

"You're right, Ian." I said. "I'll press harder."

Ian pushed his chair back and got up to leave. The remaining team followed his lead. When I suggested we meet at 10 a.m. the next day, a few mumbled about it being Saturday, including Scott. Dave Brown was reassuring and supportive. "Ann, we'll be here at 10. Thanks."

Scott asked Milton to stop by his office. I turned off the projection system, collected errant notes, and helped Dietary clear the room. Before leaving, I passed my reflection in one of the tall windows. All I saw was someone alone on the top floor of a new life.

CHAPTER 5

It was after five on Friday, a time to relax and enjoy the weekend. Todd and I used to celebrate the end of a week in Boston's North End with a glass of Chianti and a dish of pasta, our brand of comfort food. He was probably there right now, clinking glasses in a toast "To tonight" as he often did, this time with a new paramour. They'd be cuddled in a dark corner, oblivious to time and surroundings. I missed the food and Boston vibe. It was the cuddle part that made me still yearn for that unfaithful lover.

But I had Bob. I was sure he was lurking in the shadows of breaking news, ready to pounce. If I could not have Chianti, I could at least talk to someone focused on my every word. I sent him the same curt text he used to interrupt my long weekend earlier in the day. "Call me." Seconds later, my phone rang.

"Hi, Delaney. When can I talk to the big shot on campus?"

"Bob, like it or not, you get to talk to me. The board asked me to be the spokesperson, so you'll be dealing with me. I'll give you as much information as I can related to your news story." I heard a muted, "Shit," as he scratched my words in his reporter's notebook.

In a louder voice, he said, "My editors want Scott. Someone must be nervous over there if the guy who likes to rant about his remarkable medical complex is silent … hmm. I hope you know you'll be in for a tough ride if your boss won't come out of hiding."

I wanted to question his journalistic ethics, but it would only make matters worse, so I swallowed and stuck to the subject. "No one's hiding. Where did you get your info? What's the name of the patient? What—"

15

"Enough questions. My sources are confidential; you know how that works. I'll give you the name, though, since it will be a headline on Monday. The patient is, or was, Guy Lebeau. Ring any bells?"

"Should it?"

"If you followed hockey, you'd know. He's the Sabres goalie, the player everyone loves to hate. He had secret surgery that didn't go so well. Guess who his doctor was? The world-renowned advanced orthopedic surgeon, James D. Stratton, MD; that's how you describe him on your website. I might describe him differently."

Great, I thought, not only a deceased patient but a famous deceased patient. My knowledge of hockey couldn't even fill a puck. "Thanks for the information. Is there anything else I should know?"

"Nope. I'm on deadline - tomorrow at 5 p.m. Like it or not, the story runs with or without you. Your choice."

I shrugged. This news hack knew how to irritate me. "Not to worry, I'll get back to you tomorrow afternoon so you can meet your damn deadline." He didn't respond. I was sure he was smirking at the power of the press in his nasty hands.

So, what if it was Friday night? I had a few calls to make. Texts and emails about the patient would be inappropriate, knowing how this information could travel through cyberspace. Instead, I took the elevator to the second floor, walked past the ICU, down a dim, deserted hallway. I swiped my badge on the "Medical Staff Only" door lock and found Dr. Rogers alone, hanging up his white coat in the inner lounge, a place that always reeked of antiseptic hand cleaners and old apple cores. Neither I nor my news was welcome.

"Ann, did you read the sign on the door? DOCS ONLY. What are you doing here? Don't you have someone else to bother?"

"That sign is only meant to keep out the riffraff."

"Like you?"

"I have a job, just like you," I said.

His eyes rolled at that comment, then he stuffed his stethoscope in his jacket pocket, ready to leave as I moved closer. "The Milton Center's reputation is just as much in my hands as yours even though I don't use scalpels like you and the rest of surgeons around here - I use words. Words can hurt, but they can also help, and right now I need your help. The reporter told me the patient's name."

"Oh … Who is it?"

"It's Guy Lebeau. Ring any bells?"

From the look on his face, I knew hockey was a sport he followed, and this waste-of-time nuisance news story raised his bushy eyebrows a notch. "Lebeau? That's interesting … from what I heard, he died of an overdose … he wasn't even here when it happened."

"According to Mr. McCarthy, Lebeau's family is blaming Dr. Stratton. I don't know enough yet, but you could check out his case outcomes, as a peer and partner, before our meeting tomorrow morning. Now, I have someone else to bother. I plan to call Scott next."

"Good luck with that. I think I saw steam rising from that Italian stud after you told him he couldn't be spokesperson." He laughed. "You've got guts; I'll give you that. See you tomorrow."

I left him in his Land of Oz. When I passed by the ICU, a young phlebotomist came out carrying vials of labeled blood in a hand-held container, her long, brown ponytail swishing as she walked. She smiled when she saw me and wished me a good night. I noticed her name was Amanda, a pretty name for a pretty woman. I returned her wish, thankful for the work she and thousands of Amandas and Adams did each day to take care of patients. I hoped my words ultimately would make a difference for all of them, even Ian Rogers.

My office was dark, matching my mood. I turned my desk lamp on, avoiding the bright overhead lights, and called the arrogant, excitable CEO. He offered a flimsy apology for his earlier short temper and suggested going out for a drink to talk more about this Lebeau revelation; I was still miffed at his questioning my role, so I turned him down, then regretted it as I clinked an imaginary wineglass and whispered "To tonight" in an empty room.

The bio lab was my next stop. I considered Lukas one of the good guys. Even with his MIT PhD brilliance, he seemed content to answer my endless questions and loved to share scientific jargon, knowing I had no clue what he was saying. He also enjoyed my penchant for gossipy updates since he seldom left his basement sanctuary. His scruffy beard on a head with no neck reminded me of a papa gnome that used to live in a small garden at the back of our house when I was a kid, part of a family of four just like mine. This happy memory always moved into the room when Lukas and I met. He could ramble on about his research and preferred data and charts to the language of conversation. Lukas was likely fidgeting about Scott's vague assignment to "prepare a sentence or two" about the sterility of the bio lab. I walked into his basement kingdom.

Although he was a quiet man, I knew from prior visits how Lukas found his voice when the topic was research. His eyes glistened as he described the evolution of reconstructing damaged joints using stem cell pastes, bovine tendons, and porcine ligaments—revolutionary methods spearheaded by Drs. Benjamin Milton and James Stratton. The process required intricate procedures to remove antigens from these "xenogeneic tissues," Lukas said, making sure I had something to look up after I left him. Thanks to large research grants, the Milton Bio Lab had become the East Coast center for biologic joint reconstruction.

During one trip to his sanctuary, Lukas clicked an icon on his computer. A familiar TV show opened. "Ann, do you remember the "Six Million Dollar Man"? It was a '70s TV series; maybe you're not old enough?"

I laughed. "Yeah, I was young, but I've seen reruns. The show was about a guy with fictional bionic arms and legs."

"It's no longer fictional. We can do that and more; the science is amazing." He described how repairing joints from within the body eliminated infection, pain, and, sometimes, surgery itself. "Artificial joints came in limited sizes, and we adapted them to fit during surgery. The latest technology molds joints to the specific measurement of the patient, held in place with animal ligaments and tendons. They're a perfect fit."

For a man who could discuss his research with any willing listener, a summons to the sixth-floor conference room and, knowing his boss, Dr. Milton, would be there, left Lukas tongue-tied. He once told me he disliked the Center's founder, thought him aloof, even for a surgeon. Worse, he focused more on advancing profits than medical breakthroughs. Lukas preferred working with Dr. Stratton, describing him as a pure researcher.

Lukas sighed when I walked in. The call to attend the earlier meeting had sent shivers through him. "Where did the reporter get the idea of animal blood everywhere?" he asked. "This lab is pristine. I can understand why Stratton refused to show up; I think he'd prefer staying in the basement with me."

CHAPTER 6

It was after 10 p.m. when I returned to my apartment building. I'd had my fill of righteous men—the pushy reporter, nasty surgeons, and a dismissive boss. As I waited for the elevator, I thought of the spirits that still lingered in this converted 1920s office building: businessmen in wide-legged, pin-striped suits hustling to greet each other while their secretaries sported seamed hose, broad shoulders, and suffragette attitudes. It was a fascinating time. Stylish women puffed on Lucky Strikes through slender sliver holders searching for liberation, equality, recognition … and respect. They had shouted, "We've come a long way, baby." We still had a way to go.

The lights were dim in the first-floor wine bar as I passed tired waiters closing for the night. The elevator slid up to the 14th floor, opening into a wide hallway; art deco geometrics spread through the thick carpet and the metallic wallpaper. Brass numbers with ornate sconces identified the four apartments on my level. After opening my door, I looked across my small living room to the expanse of windows facing northwest. The majestic waterfall glistened against a navy sky. No matter the season, white lights illuminated the Falls at night. Winters were magical. A frozen mist clung to tree branches. Snow and ice softened the craggy rocks at the base of the Falls, turning them into shiny marshmallow mounds.

"Alexa, play smooth jazz."

The soft moan of a trumpet filled the room with strains of "Over the Rainbow." I changed into sweats and poured a glass of a crisp Sonoma white, ignored the unpacked boxes in the corner, settled into my sofa's oversized cushions, and cuddled with my laptop. Before I fell asleep, I needed to learn more about two men I'd never met. My Google guide scanned the lives of Guy Lebeau and James Stratton, MD, offering insight, conjecture, and mystery.

I took another sip of the Chardonnay, trying to piece the puzzle together, even though there were large holes. Bob McCarthy had more pieces, and he wasn't sharing. By the end of tomorrow morning's meeting, I needed to determine what the lede to his story might be and create a statement that implicated no one and gave us time to fill in the gaps. The game was on. I closed my laptop. As I dosed off, my inner monitor flashed a room filled with angry men in white coats slaying hapless skaters in a rink surrounded by marshmallow ice.

Still dressed in yesterday's clothes. I woke early under a mound of pillows, my laptop on the floor. I popped a K-cup in my coffee maker and changed into running gear. After a jolt of caffeine, I hit the gym in my building, concentrating on getting nowhere as fast as possible. The indoor run left me as ready as I'd ever be to tackle the team. Because it was Saturday, I opted for less formal business attire—tan slacks, low-heeled shoes, and a burgundy, not-quite-power-red jacket. I packed my laptop and notepad and drove 10 miles to the medical center. Summer hadn't given up. Lacy clouds drifted across a bright blue sky. The air was still crisp at this early hour, although 80 degrees was forecast for mid-afternoon.

I opened the windows in my new white sports car; inhaled the scent of dewy grass, hoping to erase a troubled sleep. But with the morning breeze, recollections of the previous night's searches wandered in: Compared to the hockey star, Stratton's story was brief: He attended medical school in Buffalo, was tenured at Mayo, and earned a fellowship in California. Gained skill and recognition in advanced orthopedics. Never married. A James Stratton, medical school student, had survived a tragic ski accident in Colorado that killed a young woman—they were both 21. Based on the date of the news item, the survivor would be 58, the same age as Dr. Stratton.

Shaking my musings, I pulled into the Medical Center's parking lot, expecting to meet the mysterious doctor at the morning meeting. I dropped off a stack of notes from the previous night's searches in my office, then headed to the Smith Conference Room, where Scott's admin Mary had arranged for coffee, tea, and an assortment of pastries. As I picked up a mug, I heard the door open behind me. A whiff of a familiar aftershave announced Scott's arrival. I turned around and saw a man dressed for golf, eager to move on.

"Good morning, Ann. Are you ready for this?"

"Scott. I could ask you the same. We need to agree on a statement to counter Bob's claims. I'm certain he hasn't told us everything."

Dave Brown, Drs. Milton, and Rogers ambled in, poured mugs of coffee, adjusted their chairs, and waited. The rest of the team entered with Lukas, settling in the same seats as the previous night.

Scott greeted each as they entered, the inveterate politician. "Good morning, thanks for coming in on a Saturday. I know you have families, outings and cookouts planned this weekend, so let's get started. Ann, where are we?"

I nodded at his request. "After our meeting yesterday, I called the reporter, Bob. He didn't share too much about his sources for the infection rate claim or the blood comment, but he revealed the patient. It's the hockey star, Guy Lebeau."

Laurie seemed shocked. "He didn't die here. I don't get it."

"You're right, Laurie. They found him unconscious in his home on Monday and brought him to Memorial Hospital. A few hours later, his heart stopped. He was 32. The media raised questions about a drug overdose, and police are investigating. According to Bob, Lebeau's superstar wife and two brothers, claimed his death resulted from surgery Dr. Stratton performed a few months ago. I notice Dr. Stratton isn't here to discuss this."

Scott put his coffee cup down and stood up. "Ann, Milt and I talked with Jim last night. He's adamant his surgery did not cause Lebeau's death. He's also angry and ready to lunge at anyone making this suggestion. We asked him not to come today. He needs to calm down and we need to continue our investigation. Let's start with infection rates. Dr. Rogers?"

Ian picked up his annotated charts and scribbled notes. "After we met last night, I looked at the minutes of our quality reports and peer review meetings. Overall, our infection rates are low compared to expected rates for all surgeries. There are a few outliers due to multiple morbidities. Even though we've seen amazing advancements in artificial joints that last longer than ever before, some patients are not appropriate for treatment. An elderly patient with debilitating comorbidities is asking for trouble in any OR."

Scott interrupted the medical lesson and asked Rogers to be more generic.

Dr. Rogers nodded in agreement. "Athletes, like Lebeau, may have underlying heart disease or, if it's true, drug interactions. I couldn't access Stratton's personal patient records, but I reviewed his overall infection rates. Lower than other docs on service, even lower than national rates."

After listening to his remarks, I tried to condense them. "So, Dr. Rogers, would it be correct to say the Milton Center quality data suggests infections to be at or below national expected rates for orthopedic surgery? I'll leave Dr. Stratton's specific rates out of the statement."

"Yeah, Ann, that sounds about right. What do you think, Scott?"

Laurie spoke up again. "What if they interview a disgruntled patient?"

Scott looked at me to answer. "We don't comment on individual patients, even if they reveal their own medical problems; we can give results in the aggregate for a procedure or anything we report to the feds since that's public," I said. "From what I know about our patient satisfaction and the reports Dr. Rogers mentioned, we're not likely to hear from other patients. We'll keep monitoring our social media channels; so far, they've been benign."

Satisfied with my answer, Scott's gaze turned to Lukas King. "Okay, let's move on to the animal blood issue. What do you have, Lukas?"

Lukas unpacked his briefcase, adjusted his glasses, and raised his bowed head. After a nervous cough, he read his statement, passing copies around the table.

"The Milton Bio Lab is a pristine development center for allogeneic and xenogeneic tissues, and cellular growth mediums for molding joints. All systems use vetted FDA-approved techniques. There is no animal blood in or around the bio lab. It is temperature-controlled, monitored, extra secure with negative pressure rooms. We are also fortunate to participate in highly competitive National Institute of Health grant-funded research and we've achieved outstanding results. Thank you."

I noticed Dr. Milton scratching out part of the statement, then he turned to Lukas. "Nice job, maybe a bit long. I suggest taking out the last sentence. You know how competitive grant funding can be, and it reads fine without it."

Lukas barely moved in his chair, agreed to the changes suggested by his boss. His soft round cheeks were getting redder by the minute. I hoped to get him to relax. "Thank you, Lukas, I think we can delete the reference to animal blood—that only repeats the reporter's false accusation. We don't want to give it any credence. You once told me you were proud of your highly skilled staff and their commitment to extreme quality; I'd like to add that to the description of the lab. When was the lab inspected?"

"Yes, you may, thank you, Ann. The last inspection was two years ago, so the next regular inspection should take place next year. However, if news stories mention the lab, the surveyors may schedule a visit sooner."

Scott pushed back his chair and stood up again, "Dr. King just reminded me about the possibility of a Joint Commission accreditation survey. Laurie, what do you think?"

Laurie glanced at me, then swiveled toward Scott. "Well … we can wait for someone to report this to the Joint Commission, or we can proactively let them know about the reporter's allegations. From what Ann's said, I think we need to prepare. During our last survey, they only found a few documentation errors, which we corrected on site."

No matter how prepared a hospital was, Joint Commission surveys were a stressful time. During their on-site visits, commission members checked everything—refrigerator temperatures, drug labeling, time outs. They also interviewed patients and even invited community members to give feedback. I turned to Laurie. "Should we note we are proactively reporting to the JC and the state? What do you think?"

Board Chairman Dave Brown sat up, pushing his chair away from the table. "Wait a minute. I'm the only board member here. If we're contacting accrediting institutions or the state, we need to call a board meeting. The quality of this institution is one of our big responsibilities. Maybe we should have brought them into this conversation sooner."

I looked across the room at Scott, waiting for him to respond. He knew a full board meeting would raise the seriousness of the charges and concerns about the strength of his leadership. "Ann, is there any chance the reporter will hold this story a few days?"

"I wish I had that power, Scott. He's already given us a few days. The story will run on Monday. Since we agreed not to discuss Dr. Stratton's patient, and we have answers to most of Bob's claims, I suggest we put a statement together, and have legal review it. Once we agree, send it to the board at the same time I send it to the reporter."

Brown nodded in agreement. "Sounds good, but I still think we need to call a meeting for some time on Monday—late afternoon, early evening."

Scott sat down and turned to Brown. "David, I agree. We need to give them a heads up about what to say, what not to say if a reporter calls."

"Good point, Scott" I said. "Thanks." I noticed a smug but warmer smile from the CEO, scoring points in front of the board chairman and the rest of us. I suggested David call each board member about our meeting, rather than email or text, to keep things confidential. I also offered to draft brief instructions on what to say or not say if talking to a reporter.

Scott suggested the group take a break while I completed the statement. As I took the elevator to my office, I noticed the quiet hallways and remember it was Saturday.

CHAPTER 7

My staff huddled in the break room, drinking coffee, talking hockey. Matt wore a Sabres jersey for the occasion, and Alice sported a Buffalo Bills T-shirt. The loyalty displayed by fans for their favorite sports always amazed me, and these guys just confirmed it.

"Hey, thanks for coming in and getting in the mood. Guess I'm a little lean on sports attire. So, what do you have? Remember, no email communication among you."

Alice shrugged and gave me a look like "I know," then walked up to the whiteboard, ready to jot down anything we could use for the statement and next steps. I suggested we add background on Guy Lebeau and wrote "do not acknowledge as patient" next to his name as a reminder with another note "express deep sympathy."

This young man's sudden death deserved sympathy. My team knew much more about Lebeau than I did. I reviewed a condensed version of my research on this rugged athlete, referring to notes on my laptop.

"Lebeau grew up on a dairy farm near Quebec, learned to skate with his brothers on a pond in his backyard, 'hooting and hollering in French and English' as one engaging sportswriter noted. He played for his high school team, caught the attention of hockey scouts, which led to a scholarship at McGill, and then he was drafted by the Sabres. The tabloids focused on his good looks, his classic broken nose, and those black curls that escaped the confines of his hockey mask often enough to attract more than his share of female fans. Just as he hit the nationals, he met a Parisian woman living in Quebec City and asked her to marry him. He was 22; she was 18."

Acting like the recent college grad he was, Matt straightened his jersey, walked up to the whiteboard, and wrote, Michelle Paradise. "She's Lebeau's wife. A stunning blond rock star. She has a throaty, raspy voice, some amazing curves, all in the right places. I could draw a few."

We laughed at his eagerness. "Not now," I said. "We get the picture."

Alice added what she knew. "Hollywood bloggers reported her parents were against the marriage. She's their only daughter. Guy's stardom never impressed them, and they predicted he would be unfaithful. They were right."

Matt added a few more details. "A justice of the peace married them, then they moved to Toronto, close to nightclubs and a flowing drug scene. In 10 years of marriage, the Lebeaus had two boys, ages 3 and 9."

Alice continued, "The paparazzi followed them everywhere and wrote about rumors of infidelities, beatings. I'm not sure any of it's true—just look at the flawless body of this high-profile mom, still breathtaking after two pregnancies. Wish I looked like that after a few kids."

"I agree; she's amazing." I pulled up photos from my previous web search. "This one shows Lebeau's arm around his 3-year-old wearing starter skates and a small Sabres jersey. It was his first skating lesson." Lebeau was smiling, his oldest in the background, skates laced, ready to join in the game. "This one is the saddest. It's Michelle, crying in anguish, as she left Memorial Hospital holding onto Guy's brother Raymond's arm."

After that somber review, I asked Matt to give us an update on social media. "He's been playing for the Sabres for five years," he explained, "so you can imagine his fans are angry that no one helped him with his drug problem. I'm sure they'll soon join his family in accusing Stratton of murder. They'll assume our famous doc gave him the deadly drugs, if that's the cause. From what I've read, they're not sure what caused his heart attack."

Everyone nodded in agreement. In the next 15 minutes we developed a statement that acknowledged compassion, clearly explained patient confidentiality, and emphasized our commitment to quality. I shortened Lukas's statement, leaving out the reference to research grants and lack of animal blood, and included a comment from Scott to show he was still in charge—a minor salvo to ease his bruised ego. I made copies and headed to the conference room.

It took a few minutes to reconvene the group. Fresh canisters of coffee appeared with finger sandwiches. Between sips and some rustling chip bags, they reviewed the statement.

"Looks good to me," Scott said, "Sounds like I'm responding positively. Any concerns?" I smiled at that remark.

Dave Brown finished chewing, then spoke up. "I suggest we simplify the language about the lab. I'm not sure we should be so specific, and others, including myself, are not sure what the terms mean."

"Glad to simplify." I scribbled the changes and read the revision. "How about, 'The Milton Center is an acknowledged leader in the development of connective tissues and blood products used to form new joints and ligaments, approved by the FDA and national accrediting agencies?' Is that still correct, Lukas?"

He nodded. "I like specifics, but it's fine. Thanks."

Jennifer reviewed the penciled-in suggestions. "Legally, it's okay, but I'm not sure where this gets us," she said. Lukas squirmed a little and asked what we would tell employees and the medical staff.

"We can share the statement after the news story is out, or elaborate once we know what's in the news," I said. "It's a morning paper and online around 5 a.m. By the time employees arrive around 7, we'll be more prepared."

I turned to Scott; not sure he was paying attention.

"Scott, I'll contact you early to make plans for the next steps. For now, I think we should clear our calendars for early Monday morning. I know this response is a little vanilla, but we don't know what we're up against until the news story comes out." As soon as they finished reading the statement, I asked them to hand it back. "I'll prepare an email with the revised statement for Bob and the board."

Mary offered to help Dave make the calls to the board members to ensure they would keep the information confidential. The team pushed back their rolling chairs and headed for home, the links, the beach—anywhere but the Milton Center on this late summer day with thick clouds forming on the horizon.

Scott slipped back into the conference room while I revised the statement on my laptop. He took a seat near me, his soft blue golf shirt and light khaki pants in stark contrast to the dark leather chair. I wasn't sure if he was here to complain, compliment, or just be smug.

"Hey, I thought you were heading to the Masters or wherever golfers go for excitement?"

"Nah, it's exciting enough around here."

"Yeah … it is." I hesitated, then thought I'd jump in, find out what was on his mind. "Are you okay … about me being spokesperson?"

"Wasn't at first. Guess you figured that out. Sorry. Nice job with the statement; hope this guy uses some of it. You're convincing, even a little foxy when you're miffed. Glad Dave's on your side. Good thing since he's my boss. Now what?"

Foxy? I wasn't ready for that response. "I'd rather you thought I was good at my job. I'll finish this update and send it off to Bob. Then we wait; won't know much more until the story hits. Could be rough for a while."

"Maybe I'll get my old shoulder pads on, get ready for a sack."

Even though I knew the tenacious reporter could be formidable, I needed to calm the CEO. "Don't worry. Bob isn't a match for you."

His ego rallied. "Thanks for the support. I don't think Bob's a match for you, either. Listen, I'm dressed for golf, but I'm ready to take a break. How about lunch somewhere?"

This guy was always ready to eat. "Sorry. I need to get this done, talk with my team—tough boss and all."

"Fine. Another time. Let me know if you need anything." I watched him leave the room, looking good in his golf gear. I felt a tension growing inside me, or maybe it was a desire to be more than Scott's spokesperson. I needed to concentrate on this job, the news story, and let Scott run the hospital.

I sent the revised statement to Bob at noon. As if on cue, I received an immediate answer. "Ann, this statement is just a PR plug. Scott's comment is so predictable and useless. It'll do for now. Talk to you Monday."

I went back to my office, filled in my team, and suggested they come in early on Monday. They had the rest of the afternoon and Sunday to relax, something I would not be doing. Entering the parking garage, I noticed Milt, Ian, and Scott walking together. Their shoulders were bent at the same angle, as if someone had pushed them down with an invisible beam. Rain clouds were forming above the pristine medical center, ready to drop unwanted sprays of patient concerns and community outrage. It was only a matter of time.

CHAPTER 8

The temperature had dropped, and the winds had picked up as I headed home. Weekend boaters tucked their vessels into marinas along the Niagara River near the North Bridge. After turning onto the parkway, the river followed me home, gaining momentum before its furious descent. Seagulls squawked, and sand flies swarmed along the water's edge into the hub of the city.

I remembered driving around on my first day back in town after 20 years away. Main Street, once a bustling avenue, looked like a tornado had swept its life away. Plywood covered the display windows of a department store where I once envied the mannequins' stylish outfits and ogled classy shoes I could never afford. The city I grew up in had a busy downtown, tourist shops, an ornate Carnegie library, schools, and churches every few blocks. Harnessing the hydroelectric power of the Falls brought chemical industries and the great Niagara Power Project of the '60s when hardworking families bought homes and spent money. When the project ended, the workers and half the population headed to new towns and cities. When I searched for the old public library, I found a crumbling community center; its books were blocks away inside a contemporary structure of heavy grey walls and skinny windows. Many of the churches and schools had closed or were converted into new uses in this city adapting to change.

My dad had never left the Falls. He was resting peacefully at Oakwood Cemetery close to the old high school. His small, flat headstone described him as a private in the US Army. I felt a gripping sadness whenever I drove by the cemetery's gates. He died years ago and would have been proud of my newspaper career as a "working woman"—even though this man from the Greatest Generation thought my going to college was a waste of time. He would often lecture from his La-Z-Boy about the state of the world as he chugged a beer and inhaled the Camel smoke that would one day kill him. He never understood my desire for higher education. "Find a good man to marry," he said. I thought I had.

If my father could have packaged the perfect husband, it would have been Todd Delaney. He shot whiskey with an expertise inherited from generations of Irish tipplers; his Blarney gift of gab and lilting laugh made even curmudgeons smile. When he strode to the dais at a healthcare conference in Boston years ago, I was at first intrigued; when he ended his session on healthcare finance, I was in love. Charm rippled out of him. While he spoke, he had this habit of brushing his sandy blond hair off his tan forehead, only for it to return in seconds. Without the Brooks Brothers suit and stiff white shirt, he would have easily passed for a surfer boy, an Irish surfer boy. I found out later he was a passionate sailor who lived for wind and saltwater spray.

After he enthralled me with finance lingo and Delaney logic, I accepted his invitation for drinks at the Ritz Carlton. We strolled through Quincy Market, consumed fish chowder at Durgin Park, and listened to an a cappella group outside Faneuil Hall. We met the next day to jog around Boston Common and along the Esplanade. In a few days, we shared more than healthcare statistics. Our physical relationship was intense, but our souls seemed to come together on a different level. Within the year, we married in a small ceremony, my mom and a few relatives attending.

We both wanted children. On our second anniversary, I had my first miscarriage. I was three months along, planning a nursery in our tiny apartment, talking about moving to the suburbs. Another year went by, ending in a second miscarriage. My doctor said not to worry; we were both healthy. He suggested hormones and explained the ideal times for sex. My third pregnancy made it past three months, then four. It was a boy. Todd was overjoyed. We lost our son when I was five months along. The doc said it was because of a uterine abnormality—my fault.

Guilt hung on me like clothes that needed cleaning. As the pain of our loss lessened, we talked about options, adoption. It took a few years and trips to China before we brought home our 1-year-old Julie. I delighted in her every move, first words, the dimples in her pudgy fingers but Todd seemed distant. This little girl was more mine than his. I don't think he ever let go of that tiny, helpless almost-son. Our souls crumbled, piece by piece.

He drank earlier in the day and late into the evening, then regretted it the next morning. The cycle became familiar and devastating. He was sober and cheerful for months at a time, then the cycle began again. His addiction was like invisible concrete—hard to see, even harder to lift. Todd admitted to a brief affair with someone not on hormones or scheduled sex, asked for forgiveness. I gave it. He sobered up, seemed to change, became more alive, advanced in his career. He was more like the man I married until the day Julie found him coming out of our master bedroom with a tall redhead, not her mom.

These memories took turns, fading in and out as I drove home. I opened the door, letting them escape, knowing they'd return on my next drive home.

CHAPTER 9

The hotel's wine bar was in happy hour mode. I was about to press the elevator button when I heard the mellow riffs of a jazz guitar mixed with wine-infused laughter. A few empty bar stools were waiting for my decision. I thought getting a divorce was a lot easier than getting single when I remembered a wise park ranger's advice—all you had to do to climb a mountain was to take one step after another. I pointed my toes in the right direction, zeroed in on a single stool, and willed my intestines to stop trembling. This was my first awkward step as a newly divorced woman into a bar alone; the closer I got, the more I wanted to run back to being married, safe, and unnoticed.

It took a few minutes to adjust to the dark navy walls and subtle lighting that created ageless encounters. Lime green velvet sofas and zebra print chairs were tucked into the room's small alcoves where tall windows framed the city's lights. I slid onto a bronze bar stool facing a mirrored wall, lined with wine bottles from around the world. The lanky bartender was wiping martini glasses with a white cloth, watching me. My reflection was terrified.

"What can I get you?" he asked.

I tried to sound confident. Martinis were not my drink. Cosmos were for Cosmopolitan readers, a publication I once read that still promoted itself as "The Women's Magazine for Sex Advice." Maybe I should re-up my subscription. I was only 48, with a fully intact libido; all I needed was a partner and some courage.

"I'll have one of your featured Chardonnays—not too oaky. Thanks."

"Got it," he said, pouring a perfect six-once measure. He placed a small white paper napkin on the glossy bar, followed by the tall-stemmed wine glass. I swirled, sniffed, and tasted. It was good. I looked up at my reflection again as a handsome man with sandy hair joined it. He looked so much like Todd, I flinched.

"Hey … sorry to surprise you," he said as I turned around. "My name's Chuck … Haven't seen you in here before."

"This is my first visit. My name's Ann; good to meet you." I extended my hand. He grasped it with a limp squeeze.

The guitarist was at the end of the bar. His music was smooth and sensuous; his tones mellow, dark and edgy. When his set ended, the room chilled and felt empty. To fill the void, my new bar mate began a lengthy monologue about his successful career in real estate law, his ex-wife, his ex-partners, and his extraordinary sailboat, pausing only for a swig of burgundy bravado and a quick look at himself in the mirror.

"You should see her; she's 42-feet-long, sleek, sumptuous white leather seats, full bar, the best teak floors money can buy. I call her C's Dream. That's the letter "C," not the word "sea." It's a play on my name," he laughed." You'd love her."

I sympathized with his ex-wife; hard to compete with a dream boat. Perhaps there was a touch of Todd in this man. "She sounds incredible. Afraid I'm not a fan of boats—any size—they make me seasick."

"Too bad, she's a beauty," he said, unfazed by my disinterest.

"I'm sure she is."

"So, Ann, what do you do?" He wasn't giving up.

"I'm a spokesperson for a hospital." I could see the question marks in his blurry blue eyes.

"Is that it? I mean, are you a nurse or a doctor or something?"

"I am something. I'm a spokesperson." I thought he might move on to the next ageless woman in the bar, but he persisted.

"So, what's it like being just a spokesperson for someone else, something else?"

"You know, Chuck, it's a little like being a lawyer. I listen to opinions, analyze information, give people advice and speak on their behalf."

"Being a lawyer is much more complex," he said, puffing up his chest. "I give advice, but it's based on years of education, multiple degrees. I have an undergrad in sociology, a Master of Laws, and Doctor of Juridical Science—that last one from Harvard—plus years of experience. I tell my clients what's best for them, how to win. That's what I do. And I'm paid very well ... more than a spokesperson. Uh ... no offense intended."

I could not help but wonder what this self-enamored, master of the universe was doing in downtown Niagara Falls, NY, cruising a low-key happy hour. I was no longer anxious. I was pissed.

"You know, Chuck, I'll admit there's one difference. I don't boast about me; I boast about them."

The over-educated, overpaid buffoon was silent. I finished my six ounces, paid the happy hour rates, left a hefty tip for the man wiping glasses, still watching me, and said goodbye to my ex-bar mate. In the empty elevator, I shouted, "What a jerk!" and smiled. I had made it through the singles bar scene—or at least had taken the first step.

CHAPTER 10

After my precarious attempt to ease into the singles bar scene, I escaped to the comfort of my temporary home on the 14th floor. I had my laptop and a Chardonnay of unknown provenance to keep me company. My phone vibrated in my tote bag. Scott must have known I'd be at home alone, brooding. I smiled before I answered, hoping to sound cheery. "Hi, boss."

"Hey, Ann. I wanted to thank you for setting up the meetings and getting the statement put together. How are you feeling about this whole thing?"

The sound of his voice had me sensing things I wasn't ready to face. I forced myself to stick to business. "We've done everything we can until we read the story on Monday. I'm trying to get more background on the hockey player. I'm also concerned about Dr. Stratton. Never met him. His reputation seems good. On surveys, some patients describe him as aloof; most praise him as an excellent surgeon."

If I kept talking, maybe I'd stop feeling. "I unearthed a Facebook comment from a few months ago, around the same time Lebeau was a patient. An A. J. Smith wrote, 'Stratton's a butcher and needs to go.' Our response at the time had been to suggest the sender contact our patient rep. That was the last we heard from him or her."

"Can't you take the comment down?" Scott asked.

"It's a little late. As much as it stings, comments like these show our efforts to be transparent. Our 4.5 rating is strong, not perfect. If I know Bob McCarthy at all, he's downloaded the comment for future use."

"Hmm …"

"Has Stratton ever come up for a case review by the medical staff?"

"Not that I remember. The board reviews lots of cases. I'll have Jen Newton check. Hey, you up for a late dinner? I'm just walking around my empty house and could use some company."

Even though I found him charming and part of me wanted to get out of my dour mood, drive down to the escarpment, and check in—for the night—with the slightly inebriated CEO, I knew better. "Scott, I'd love company too. It's late. I've been sipping Chardonnay for an hour, shouldn't be driving. Sounds like you shouldn't either, and besides, what would we do?"

"Do? Um ... talk, drink some more? See what happens."

"Scott, nothing will happen; you're my boss."

"Hey, sorry. Bad idea. Forget I said that."

I felt sorry for him. And me. "I'm kind of glad you called. I get lonely. It's hard adjusting to a single life. I had a drink in the downstairs bar tonight and met a jerk named Chuck. He was—"

"You met a guy in a bar? That's crazy. It's dangerous."

"Not sure it was dangerous. It was crazy, though. He's a lawyer with a big boat."

"Jesus, Ann, what happened?"

"Nothing. I left. I can take care of myself."

After a long silence, Scott said, "You're right Ann; you can take care of yourself but sometimes ... never mind."

"I'm glad you're worried about me. I need to get some sleep. How about brunch tomorrow?"

"Sure, love brunch ... love company more."

"Scott, let's talk about brunch."

"Yeah, sorry..."

"There's a little restaurant near my apartment, The Red Coach Inn. I've wanted to visit since I moved back here. It's another piece of Niagara Falls history. Ever been?"

"Never heard of it. Is it still open?"

"Yeah. I've walked by a few times. We can get a table near a window and talk about next steps. They still have a doorman and a long, red-canopied entrance. Looks like it did years ago."

It was a special place when I was young. My favorite aunt used to take my sister and me to lunch at the Inn on our birthdays. We wore crinkly taffeta dresses, white nylon socks, and black Mary Janes. Our mom tried her best to arrange scraggly curls, hide our scuffed knees and dislodge the dirt under our fingernails, knowing my aunt had frequent manicures with bright red polish. She also wore furry animals around her neck and diamond rings from past marriages. The menu was always the same.

"Ann, are you there?"

"Sorry, I was just remembering how much my sister and I loved to go to lunch there with my aunt on our birthdays. We always ordered grilled cheese sandwiches, cherry Cokes, and hot fudge sundaes. I'm sure they have a few tastier options."

"Do they have mimosas?"

"Don't worry. They have a full-service bar. Get some sleep. See you in the morning around 10 a.m."

I sunk into my sofa's cushions, pale ivory and soft like all the other surroundings the Simply Soft boutique offered. The salesclerk asked me if I had children or pets when I chose the cream-colored furnishings. "Not yet," I told her, I really loved dogs, big fluffy ones. This was no home for a canine, maybe when I found a new house. I could always sell the furniture. A good dog was almost as good as a good lover, maybe better.

Scott's big heart and big ego often collided; add some tough news and a few fingers of liquid refreshment—and I became his best friend. Maybe I was. He was an attractive man with liquid eyes and warm embraces, ready for a willing victim to consume. I was glad I had declined a late-night visit. I still thought of him as a married man. His ex, Maria, was as stunning as he was handsome. We had met a few times in Boston. Even though she was out of the picture, at least in geography, I was jealous of the tall beauty with dark chestnut hair that never frizzed or drooped. She played tennis every day in the summer, did yoga classes year-round, lunched with friends in designer duds, and never ran a vacuum or weeded a garden.

Scott seemed pleased to be a bachelor, boasting about his two black labs, his college-age boys, and his golf game, but never mentioned dates or other women. I had visited his home at an exec team celebration of the Milton Center's designation as one of the top hospitals in the country for orthopedics. Interior designers had transformed the rambling ranch into a showplace filled with glossy surfaces, fine art, and expensive rugs; the windows were so clean they didn't seem to exist. I knew his summer sons had gone back to college. Perhaps Scott was feeling melancholy, even worried about the Center and his reputation as its leader. This was more than a preseason football game; it was as if the playoffs just started, and the clock was ticking down to an unexpected end.

After a night of fitful sleep and dreams of front-page news stories, I got up early, hit the gym, showered, and dressed. I wore light peach linen slacks with a linen knit top, a long silver chain with an opal pendant—simple, elegant. My expensive hair, highlighted and trimmed to shoulder length was another post-divorce extravagance along with my white sports car and puffy white furnishings, covering my past in a spray of soft, pale immunity. I ran my hand over my empty left ring finger (an old habit), thought about my aunt and her collection of diamonds. and sighed. This was my new life. I headed to the elevator and walked to the Inn.

Scott was in an animated conversation with the young hostess, who seemed fascinated with the tall, dark-haired man. I wondered if he'd carefully planned his casual attire or yanked a few things in haste from his bachelor closet. Dressed in ivory slacks, soft leather loafers, and a short sleeve, dark-blue silk shirt, he was captivating—and he was my date. I tried not to forget he was my boss.

He spotted me quickly, grabbed me in his arms, and said, "Good Morning. This is such a great idea. Thanks."

I unwrapped from his clutches and tried to look relaxed. "Good morning. Scott. You're in a good mood."

"Why not, it's a beautiful day, and I'm with a beautiful woman."

I wasn't sure if he meant the hostess or me, but we both appreciated his compliment. She escorted us to our reserved table with a panoramic river view. Local culinary students worked in the trendy restaurant on weekends, and the meals were often exceptional. After our late-night phone call, I felt awkward and spent more time looking over the menu than necessary. Scott did the same. He ordered mimosas for each of us. How dangerous was drinking with the boss on a Sunday morning? My fleeting concern dissolved when the waiter returned with the bubbling elixirs. We clinked glasses, said, "Cheers" and lost our voices.

As the champagne softened our anxiety, we laughed, talked about the weather, and realized we were ravenous. It was an odd, romantic morning.

"Ann, about this Facebook comment, what should we do?"

"Scott, I wish I had all the answers. For now, I think we'll let it be. The bigger problem is the news story coming out tomorrow morning. If I know Bob, it will be at the edge of reality, pulling heartstrings for the sad family. He'll say Stratton and the Milton Center were the cause. The truth will be hard to find in this first news piece. We have to let this run out."

Scott sat back in his chair, his dark eyes searching the room, the view, then me.

"Ann, you seemed so confident in the meeting yesterday; what happened?"

"I've read a lot about the hockey player and his family since then. If I were writing this news story, I'd play up the tragedy, fill it with emotional quotes and accusations. We can expect a lashing. Are you ready?"

"I thought I was. I hope our reputation is strong enough to withstand this lashing."

"I'll put my money on you and the team. Milt must be on board. I hope Stratton can challenge this story without compromising patient confidentiality."

Scott seemed lost in thought, looking at the river hurling across the rocks in the distance, then turned to face me. "Stratton is the Center's big draw. He attracts top athletes, the rich and famous. Milt recruited him. I hope he knew what he was doing."

"This hospital's success is resting on your shoulders too, Scott. I'll try my best to keep its reputation as sound as possible. It may require tough decisions on your part."

"I know," Scott said as he sat back again and watched a group of tourists crossing into the park. The tour guide warned the parents to keep their youngsters away from the churning water; the children were eager to test their boundaries. He smiled at them, at me. The waiter took our order of eggs Benedict with a sauce of creamed shiitake mushrooms in brandy, not my usual morning meal. After a few more sips of our mimosas, Scott mentioned his meeting with Milt and Ian.

"Ann, Milt's worried about the board. He's its only physician, and some board members may not understand the surgical realm; it's another world, especially the intricate research done in our lab. I must admit I'm concerned about the board's trust in me as CEO. You wanted the spotlight—are you ready for this?"

I watched the champagne bubbles swirling in my mimosa, knowing Scott was waiting for some words of wisdom or at least reassurance. I looked past him, at the mist rising in the distance—it was a beautiful a new day. "Scott, I'm ready. I believe in your work, in your vision, if we are open with each other. I think the board will rely on your confidence."

He took my hand, his fingers tracing mine. It was a tender moment. Keep this professional. I was still recovering from a broken heart; I didn't need more damage. He took his hand away as if he could read my thoughts. "Ann, I understand. How about another round?" He signaled to the waiter who hurried off to the hidden bar, then looked back at me, changing the subject. "So, how's Julie doing?"

I'm sure my face lit up at the mention of Julie. "She's smart and funny and the love of my life. I miss her. Not sure she misses me—too busy enjoying her travels in Europe, meeting new friends. They stay at hostels, eat simple meals, say, 'magnifiqué' a lot—it's her new word for food, wine, and men. I'm happy for her, worried too. I can't turn her back into a whimsical 5-year-old, learning to read, climbing trees, sledding with her dad ..." I looked away, the memory raw, the mimosas exaggerating my emotions.

"Sorry, it must be hard. When Maria and I split, the boys were in high school. They blamed me for the breakup. I never told them their mother was in love with someone else for a long time. I suspected for a year or so until I finally confronted her. She didn't deny it. It wasn't until after the divorce was final that the boys forgave her and me. We seem to get along now. The boys come here all summer. Maria has them during the school year. Before we know it, they'll be off to see the world, like Julie."

Listening to Scott, I thought of how we both filed flight plans for similar life journeys. Unexpected turbulence changed destinations, turned us around. Despite plotting new directions, I was in the dark about the future; even Scott seemed adrift.

He talked about his boys, showed me phone pics of their touch football games, his dogs chasing tennis balls, and, finally, looked up, like he wanted to say something then changed his mind. He took my hand again. "Ann, thanks for everything. I need to get going. That little white ball is calling my name. I hope you have a good day… see you in the morning."

He left. I lingered on, finished my drink, watching wispy clouds and texted Julie. "Miss you. Love you. Mom."

CHAPTER 11

After a troubled sleep, I clutched a "Milton Center" promotional mug filled with black coffee and opened my laptop. The Buffalo News online feed was updating. I sipped the dark liquid, staring at my monitor. Google updates were focused on the presidential elections, the most unusual in my lifetime and apparently in anyone's lifetime; five minutes later, the feed came through. The headline screamed. I was sure it was 40-point type and top of the fold in this morning's print edition.

Lebeau's family claims hockey star's death due to Milton Center surgery; secrets abound
by Robert McCarthy, Buffalo News Investigative Reporter

Just days since his unexpected death, the family of Sabres' ace goalie Guy Lebeau is accusing the Milton Center for Advanced Orthopedic Medicine and surgeon James D. Stratton, MD, of murdering this vibrant father of two young boys, leaving his famous wife in agony.

Williamsville police continue to investigate Lebeau's death, waiting toxicology results. As friends mourn, some suggest his old drug habit may have returned.

Rescuers found Lebeau gasping for air last Monday in the bedroom of his home in Williamsville. His wife Michelle had just returned home from a photo shoot about 6 p.m. Their sons were staying at the summer home of friends for the week. The hockey star drew his last breath on the ambulance ride to Memorial Hospital. The medical examiner determined the preliminary cause of death was heart failure. Police said toxicology results will take several more days.

The News tried several times to contact the CEO of the Medical Center, Scott Marino, without an answer. Spokesperson Ann Delaney, a new member of the administrative team, issued a brief statement touting the medical center's flawless reputation and their requirement to maintain patient confidentiality. Until his death, Lebeau had been a healthy, rugged sports icon, leading his team to victory. Two months ago, Lebeau was admitted to the medical center for a standard knee repair to replace a damaged ligament. Stratton, purported to be a leading surgeon in his field, performed the surgery using pig tendon and other unidentified tissue produced from the bio lab at the medical center.

According to Raymond Lebeau, Guy's younger brother and family spokesperson, the surgery was highly experimental, and rejection of the animal tissue was possible. "Guy just wanted to get back to skating and agreed to have the surgery. It was one of those same-day procedures, and he was home a few hours later. It was too soon. He was in horrific pain, kept popping pills given to him by his doctor. Nothing seemed to help."

The hockey star tried to ignore the pain. "He was so stubborn," Raymond Lebeau said. "He called Dr. Stratton, who told him to be patient; the wound would heal, and he'd be fine. He wasn't fine. One day I came over, he was limping badly, and his speech was slurred. The pills were just making it worse. I think he had a major infection, and the drugs covered it up."

Stratton could not be reached for comment. A source close to the Milton Center told The News Stratton was angry and defiant. He was about to be ousted from the orthopedic specialty center for his arrogance following a confrontation at the medical ethics committee. Since Lebeau's surgery, the medical center has installed high-security surveillance systems, and security guards are visible outside the perimeter of the building.

Neighbor Jake Leone told The News he thinks the center is doing something illicit. "I'm not sure what they are up to, but it's not good," he said. "I noticed bloody bags of animal parts or who knows what carted away in a van at the rear of the hospital. Security is everywhere. This was beautiful farmland; now it's like Los Alamos—they're performing secret experiments in that lab."

Leone, an animal rights activist, has been a strong opponent of the medical center's construction on land taken by eminent domain to expand roadways next to his home, roads ultimately built to access the medical complex.

According to the statement issued by Delaney, "The Center conducted an internal review of documented infection rates, peer review analysis and a physical tour of all areas of the hospital." Apparently, all was in order, the statement read. "Reviews by the Centers for Medicare and Medicaid Services (CMS) consistently show the Medical Center's rates of infection to be in the normal expected range and in many instances, the lowest in the nation. Cleanliness rankings by our patients through Gallup surveys rate the Milton Center at the top of the rating system."

Delaney also cited the center's additional recognition for the mysterious lab activities. "The Milton Bio Lab is an acknowledged leader in the development of connective tissues and blood products used in the formation of new joints and ligaments, approved by the FDA."

Her statement ended with high praise for the staff without addressing the issues of Lebeau's excessive pain caused by one of its leading surgeons.

Meanwhile, the Lebeau family members are grieving, and are convinced Stratton and the Milton Center took the life of their beloved husband, brother, father.

Grand Island police also are involved in the ongoing investigation.

I let out the breath I had been holding while reading. Bob had filled this story with disparaging and false conclusions. He was manipulating facts and inserting the angry neighbor's claims, the same irrational neighbor who was the reason security was so intense. The Milton Center installed extra security systems years before Lebeau's surgery, when Jake Leone tried to ambush Scott coming out of his office on the sixth floor. Bob's fact-twisting was alarming. I knew he was unhappy dealing with a spokesperson, but he should have asked me about the neighbor and the family's concerns. He said Lebeau's wife was talking, yet his only quotes were from brother Raymond. Where did he get the info on Dr. Stratton? Who was this "close source"?

I warned Scott it would be rough. I thought of calling him then realized how early it was, so I texted instead. "Call me after you read the story. It's not good." My phone rang minutes later.

"Ann, what the hell! There are so many things wrong. It's slander; it's defamation; it's outrageous. I can't even think straight. We'll sue the paper, sue the reporter. Stratton will explode. God, this is awful."

The phone almost shook from his rant. "Scott, slow down. The family's interpretation is one thing … the police will work on that part. And our outlaw neighbor is another problem. I think we can get that under control. My real concern is the "unnamed source." Who is this?

"Ann, I haven't got a clue. I need your help with an internal memo, something reassuring for our team and the community. We've got to get our hands around this."

"I agree. I'll set up a meeting with the original team for 7 a.m. Does that work?"

"Yeah. Thanks. See you soon."

My morning run and breakfast were out of the question for now. I needed Alice and her organized brain. My call woke her up. It was only 5:30 a.m. She agreed to set up the conference room, get coffee and something for the team to eat. I emailed the key players about the meeting and forwarded them the news story.

By 5:45 a.m. I had multiple text messages from local TV news reporters wanting to get on the air for the 6 a.m. news cycle. I quickly responded. "These accusations are unfounded. We will provide more information after we have had time to review the blatantly false information and exaggerations in this news story."

I showered, pulled my wet hair into a ponytail, dressed quickly, not sure anything matched, packed my hairdryer in my tote bag, and sped to the medical center, my stomach growling all the way. Alice greeted me with steaming coffee and a cafeteria egg sandwich. She knew I would be fuming and not thinking of food. She also had the morning newspaper in hand with the damaging headline.

"Here's the hard copy," she said.

"Thanks." I read the whole thing once again. The impact of news in black and white was always more powerful. I threw the skanky newspaper in the waste bin, along with my half-eaten egg sandwich, wishing I could trash every copy of The Buffalo News.

The conference room was ready. We pulled our group together and headed to the sixth floor. Channel 7 ran the story at the top of its 6:30 a.m. newscast, liberally quoting The News piece and its manufactured facts. The slick morning news anchor, in his sternest voice added, "Spokesperson Ann Delaney provided a terse reply for a request to get the Milton Center's version of the story."

The smug newscaster hopscotched around the truth, omitting the "blatantly false" part of my statement from his morning report. The original Friday team slowly moved in; some seemed more shocked than others. Scott continued his rant from earlier this morning, stirring more than his coffee.

"By now, I believe you've all read the morning slander sheet. I'd like to put this Bob McCarthy guy on the football field and bash him into the ground. I can't believe the editors over there would let this run in any form, especially as the top story of the day. Ann, are you sure you want to be the spokesperson? I'm ready to take him on."

There it was: Scott questioning my ability with the rest of the group silent, sipping coffee, not looking at me. Here was the guy who hired me to do this job, shared late-night ramblings, mimosas, and friendship, convinced me to move away from everyone I knew. Now he was vacillating. I took a deep breath.

"Scott, I understand your concerns. I knew the story would exaggerate the facts; it's dripping with vitriol. We have to decide where to go, how to get there. I'm willing to turn my role of spokesperson over to you or the board chairman, be as supportive as I can be, but I have years of experience talking with media. It can get dicey. For now, let's be objective about a response plan. We'll need to send a message to our staff and patients."

He mumbled something in Italian under his breath. "Fine. Let's get started."

While I was speaking, Alice downloaded the news story into a word document and separated the sections, numbering each, then projected it on the screen at the end of the conference room. Her teeth were clenched, and she almost knocked over her coffee. I smiled, hoping to ease the tension in the room, wishing I had not gulped down half an egg sandwich.

"Thanks, Alice. Let's look at each issue. The first section deals with the family's accusations that Dr. Stratton did surgery with animal tissue that potentially produced an infection or rejection that led to excruciating pain. Then, Dr. Stratton prescribed strong medication to obviate the pain. An overdose of the meds plus the potential infection led to a heart attack and death. Is there any truth in here?"

Everyone in the room looked at each other, reluctant to share that they even knew the rather bullish James Stratton. Apparently, he was guilty of poor employee relations but, I hoped, not poor patient care. Finally, Dr. Rogers spoke up, referring to a chart on his laptop.

"I haven't talked to Stratton about this, but I went through the medical record. This is confidential, for this room only. He performed an ACL repair—replacing the torn ligament with a pig ligament—a procedure he has done hundreds of times both here and at other medical centers. This method has become almost a standard, although sometimes thought to be experimental." He caught his breath and our attention.

"According to the record, the anesthesiologist administered a medication during surgery that would have quelled the pain after surgery and for about three more days—one of those new, approved, long-lasting meds. They excised the torn ligament, cleaned the knee cavity, and prepped and attached the new ligament. The procedure was 47 minutes long, the patient went to recovery, and was conscious and alert within the next hour. He did not complain of pain, said he was starving. He was given apple juice and crackers—also standard. By 5 p.m. that evening, he had had a full meal, was up walking, with crutches, and was discharged. One of his brothers picked him up and thanked the staff for great care."

"Is there any mention of infection or rejection?" I asked.

"I don't have Dr. Stratton's personal records, but if there was any infection, it would have happened within the next week. He would have returned for additional surgery. There's no record of his return. Regarding the ligament used, I think Lukas may have more information."

Lukas seemed uneasy, but he offered some information. "Our bio lab is a pristine place. I know I've said that before, but I can't say it enough. All animal tissue used in the lab is put through a rigorous cleansing system that prevents rejection but maintains function. And, Ann, there are no bloody animal parts anywhere—we carefully package and preserve everything. It is a delicate process, one we've mastered. Actually, it's the hallmark of our institution. I believe Dr. Milton will attest to that."

Milton pushed his chair back with his long, thin fingers, thanked Lukas, and expressed his view. "Based on the facts that the patient did not return within that week with evidence of an infection or displaced ligament and, based on my own conversations with Dr. Stratton after the procedure, it was successful—one of his best outcomes, as he described it. I spoke to him earlier this morning; he was fuming. Reporters have tried to call him. His staff are running interference. He's also concerned they may come to his home, follow him. I hope, for his sake and theirs, that doesn't happen."

Scott stood up and went to the far end of the room, gesturing to the talking points. "Let's leave Dr. Stratton for a moment and go on to the other points here. We've met Jake Leone and his wife Claire before. They're the reason we are hyper about security here. For a time, Jake drove his pickup over the island with a hand-printed sign on the back tailgate that said, 'Milton kills animals and people.' We tried everything to get him to stop. It all came down to his First Amendment rights. They're card-carrying members of an animal rights group. It's odd since their family once owned a cattle farm. All that's left are fields of hay."

"Thanks, Scott," I said. "I believe the real reason behind their bullying is the loss of their land. It happened before Milt bought the land for the medical center. The Island wanted to expand the highway to bring business and revenue to the town. The Leones blame us."

My inner Pollyanna had thoughts about placating Jake. It was worth mentioning. "Scott, I think Jake will use this accusation of murder to vent his anger with his failures in life. I suggest we ask Jake and Claire to come in to discuss their concerns, take them on a private tour, see what we can do to support them."

Board Chair Dave Brown spoke up. "I think he's just a kook. I'm not sure it will help. It might make things worse. Scott, you've met him once. What do you think?"

"I did, but it wasn't a friendly meeting. He came to the dedication ceremony in his grubby overalls and work boots carrying another sign that said, 'Milton Center is a group of high-priced trespassers.' I stopped my remarks and asked him to be quiet. He got even louder. I had security take him out."

"Have you talked to him since?" I asked.

"A few times. Jake's a complex, angry man. He once told me he fought in Vietnam. They drafted him and some close friends. Jake was the only one who came home; he got a chilly reception from an anti-war nation with no thanks for his service. I guess some wounds haven't healed."

We needed to move on. Our next concern was the anonymous source. As I pointed to this section of the display, Scott said, "Stratton is a member of the ethics committee—that's public knowledge. They all sign a confidentiality agreement. I doubt anyone of them would be the source."

He explained the structure. "The chairman of the ethics committee reports to the president of the medical staff. If needed, they can bring in other members of the staff, clergy, even family members to get more information."

Milt spoke up after weighing everyone's contributions. "I don't believe the ethics committee has dealt with issues surrounding xenogeneic implant. If it helps, I'll talk to the chairman. I'm sure he's aware of the story by now."

Jen reminded the group of our legal responsibility to patient privacy and security. Without cause and patient permission, even docs and medical staff leadership should not access patient records. We needed to be careful. The meeting ended after we agreed to reconvene at 2 p.m. In the meantime, I would work with Scott to compose a letter to our employees for distribution via email at noon, attach the letter with the lunch menu for visitors and post it in the lobbies throughout the building. A heartfelt message from the CEO could mollify the accusations in the morning news and give Scott a spokesperson's role in the next news cycle.

CHAPTER 12

Scott and I walked down the hall to his office, heads bowed, each of us thinking about the Milton Center's reputation and our own. Our employees and patients needed the truth. Every word counted. Scott's confident air and inner bully faded as we entered his office. His actions or inactions were already being scrutinized. Twitter feeds were challenging his leadership, suggesting arrogance, even cowardice. Reviews on our Facebook page were still in favor of Dr. Stratton's expertise, something I thought we could use to our advantage. The negative comments from Jake's animal rights comrades were matched by outraged pet lovers.

It was only 9 a.m. on Memorial Day. Most folks were heading over to the nearby state park for family outings and cookouts. The outside temperature was rising. I could see a clear sky and bright sun across the Island spreading rays of light across Scott's laptop screen. Slumped in his executive desk chair, he scanned the news story once more and asked, "What now?"

"Let's work on the letter to patients and staff. Ideas?" I asked.

"This story is pure fiction The newspaper doesn't give a damn about the truth. Looks like sensational headlines and misleading information sell papers—a dying industry, by the way," he yelled at the walls.

"That might not work," I said, raising my pen from the still blank page in my notebook. We needed to reassure employees and patients about our high-quality care, a fact the news story neglected. Fighting back with our quality data was useless; even a list of hockey stats would have more impact. After a few scribbled notes, I looked up to see Scott glaring at the headlines on his computer screen.

"Scott, the most important thing you need to do is sound sincere and troubled by the wild accusations dished out by The News. While the story talks about ethics, the entire article is an unethical attempt to diminish the character of this institution."

"What about Stratton?"

"We can't discuss details of the patient's care. We can emphasize Dr. Stratton's strengths as a surgeon treating players from major sports, Olympic athletes, and weekend warriors."

Scott got up and walked toward the windows without speaking. He rubbed the back of his neck, shrugged his shoulders, then faced me with a look of concern. "Ann, what if Stratton did something irregular in surgery or gave this hockey player oxy or worse? What if he contributed to his death?"

His questions left me reeling. "Do you believe that?"

"If I can question his actions, what do you think our employees, patients, the press, and the police are thinking?"

He was right. We needed to be cautious not to judge him and, at the same time, not claim his innocence. I needed to sharpen my word choices or rather his word choices. "I think we can say we're confident any accusations made about his care of patients will be inspected by local law enforcement, the medical staff, and regulatory agencies."

Scott didn't respond, sat down, and scrolled through the story again. News vans and greedy reporters were lining up outside the hospital entrance; we needed to get this letter done. I suggested I take a stab at writing it up and come back with a draft in half an hour for his review. Scott nodded and agreed to call Milt and Dave Brown about our plans. I left him brooding in his dark leather chair.

Thirty minutes. Fast writing was a skill I learned as a young reporter when deadlines were minutes away. An anxious editor once told me when I was staring at a blank screen too long, "Just tell me the story."

To all employees:
This morning in The Buffalo News, a reporter wrote a front-page story attacking the Milton Center for Advanced Orthopedic Medicine. I read it at 5 a.m. and fumed.

My first thought was, "How could this happen?" I have never read anything so biased, misleading, and filled with egregious errors. The story seemed to attack the very heart of this great hospital, filled with caring staff and expectant patients, patients who want to go home, better for coming here. I know the great work we perform every day.

Regarding Mr. Lebeau, we mourn with his family at his death after an amazing career. Information regarding his medical care at Milton is and will remain confidential. An investigation by police is ongoing and should proceed without conjecture.

Our neighbors, Jake and Clair Leone, have been vocal about their personal opinions before and since the Milton Center opened. We admire their commitment to strong beliefs; however, we know our approach to using animal tissue in human joint repair has had powerful benefits for our patients. Our center is proud of the work of Drs. Stratton, Milton and King in establishing a pristine Bio Lab. Patients come from the entire East Coast to receive the innovative techniques that curb pain and produce amazing results.

Another troubling aspect of today's news story was the reference to an unnamed source. We admonish The News for using unnamed sources—a practice they once criticized other news media for adopting. It is sad to read such a twisted version of the truth, smearing reputations without proof of wrongdoing. We are proud of the work of our Ethics Committee that serves as a sounding board for patients and staff to raise issues, discuss consequences and determine next steps in a process. We will not discuss Ethics Committee sessions nor their outcomes. As patients and community members that may someday have ethical questions, we hope you understand the value of this committee and the need for privacy.

We welcome your questions and comments in response to today's news story or future news stories and have set up a special email address and phone number below. My sincerest thanks to all our compassionate staff and our patients who come to Milton for care. - Scott Marino, President & CEO

I read it over, made some grammatical improvements, and handed it off to Alice and Matt for their first reactions. They thought I spent too much time on ethics and not much on infection but otherwise agreed it was heartfelt. I adjusted the letter making sure it was only one page. Before heading to Scott's office, I stopped by security and asked them to corral the media into an area away from the main entrance with a visual of the nameplate across the front door. I remembered being shoved around as a reporter, placed outside a hospital looking for a good photo background other than a parking lot or blank cement wall.

As soon as we approved the letter, sent it to the board, and printed it for patients, I planned to distribute it to the media at the press conference. I saw Bob holding court at the gathering and thought it might be a good idea to let him see the letter first via email. I also thought I might meet with him in private. I hoped he wanted the truth just as much as we did. Since the weather was warm with a light breeze, we set up an outdoor press conference.

CHAPTER 13

Scott's manicured football throwing hands held on to the letter like a lifeline to his future. He took his time, nodded a few times as he read it. "Ann, nice job. I sound caring and in charge. Don't know how you do it. Hope it does some good. Thanks."

I could see some of his angst melting and noted a faint smile perhaps, or maybe it was just a sigh of relief. We inserted his signature in the digital copy and began the email process. The board received it first, followed by all staff. We distributed a printed version to all departments and nursing units for patients; an enlarged copy was attached to poster boards displayed at all entrances. Alice took charge of creating a special email address mentioned in the letter and implemented the "hotline." I sent a copy to Bob, then opened the door to the media frenzy. ESPN pushed their cameras in front of the local TV outlets, convinced a murder had happened here. Security had set up a podium and sound system at my request a few minutes earlier.

"Good morning, I'm Ann Delaney, VP of Public Affairs for the Milton Center. I have a letter to distribute this morning from the CEO Scott Marino; the same letter we gave employees and patients in response to The Buffalo News story reported by Bob McCarthy. To maintain a consistent flow of information, Mr. Marino and the board asked me to represent the hospital as spokesperson regarding the issues raised in this morning's news. Blatant errors and unfounded accusations filled this front-page story constructed to sensationalize the sad loss of a well-known sports professional. I appreciate your quest for the truth and will answer your questions as accurately as I can, within the limits of patient and staff rights to privacy. Please move away from the main entrance to allow patients and families access for care. Thank you."

The ESPN reporter yelled out, "Mrs. Delaney, tell us more about animal blood and what happens in that secret bio lab?"

"It's Ms. Delaney, thank you. I will be glad to set up a tour of our facility, including the bio lab—at least the exterior. The walls are glass, and you can see what our scientists are doing. It is a sterile environment. You can also walk around the perimeter of our hospital. I'm sure our exterior is as spotless as the hospital is on the inside. Thank you."

Just as I finished, I noticed pings and rings with reporters pulling out their vibrating phones. From their conversations, I understood a preschool bus filled with kids had crashed on Main Street in downtown Buffalo. Traffic was being diverted. Except for ESPN and Bob, they dashed off to cover the next catastrophe. They'd return when the chase for that story was over. I was thankful that the Milton Center was a specialty medical facility without an ER although we were equipped to manage orthopedic trauma.

I remembered covering a story of a crash on I-90 years ago in Tonawanda. Several people were injured and sent to Kenmore Hospital. Their ER was chaotic. Security never noticed when I slipped into the center of the action. They brought in a little boy, maybe 3 or 4, sobbing, with blood dripping in rivers down his tiny face. He wanted his mom. A terrified woman with a badly broken arm ran down the hall to him. "Hey baby, you're going to be okay; everything will be okay," she said, even though she knew his dad did not make it. I wrote that story with my eyes blurry from crying.

Jake and Clair Leone were milling about with a small group of people, ready to step up to a mic, any mic. Most of the media left before they had a chance. From prior encounters, Jake knew the rules about trespassing on private property. I doubted he shared them. The plotters clustered near the remaining journalists with their heads bent, as if they were in a huddle planning the next play.

Alice stepped up to the podium, flustered by the magnitude of this morning's news. "Ann, this hotline is overwhelming us. We need more extensions and some tips on what we should and shouldn't say."

Alice's feet were on the ground when mine were barely touching. "Sorry. I'll be right there. Look at the Leones—they're up to something. I guess we'll find out soon enough."

Alice and I cobbled together some talking points for the staff answering calls related to the news story. I blurted out my thoughts as she typed away. "The information regarding the Milton Center and allegations concerning Mr. Lebeau are blatantly false. The rest of the news story is misleading and inaccurate. We appreciate your concern and assure you our patients and families are receiving the best possible care for their orthopedic issues. We invite you to address your concerns, in writing, to The Joint Commission, our accrediting body. Thank you."

Laurie and the quality team might cringe at my suggestion to contact The Joint Commission, but I knew most people would not take the time to write them and, if they did, it was important to address each one.

The reception desk phone rang when we entered our office. The digital readout said, "Executive Office." Alice answered the call. "Ann, Scott's on his way down. You need to turn the TV on."

My office was equipped with an HD TV to monitor breaking news, although it was seldom used. I found the remote in a bottom desk drawer. As I pressed the 'On' button, Scott walked in. He twirled my guest chair around, grabbed the remote, and turned up the volume. They were broadcasting Lebeau's funeral. It was barely a week since his death, yet it seemed like months ago. April Martin from WKBW Channel 4 was outside St. Barnabas Cathedral when the family of Guy Lebeau exited the funeral service.

Michelle Lebeau, in a form-fitting black suit, black hose, and large-brimmed hat, gripped the shaky hands of her two boys. They looked so young and vulnerable. Their dark curls and deep-set eyes mimicked their famous dad. The cameras were merciless, zooming in on their tiny distraught faces. The boys did not know where to look nor how to escape the media horde and throngs of well-wishers. Behind Michelle were Guy's brothers, Raymond and Pierre, hands clasped in front, wearing dark suits, dark shirts, black ties; their eyes scanned the sidewalk for comfort or distraction.

April's whispered voice filled my small office. "Now, coming down the church's steps is the entire Sabres hockey team. It's an amazing show of support for Michelle and her family and a very sad day for Sabres fans." The station's sports reporter joined April in calling out the names of team members as they passed, even though their names were emblazoned in broad letters on the backs of their blue and gold jerseys. Coaches and an unending line of family and friends followed.

The scene shifted to the Milton Center's front entrance and April's earlier report. She read from Scott's letter to employees. "Regarding Mr. Lebeau, we mourn with his family at his death after an amazing career. Information regarding his medical care at Milton is and will remain confidential. An investigation by police is ongoing and should proceed without conjecture.

April added, "As you can see, the Milton Center denies wrongdoing in the death of Guy Lebeau."

I turned the TV off. "Whew! That was better than I expected. They even used a quote from your letter and didn't editorialize."

Scott leaned back. His fingers combed through his hair, and his dark eyes were distant. 'I guess you're right about the letter—so far. I don't like the drama of a funeral attached to any reference about the Milton Center."

"Those little boys look so much like their dad," I said. "I can't imagine how Michelle keeps them from falling apart; they were so stoic. And the team … in jerseys. Pretty powerful."

Scott nodded. "Those boys remind me of my own sons when they were younger, keeping them still for a moment was hopeless. Those little guys barely moved."

Scott spoke up first, asking me what to expect next. I filled him in on the phone line and the Joint Commission notification. I could hear Alice behind me, clearing her throat to get my attention. I turned away from the TV and motioned for her to come in.

"Ann, security is looking for you. It seems our friends the Leones have some big signs. They're picketing outside the hospital entrance."

"Great, that's all we need," Scott said, jumping out of his chair. I smiled at his reaction, understanding why the board chairman had agreed to give me the spokesperson role.

"Best if I work with security for now, Scott. We can meet with the Leones when things settle down," I said, unsure when that might be.

CHAPTER 14

Picketing seemed like such an old-fashioned method of raising a stink. With instant news through Twitter, Facebook, or live video feeds, complainers had so many more ways to communicate. Yet, I had to admit handmade signs carried by disgruntled activists would get attention. In a way, it was better. Social media was too hidden, anyone could open an account in a fake name, rant and rave and stir emotions while remaining invisible. Jake and his pals craved publicity. I was fairly certain their picketing action would not turn into a major protest. Most families I knew had pets, ate meat, and were not concerned about saving whales or polar bears from extinction; they loved cholesterol-packed bacon and eggs, if only on Sundays. I wasn't sure of the depth of Jake's activism, so I asked Matt, my cyber guy, to do some deep-dive research, then I called security.

About eight people were milling around, not sure what to do, carrying poorly lettered signs "Milton bleeds animal blood," "Million-dollar CEO hides from truth" and "Come to Milton to die." I asked security to call the police and have them escort the pickets to public property outside the hospital entrance and let them know they could not obstruct traffic. I also asked security to monitor the employee entrance and check on the helipad. As a referral center, most of Milton's patients came from long distances, often by air. A Milton Center helicopter service picked them up at the airport in Cheektowaga and flew them to the center, a 20-minute flight. The helipad was on land owned by the Milton complex.

Out-of-town family members were invited to stay at the Milton Inn, adjacent to the main building. It's Fresh Restaurant, open to the public, was a farm-to-table venue, featuring an array of local produce. Ice wines from Niagara-on-the-Lake and local vineyards shared a separate menu. Due to earlier concerns from the Leones and other vegans, the restaurant did not offer beef or pork dishes. It did concede to using animal products produced locally by grass-eating cows and goats—yogurts, cheeses, milk, and eggs from free-range chickens. In the past three years since the restaurant opened, it had earned awards and weekend reservations were a must. The Best of Buffalo food critic gave it a "thumbs up" in a Buffalo News feature, highlighting its gluten-free specialties. I guessed the pickets didn't care.

After Scott left, I slumped into my desk chair and dropped my head into my hands. What a day. Murder in the morning, a funeral in the afternoon, and pickets brandishing "bloody" posters warning patients they could die. It was all bizarre. When my phone rang, I was relieved to see the caller was George Gonzolas, our chief security officer. A sweet man with a tough exterior, he was the only guy on campus who called me Annie, just like my dad once did.

"Hey, Annie, are you okay? Wasn't sure you were there."

"Hi, George. I'm fine. What's up?"

"Sgt. Burke from the Grand Island Police is on his way to your office."

"Thanks for calling in the police." I was worried about our patients and employees seeing those cardboard signs about blood and dying. I looked up to see a young police sergeant, hat in hand, knocking on my door jam.

"Ms. Delaney, I'm Sgt. Charles Burke from the Grand Island Police. We actually met once before in a security training session. We were doing an 'active shooter' in-service."

"Yes, of course. Please come in." He was so young. I could tell from his smile, he sympathized with us. He wore pressed blues, a black leather holster, and his shoes reflected the lights in the room; he was the antithesis of Bob McCarthy in so many ways. I stood up to shake his hand, aware of the gap in our ages. When he pulled out a chair for me at my small conference table, I knew his mother had taught him good manners, reminding me I was old enough to be his mother.

"Please call me Ann," I said to reduce the formality and years between us.

"Interesting day, Ann. This whole thing about Lebeau is shocking. Chief Schuller is working with the Williamsville Police on the preliminary investigation. Looks like drugs were involved in some way, but we don't know yet. Lebeau was such a great goalie. The Sabres and their fans will miss him. As far as Mr. Leone's concerned, we've dealt with him before. I think everything's under control."

"Good to hear."

"The protesters were a bit grumpy," he said. "They moved onto a public road, just outside the entrance; only a few are left right now. That could change, of course. Some TV vans came by, took some video. I saw a guy with a press badge talking to some of the protesters, Buffalo News, I think it said."

"That would be Bob McCarthy; he's a stealthy one. You might want to watch out for him."

"No one else stopped, although I did see an employee in a nurse's uniform shout out to them: 'Go home - this is a great hospital.' I had to laugh, and I agree too. Did some damage to my ankle last year, and Dr. Stratton straightened it out. I was back to work in no time." He looked a little embarrassed for being so candid, grabbed his hat, and stood up. "I can't imagine this protest will last too long. We'll keep an eye on it."

"Thanks, Sergeant. I'm glad we can call on you. I hope it doesn't become a big problem."

We shook hands and he left.

As I walked into the main hallway, I noticed my nemesis loitering near the main elevator banks. "Hey, Bob, can I help you?"

"Oh hi, Delaney, I was … er, just visiting a patient," he said, in a quick but not too smart response.

"Really? What room is he or she in?"

"I'm not sure. I think it's on the sixth floor."

"You should know our sixth floor is the administrative area. Does that patient happen to be Scott Marino?"

"Okay, okay. I thought I'd see if the old quarterback might be in. You know his letter is a puff piece. I need some real reaction to this Lebeau murder."

"Listen, Bob, I could call security, but let me buy you some coffee instead. I could use your help."

"Love to have some of that pricey Starbucks stuff you sell here."

It was close to 3 p.m. and the lunch rush was over. The dietary staff was cleaning up, moving chairs and tables into place. Bob seemed grateful for the attention and free coffee. He poured packet after packet of sugar into his cup as I watched in awe. It was probably the only calories he had all day.

"Look Bob, I want to work with you, not against you on this Lebeau story. I'm sure your bosses are pushing hard to get more. I understand."

He looked up, more interested in the coffee than me. "So?"

"We took the piece you wrote this morning apart, piece by piece. Lots of fiction, especially the animal blood. Really?"

"Hey, I have my sources," he said, not too anxious to share more.

"It's completely false. I bet those sources are the Leones and their groupies."

He added more sugar and kept stirring. "So, what if they are?"

"You covered the original meetings when the Island decided to expand the highway, take some of the Leones' land. I read your stories—not too biased like the stuff you wrote today. Do you think their land loss is the real reason they're making this fuss?"

"Thanks for the journalistic accolades. They're out there now, marching, so it's a news story—no fiction involved."

"Are you covering it?"

"Yeah, so…"

I nodded as he finished his syrupy brew and looked up.

"The News is not keen on covering pickets," he admitted. "It's boring. I predict it'll be over soon. Not sure Jake is going to be quiet. He'll find other ways to anger the big boys running this show."

"Thanks."

"Del, this doesn't stop the story on the hockey star and his untimely death. That bioethics claim is real. Stratton's in serious trouble. Heard he cancelled all his cases today. Maybe he's feeling ill. Killing people can do that to you."

I was amazed at Bob's insider knowledge. Who was he talking to? I sensed Scott and Milt were holding some things back. If they wanted me to be spokesperson, I needed more information and their trust. It took me years in my last job to get that level of trust. What was I thinking when I agreed to leave it all behind, taking on this new challenge? I almost forgot Bob was still sitting there.

"Hey, remember me? Did you see those small boys at the funeral service? They need to know how their father died. I'll keep pushing until we have the real story. Thanks for the coffee and sugar. I'm on deadline."

CHAPTER 15

I dialed Scott's direct line. It was after 6 p.m. Secure in his inner chamber, he picked up after the first ring. "Scott, I need to see you."

"Sure, come on up, I'll unlock the front office door."

The sixth floor was deserted. The rest of the team had left for the day to head home, stop for dinner fixings, open doors to warm surroundings, giggling kids, and welcoming hugs. My family wasn't home anymore, even though I carried them around in my heart. I swallowed my melancholy and opened the door to Scott's office.

He was marching around, leaving deep footprints in his thick rugs. He stopped when I walked in. I thought for a moment he might give me one of his bear hugs, maybe I wanted one, needed one. He smiled.

"Tough day, huh?"

"You could say that." I moved over to the window; traffic had slowed down; the sky was the warmest shade of blue hinting at sunset. He moved next to me, quiet, waiting.

"So, what's up?"

I turned to face him. "Scott, I need to know what happened in the bioethics committee."

"Is this about the unnamed source?"

"Yes, and more. I need to know what you know. Scott, you can trust me. I can keep a confidence. This is serious. Someone in here—at prestigious Milton Center—is filling Bob McCarthy's battered notebook with confidential information."

He motioned for me to sit in one of his guest chairs as he sat on the opposite sofa. "You're right, Ann. I should have been upfront about this.

We have two problems. One is the confidential nature of the committee; the other is the person leaking this information. And, for the life of me, I can't connect any of this with the death of Guy Lebeau."

"Let's start with number one."

Scott filled me in on Dr. Stratton's review before the committee. It happened soon after he began his practice at the medical center. During his credentialing process, Stratton provided information to the medical staff committee about an accident he'd had while skiing in Aspen in the '80s. Scott looked up, his dark eyes shadowed from the lingering brightness behind him.

"Jim was on a semester break from medical school. He went skiing with some friends and his fiancée. They hit some slick ice, lost control, and careened down the slope. He ended up with a massive compound fracture of his left leg. His fiancée swerved off the trail to avoid hitting him, smashed into a tree, then hit her head on a rock; she didn't make it. Jim lost a lot of blood waiting for the ski patrol. He would have bled out, but a Medivac team rushed him to the nearest hospital. It's amazing he survived. He had the best orthopedic care available at the time and a transfusion to keep him alive."

"What a tragedy."

"That accident is probably the reason Jim spews so much vitriol, seems angry at the world. It's why he changed his specialty track from radiology to orthopedic surgery. The transfusion is also how he contracted HIV… AIDS," Scott said.

I looked up from my notepad, stunned by this late-breaking news. "I had to ask you about this? You never thought I might need to know about the accident, the AIDS? Scott, what were you thinking? Bob knows this or at least he knows somebody else who knows. Jesus."

Scott turned away, looking out at the dimming skyline, not sure what else to say. I wasn't sure of the implications of an HIV-positive orthopedic surgeon on our staff, I'd look that up later. Who had raised a concern? Was it a patient? A staff member, a surgeon? The possibilities kept colliding in my mind.

"Scott, who complained to the bioethics committee?"

He looked up, rubbing the dark stubble along his chin, as if considering his options when there was only one answer.

"I did."

"What?"

"Ann, listen... it wasn't really a complaint; it was more of an ethical concern. I was the new CEO here, needed to get the committee's reaction. Not so many years ago, we considered AIDS highly contagious. It is blood-borne. If a surgeon cut his hand during surgery ..." He paused.

"Don't stop there," I said.

He got up and trudged around the room. "Ann, please ... just listen."

I sat back, crossed my arms in defiance. "I'm listening."

"A lot has happened to treat AIDS in the last 30 years. The new medications are close to miraculous. Many people, including Stratton, have no detectable virus left. I know he can be gruff, but he was straightforward with the committee."

I still had a look of disbelief on my face. "Wow. You hired me to put this center in a positive light—get good stories. You know, I have no trouble telling the truth; it's the damn lies that bother me."

He walked over to the window, looked away. "I haven't lied to you. God, I never thought. This AIDS issue has nothing to do with Lebeau or the lab. That ethics meeting was a tough one. Stratton was so cold, measured, giving us the most private details of his life until he mentioned his fiancée. He sat there, whispered her name, got up and left."

I could almost forgive the righteous CEO for his omission after hearing a trace of emotion in his voice. "For what it's worth, Stratton must have recognized your need to know or he would have walked out the door and the medical center that same day. I doubt he's the one talking to the reporter."

"I agree, makes little sense. I'm baffled. Everyone impressed me on the committee. That was three years ago. I don't know how this became public or who blabbed to the reporter. Believe me, Ann, it wasn't me, either."

"I believe you. Guess I'm just disappointed and confused."

Something was still missing. I asked Scott to get me a list of all members of the ethics committee since the center had opened. Scott assured me he would follow through.

"Ann, sorry for not thinking this through. What else do you need?"

I stood up and moved across the room to the door. "I need you to trust me; give me the whole story, not just bits and pieces. It feels like I have to pry things out of you."

"Sorry."

"I get it. I'm sorry too. It's been a long day. I'm sure Bob's covering the funeral and the family's accusations again in tomorrow's story. I need to get out of here for a while."

"Would you like to have a drink somewhere?"

"Not tonight. I have a lot to think about. Good night."

Even though I was furious with the not-quite-so-charming CEO, I kept thinking about the man I'd never met. Jim Stratton was an enigma. He must have had a tough time in medical school dealing with AIDS, an untamed contagion associated with men having sex with other men. No wonder he was quick to react, protective of his reputation. The first AIDS positive patient treated at my former hospital years ago had everyone anxious, especially the direct caregivers despite standard precaution vigilance. The nursing supervisor called me one day to let me know we might get a media inquiry. It was a reportable disease, and we assigned our hospital a "1" after the number of cases being tracked by the CDC in our state. I did not want the patient's name, thanked her for letting me know. It wasn't long before "1" became "2" and "2" became "4". Other area hospitals had similar counts. As the medications expanded, the inquiries diminished until, at some point, no one asked. I hoped they would not ask again.

It was getting dark as I left my office. The sunset was deep in the sky ahead of me as I drove on the Niagara Parkway to my snug apartment where wine and chips would tide me over until the next morning and Bob's story of the day.

CHAPTER 16

After a restless night, I got up about 4 a.m. The sun hadn't made its way above the horizon yet. I booted up my computer, checked The News website, nothing. I made coffee and toast, checked again—it was the top story of the day.

"Milton denies involvement in Lebeau death while family mourns loss," the headline read. The story began with a dramatic description of the bereaved family and the young boys "looking so much like their dad," and continued with more drama. "Michelle never lifted her head as she clutched Raymond's arm." Bob had somehow grabbed a new quote, or had one in his pocket, from Guy's brother.

"We blame this on that arrogant surgeon," Raymond said. "He can't even fix his own limp." I would have written the next sentence the same way. "The entire Sabres hockey team, dressed in blue and gold jerseys, stepped in time to the young family leaving the church awaiting a long line of black limos."

Once again, Bob mentioned Scott's hiding behind me and quoted parts of Scott's letter. The picketing story was a sidebar. The photo of the Leones holding inflammatory signs ran across two columns. Bob's story was brief; the photo said it all.

Near the end of the piece, he zeroed in on Stratton. "Dr. Stratton has refused to talk to The News or have the spokesperson offer excuses for him. A source within the hospital said the accused physician canceled all his surgeries yesterday. The hospital has not addressed Dr. Stratton's ethics committee review, citing confidentiality issues. Their silence is alarming."

Bob was the hero of his own make-believe world. His dramatic descriptions, arrogant questioning, and use of "accused" instead of "alleged" made powerful copy. He was standing at the top of a slippery libel slope. There must be legal action we could take. Scott called. It was 5 a.m.

"If I didn't know better," he said, "I'd have cried at the sad story. What do we do now?"

"We need to plan an offensive move, not sure yet what it is. I think we should use patient letters, some positive Facebook comments. We have lots of patients praising the good doctor. I really need to meet this man. I'll stop in after I gather more information for a statement."

I texted my team to find positive patient quotes we could use before heading out for the day. When I arrived at the center, I walked past my office and went down the hall hoping our compliance officer, Laurie was in early. Besides Scott, she was the only person on staff I knew before I joined the team. We had met years ago when she was a practicing family doc, and I was a fledgling journalist writing clumsy healthcare stories in and around Buffalo. She taught me a lot about medicine and how physician choices in meds, tests, and procedures could make a difference in the health of a community. I couldn't believe this pixie of a woman was a nationally recognized leader in quality data analysis. Scott had worked his magic recruiting her to the Milton Center. She had access to internal files and meeting minutes, and she headed the information systems security department.

As I entered, she adjusted her frameless glasses and scooted back from her double, flat screen monitors to give me a warm smile. "Ann, how're you doing? I read The News this morning. Lots of accusations, not much proof."

I nodded. "I'm fine, thanks for asking. The reporter pushed the emotional side of the funeral. I would've done the same thing. The problem is the way he blames us for this hockey star's death. Like everyone else, I wished the investigators had the results of Lebeau's drug tests. Do you know Dr. Stratton well?"

She motioned for me to sit and closed the door to her small, neat office. It looked like she never used paper, although she had a tall file cabinet behind her gleaming desk.

"Not sure what you want to know. I met Jim three years ago when we opened the center. He's highly qualified. I think he's always trying to be better—better than anyone. His surgical methods are innovative, and his outcomes are outstanding. He works closely with Lukas in the lab, perfecting implants and creating probiotics."

She paused briefly as if not sure how much to reveal. "Personally, I think he's not really a social animal. I've never seen him linger in the physicians' lounge or go to the café. He only attends medical staff meetings to give a report, then leaves. I guess you could say he's a loner. He can turn the air blue swearing. He may be a Jekyll and Hyde because his patient surveys paint him as a kind and gentle man. Not sure I'm helping here."

"I've already experienced the mean, angry Dr. Stratton, thank you. I don't think he's impressed with anyone without an MD. I think he's only impressed with himself. He told me he was the 'best god-damned surgeon' in this place, then he hung up. It would help me if I knew more about our esteemed doctor."

Laurie seemed to hesitate a moment, then pushed back her chair and took out her key ring to open the file cabinet. She lifted a manila folder and placed it on the desk between us. I could see the name "James D. Stratton, MD" on the label.

"Ann, I trust you will use this information carefully. You cannot quote, copy, or remove anything, but it will give you background."

"Thanks, Laurie. I assure you I will be very careful. Is there anything in here from the ethics committee? Scott already told me about the ski accident and HIV."

She seemed surprised. "He must think it will get out or has already. That meeting happened about three years ago. Only a few members of the medical staff were there and, as you know, sworn to secrecy or I should say committed to confidentiality. I don't think too many people around here know about it. Jim was no longer considered a transmission threat." Laurie leafed through the file. "The ethics committee agreed he didn't have to reveal his background to patients or staff, wanted nothing to impede his practice at our center. As far as I know, his secret's safe; he's been under treatment for many years. I think we based his crankiness on latent anger about the accident."

"Scott mentioned his fiancée died. One of the happiest days of their lives ended in a tragedy."

Her voice softened. "I think part of him died, too. I'm frankly surprised he continued to pursue a medical degree, especially one so invasive. He's treated an impressive list of athletes and entertainers who've come here for his surgical expertise. Most of the time, we don't even know they're here. At their request, we give them fake names. Not that unusual."

Laurie explained the Milton Center's discretion policies. "Patients may sign in with an alias—a practice not really that uncommon, even in community hospitals. The Milton Center is almost paranoid about patient privacy. That's why we attract so many famous or soon-to-be famous athletes. It's rare to have someone like an Angelina Jolie be open about surgery."

"I understand. At my former hospital, we had a few 'John Doe' patients, usually because they were politicians or prisoners."

She laughed. "We get the famous and infamous too. They sign a contract with the treating surgeon, who agrees not to use their real name. Their actual patient records and insurance forms have the correct information, a unique patient number—but patient-list-boards use the alias."

"Laurie, I understand the need for confidentiality; that should apply to the ethics committee too. How is this reporter getting insider info?"

"The only people who get the meeting minutes are the committee members, the CEO, and the board's quality committee."

"Who's on the quality committee?"

"It changes every few years. When we started it was Dave Brown, the board chairman, Dr. Milton, Dr. Rogers, Scott, and me. We invite others based on the agenda. I feel like I can rule everyone out. There's no way Scott would do this. Dave doesn't have a medical background. Milt surely doesn't want bad news, besides he's Stratton's partner. And Ian—he's been willing to step in to find the culprit. I'm at a loss. Sorry, Ann."

When Laurie turned around to read through her emails, I looked through the file and found the minutes of the meeting in which Stratton explained how he had acquired HIV. Scott was there, Ian Rogers, and Jennifer from legal was a guest of Dr. Stratton. Milt chaired the committee. They turned the agenda item, entitled "surgical update" over to Dr. Rogers. He told the committee the CEO had made a request to discuss Dr. Stratton's background and potential ethical issues that could come up during his tenure. Dr. Stratton circulated a 1984 medical record from Denver

General Hospital, covering his emergency treatment of a complex compound fracture and the administration of two liters of blood. Blood tests had not yet been developed to identify HIV. He then passed around a 1985 medical record indicating his blood had tested positive for HIV. As medication cocktails were developed to treat the disease, Dr. Stratton said he could produce subsequent medical records showing his HIV levels had tapered off and no longer registered in a blood test. He left the meeting following his emotional testimony.

Jennifer reviewed state rules and regulations regarding health care workers and HIV. In 2011, New York state did not require physicians to inform patients or colleagues about the infection—it was a voluntary process. The members of the committee briefly discussed Dr. Stratton's circumstances and unanimously agreed on his admission to the medical staff with full privileges.

I closed the file on the mysterious Dr. Stratton and handed it back to Laurie.

"Thanks. I can see how this information could get out of hand if Bob or any other reporter got a hold of it. Bob's curious and sneaky enough to do some undercover work, stir things up. Maybe he's trying to show how Lebeau contracted HIV from Stratton during a surgical mishap. Is that even possible?"

"I doubt that. Even if Lebeau tested positive for HIV, his history of drug abuse would likely be the cause."

"You're probably right." There was nothing I could use to distract Bob from this part of the story. I wanted to know his source; it was a problem almost as concerning as who caused the hockey star's death. "Is there anything else you think I should know?"

"That's the only file I have on Stratton and ethics," Laurie said. "They only discussed it at that one meeting. And speaking of meetings, I have one shortly. Are you all set?"

When I'd first entered her office, she seemed content to chat. Now she was a little uneasy, shifting in her chair, looking past me at the door. She straightened up the papers in the file and placed it in her secure locked cabinet. I thanked her, suggested we have lunch in a day or two, and left.

She knew something, or suspected something, but she wasn't ready to tell me.

CHAPTER 17

The Facebook comments were too good. "Dr. Stratton is remarkable; thought I might never run again after a knee injury..." "Thank you, Dr. Stratton and the Milton Center. I could barely walk from arthritis—now I can move without pain—a miracle." "5 stars - U R best."

It was as if we told patients what to write. I checked the names with medical records and asked the supervisor to get me their phone numbers. After a few calls, I realized the patients were real and still gushing with accolades about Dr. Stratton. A few complained about long waits: "I waited hours to see Dr. Stratton. He may be the best but if you can't get in, it doesn't matter." "I gave up and flew home—very disappointed." Most of the patients who were unhappy had returned, but no longer shared their feelings on social media.

My team tabulated the scores for Facebook comments about Stratton, and came in at 4.7, higher than any other surgeon on staff. We then looked at his patient satisfaction scores—consistently in the 90th percentile, far above other docs on staff. Written comments were similar but unidentified because the survey participants were confidential. Surveys often brought out the most-satisfied, and the least-satisfied patients; people in the middle rarely commented or even returned their surveys.

I gathered my ammunition to craft a statement of support for Dr. Stratton, trying one more time to reach him. His office staff treated me like the enemy; I was not even sure they understood my role at Milton. One staffer even told me not to call again. "We're not helping anyone tarnish his reputation," she said before hanging up. For some odd reason, they believed

I was looking for a scapegoat, a way to blame Stratton while still praising the Milton Center. I tried one more time with another angry loyalist. "Leave Stratton alone," she said, "without him, your precious Milton Center is done."

A veteran reporter like Bob would scoff at a news statement loaded with solicitous social media comments. He could read our Facebook page and Twitter feed on his own and probably had. None of the comments would stall his propaganda. My thoughts floundered for a few minutes until I considered calling Dr. Milton. It was risky. Even though he was Stratton's partner in practice and founder of the center, Dr. Milton had not impressed the local media. They called him "arrogant" in one older story and "secretive" in a feature on the bio lab. One described him as, "Darth Vader without the black cloak and light saber."

Calling the office, he shared with Stratton was useless. They'd already given me the runaround. They probably wrote my name on post-it notes with a message, "Do not put Ann Delaney through." Maybe, if I scheduled a knee replacement, I could get their undivided attention. Since my knees were still in good shape, I asked Scott's administrative assistant Mary to have Dr. Milton call me. A few minutes later, he phoned to let me know he was in the lab completing a project. He would meet me in my office. An hour later, he slipped through my open door and paused until I looked up. His voice was barely audible.

"You wanted to see me?

"Dr. Milton, yes, thanks for coming down. I need your opinion and some help. Please come in."

He seemed tense, plunging his lanky fingers into the pockets of his starched, white coat. "Sure, what can I do?"

He nodded when I asked him if he had read The News story but did not offer a comment. After a few awkward moments, I tried again. "I spoke with Scott earlier—5 a.m. We need to come up with a positive statement about the center and Dr. Stratton's work here. My team assembled some recent Facebook and patient survey comments," I said, spreading out the comment sheets around the table.

He read each one, then looked up. "What can I add?"

"Dr. Stratton gets remarkable scores, even higher than other orthopedic docs on staff, and his patient volume seems higher too. What makes him so different?" I asked.

Milt sat down at the table, joining his hands, looking like a man about to pray. After thinking about what he would say, he asked to review anything I would use from his comments. He preferred I take notes rather than record our conversation. I agreed.

"Dr. Stratton and I studied at the Stanford Clinic in California. That's where we practiced some very innovative techniques. They challenged us to treat orthopedic medicine like the next venture into outer space," Milt said, pausing again to gather his thoughts. "After we completed our fellowships, we went in different directions until I recruited him to work here. Jim created new surgical procedures, new medications and herbal uses, even new ways to implement mind over matter. He takes risks, but they seem to be worth it."

He looked back down at the comment sheets, then continued his narrative. "My path took me into the realm of research, seeking ways for the body to repair itself; it is amazing science. Alas, it takes me away from the surgical suite too often." He paused again, then continued, "I guess you could say Dr. Stratton is a skilled surgeon who looks at arthritis and joint injuries as challenges to overcome, not just treat to relieve pain. He transforms these troublesome maladies into highly functioning systems within the body. It's quite remarkable."

Dr. Milton spoke with an underlying cadence, as if assembling a fine piece of music, note by note. I hoped I could read my scribbling after he left.

"Thanks. Your last few sentences will be perfect for this statement and reassure patients and their families we care about them. And, we don't murder people here."

"Do you think this will appease that reporter, Bob, right?"

"Yeah, it's Bob McCarthy. This will help. I'm afraid the story will go on for a while. I'm also concerned about the inside source the reporter wrote about. Do you have any idea who that might be? Why he or she would do this?"

"Ah. Another topic. Sorry. My expertise is all about bones and joints. I really can't help you there."

"I understand. Thanks again for coming down, helping me out. I really appreciate it."

"No problem. Thank you for doing your best in a difficult situation."

He slipped out as silently as he'd entered and left me with a rare compliment. He was as mysterious as Dr. Stratton, but at least he did not berate me, swear, or refuse to help.

CHAPTER 18

It took a few hours to get Scott and Milt to approve the newest statement before emailing it to Bob and other media outlets. Milt wanted to be referred to as Dr. Milton on second reference rather than Milton. I complied even though I knew the editors could change it to his last name only. I had run into this early in my career with a general surgeon who called me at home around 11 p.m. to let me know he was a doctor and should have been referred to as one throughout a news story highlighting his new surgical procedure. I told him I would forward his concern to the editor. Ego is a powerful thing that doesn't care what time it is or who it browbeats. About 10 years later, after a difficult news series about a young woman's claims of sexual harassment by a male physician were found to be false, I convinced a reporter to write a story exonerating the physician. Dr. Ego, the senior partner in the accused physician's practice, stopped me in the hall, months later, bent down, and said, "Ann, you did a great job handling that story—they don't all turn out that way. Thanks."

He walked on. I stood there amazed and still cherished the moment years later. I wasn't sure Dr. Milton was as enamored with my journalistic genius even though he approved the rest of the news release, including his description of Stratton as a remarkable man. I guessed Milt knew how to do some PR hustle when needed. His name was on this facility. I'm sure he wanted this news event to melt into history.

The pickets continued to mill about the center's main entrance road, their tattered cardboard signs still readable and accusatory. Only a day old, their righteous showdown was in slow motion. Scott Marino could walk rings around these guys. How quickly they became background. I wondered how long their outrage would last.

I passed admitting on the way back to my office. Unlike years ago, when patients provided personal health information in teller-like lines, the Milton Center's admission department offered privacy in a secluded area, connected to our helipad via a frosted-glass walkway. Patients could wear Milton Center hoodies as they departed the flight to access the tunnel. Patients arriving by car accessed the center via another tunnel with a proximity parking gate operated by a special phone app. Although Milton did care for a few trauma patients suffering multiple fractures, it did not have an emergency room open to the public; all patients were pre-admitted using a unique form containing their thumbprint and patient ID number.

The Milton Center relied on such technology to streamline patient care and assure privacy. I thought about my conversation with Laurie earlier and wondered if Guy Lebeau had been one of our covert patients. Dr. Milton knew more but wasn't sharing. Even though Laurie seemed to know a part of the story, I thought it best to check with Jennifer, our in-house lawyer. I texted, "Can we meet around 4 or 5? Need info on patient contracts."

"Sure - stop by around 5."

Jennifer welcomed me to her sixth-floor haven, not far from Scott's office. The wall behind her desk displayed a Columbia law degree surrounded by multiple awards in thin black frames. Photos of her three children and smiling husband covered a long walnut credenza behind her desk. She loved them deeply, often proclaiming, "I'm so blessed," although her blessings came with some regrets. In a rare moment away from our offices a few months ago, we had skipped out of a boring legislative session on right-to-know laws to enjoy margaritas at a nearby restaurant. I shared my family saga, efforts to get pregnant, the sadness of all the losses, the joy of adopting Julie, and the ache of leaving Todd.

"You know Ann," Jen said, "when I graduated, all I could think of was a career as a defense attorney. Marriage was out of the question until I met Rick. He was a prosecutor—well known and respected. We married after living together for a few years. Never wanted children, just the good life, whatever that was. Once I started in health care law defending docs, my income soared. Rick's barely moved, yet his workload grew heavier. Somewhere along the way he changed his mind, wanted a family and offered to be a stay-at-home dad. It took a while, but I finally agreed and, well, now I have three reasons I keep working and he stays home."

"I'd say he's a keeper. I wish Todd had that kind of commitment."

"Rick's a special guy, but deep down, I worry. Does he regret ending his career for mine, or worse, will I regret it?"

"I hope that never happens. I regret leaving Todd sometimes but couldn't live with some of his decisions, so now I have to move on."

"You're right. We both need to move on. I wonder if they missed us in that stuffy meeting. Glad you're part of our team, Ann."

Grateful for her recent friendship, I was impressed with Jen's expertise in medical malpractice, having spent half of her career on the other side, defending docs against hospitals, against patients, against each other. The board understood the need for an in-house lawyer to manage intricate research contracts and to defend the center's innovative procedures and bio lab breakthroughs.

I closed the door behind me and sat across from Jen and her family photo.

"Thanks for meeting with me. I know it's late. I don't want to keep you from dinner, homework, kid baths, and, oh, that hunk of a husband."

"He is good looking—and mine, by the way," she said, turning to smile at the precious pics.

"Don't worry. I get into enough trouble around here on my own."

"So, what's up?" she asked, once again the consummate professional.

"I have a few questions on our admissions and patient contacts. I'm familiar with the standard HIPAA requirements and patient security promises. We go beyond that, am I right?"

"We do, and I'm sure you want to know why," Jen said. I nodded in agreement.

"As you know, we're a not-for-profit medical facility, open to treating anyone with an orthopedic-related medical problem. We don't accept walk-in patients, although we would in extreme circumstances. That gives us the ability to get more information ahead of an admission from their treating docs or the patients themselves. When Dr. Milton created this advanced center, he put in some extra steps to make sure we had the most secure patient environment we could. Too many hospitals are targets for ransomware hacking and resulting blackmail. Most of them pay up, too."

Jen admitted patient privacy was a quagmire. Even though paper records were tedious and often misplaced, electronic records and errant laptops seemed ripe for hacking.

"We believe the Milton Center's uniqueness is a model for other hospitals. A digital admission application uses this information to schedule tests, office visits, surgery, and the discharge process before the patient ever arrives on campus."

"I'm impressed."

She explained the steps involved, if I needed access to the electronic system information. "After I review the patient contract to determine if your access would be appropriate, I would contact our forensic technicians to set up a review session."

She noted the contract is both oral and written, included fingerprints, and, if patients approve, a video conversation with the treating doc before agreeing to treatment or surgery and after treatment to discuss the healing process.

"We can use portions of this contract video, with patient permission, for marketing/PR purposes."

"How do you keep track of patient identity?"

Jen shifted in her seat, ready to delve into this area. "Some patients—well-known athletes, entertainers, TV hosts—are people who don't want the world to know they are having a new hip or knee joint or any of the degenerative issues associated with aging, especially if the world thinks they are on top of their game and 10 years younger."

I understood their motivation for secrecy and their willingness to do anything to stay the aging process for a few years. "So, Jen, how do staff handle this?"

"Well, all patients get an ID number, some use a unique name, not all are Jane or John Does. The lab, nursing, techs, therapists always use the admission name when addressing the patient and may or may not know if it's fictitious. They may recognize the person, but they use the name on the patient list; it's part of the agreement to protect patient confidentiality."

"This system may be one reason we attract so many people from outside our area."

"Exactly. It underscores our core business," Jen said. "We offer advanced healthcare from admission to discharge. How's that for a marketing message?"

"Not bad. I'll keep it in mind."

Her friendly smile vanished. "Ann, let me ask you a question. Why do you think The Buffalo News is so intent on discrediting the Milton Center and Dr. Stratton?"

"I'm trying to find out. Since you mentioned Dr. Stratton, what do you know about him?"

Jen sat back in her chair, looking unsure about how much to reveal. "He came to us with glowing recommendations from former medical practices and in particular from Dr. Milton. They're old colleagues. He brings in lots of revenue. Patients love him. Odd too, if you've met him; he would seem very hard to love."

I only knew the hard-to-love part. "I've only talked to him on the phone. Told me to leave him the 'f' alone. I've tried meeting with him since then and planned to wear my flak jacket, but his office staff was uncooperative. I don't know if he has a lawyer; he probably should—someone like you even."

"From what I hear, he has a lawyer. Not sure he's listening to him. Looks like he's trying to ride this out. I don't think the media will let him."

"There's a lot more going on here. I doubt he's responsible for the hockey player's death."

"I hope you're right, Ann."

Jen checked her watch, I knew my time was limited, but I had one more question. "Do you have any idea who the unnamed source might be?"

She leaned forward. "Damned if I know. Everyone on the ethics committee is solid. Could be a staffer or a disgruntled OR nurse. Don't know."

"Maybe I can get the reporter to give me some hints."

"Good luck with that."

I picked up my notebook and pushed back my chair. It was time to leave. "Thanks for seeing me, Jen. Give Rick my best."

"Out," she said, a frown mixed with a smile, as she got up and opened the door.

"Not to worry. I appreciate your help. I've one more stop before I get out of here today."

Her happy, intact, family photo seemed to smile at me as I left, reminding me of my family, torn into three pieces. The best photoshop in the world could not put us together again.

CHAPTER 19

Before heading out for the day, I swiped my ID badge to enter the security office. George was scanning the center's parking lots, watching the picketers. A few were walking around, holding signs, trying to engage visitors. He sent two uniformed men to escort the animal righters off Milton land, packing copies of the rules for picketing.

George hid his fearlessness in a short, round frame I knew was more than capable of dissuading a wrongdoer. His strengths were personality, smiling eyes, and charming women, especially his newest granddaughter. He was my tour guide on my first day at Milton, showing me all the public and private spaces, including the OR suite, oblivious to the hustle of stretchers and carts being wheeled around us. He knew his way around. I trusted him to guide me.

"Hey, Annie, I can't believe these guys. They know they're not supposed to be on private property. If they don't stop, I'm going to ask the cops to set up a perimeter; it may be costly, but this is getting out of hand."

"I'm sorry. I feel like I'm responsible. Do you have a minute to talk?"

"Anything for you. What can I do?"

We moved into his cramped office, where computer screens surrounded his desk. He shifted stacks of paper from two metal chairs onto the floor so we could talk, then closed the door. Static and security jargon filtered into the room from officers checking in from their outside rounds. The bank of monitors alternated between camera feeds covering the exterior entry points and interior hallways. George seemed oblivious to the sounds and sights around him.

"Do you know the last time Guy Lebeau was a patient here? His name doesn't show up on patient lists."

"He was probably using an alias," George said. "I don't blame him. Hockey players injured during the off-season are not a coach's dream. I remember seeing one of his brothers coming in from the visitors' parking lot one day a few months ago, May or June. I'm not sure. I thought it was the younger brother, Pete, or Pierre. He's a little shorter."

"This wasn't a hockey injury?"

"I doubt it. Last season was over and this one hadn't started yet. He was an amazing goalie. Hard to believe he won't be playing again."

"I've heard that a lot," I said. "What's the best way to get more information on that admission? The reporter isn't sharing."

He shook his head. "It might be tricky. You know—HIPAA and all. I guess you could check with Laurie or Dr. Stratton, even though he hasn't been here for the last two days. Who do you know who can get you access to medical records?"

"Scott?"

"I doubt he can get them. He'd have to work with someone from information systems."

"Thanks. I'll check with Laurie. How old is that little one now?"

His grin made me smile. "She's 6 months—a real beauty. Thanks for asking."

I left the building, grateful we did not have an ER, a place I knew was rarely empty and too often chaotic, filled with emotions and held breaths. A nurse once told me working in the ER felt like a choreographed dance; everyone knew their places, where to stand and when to move. Patients may miss the eloquence of it all, but even they played a role in every unfolding scene, some without happy endings. The Milton Center had its own stage and players, with electronic systems replacing people found in traditional hospitals; yet people like George and Laurie, and so many others, understood the nuances of protecting and caring for patients—something on-screen forms could not capture.

I passed the men in blue as I crossed to the employee parking lot. Our protesters were gone, for now. Before starting my car, I checked my emails and text messages. Bob sent me a terse "thanks" for sending my earlier statement with another request to talk to Scott or Stratton—anyone but me. I needed to know what Bob knew about that accident that injured Lebeau.

The setting sun cast shades of pink and purple across the sky. The evenings were becoming cooler. September always felt like a new year. Kids were back in school, the lazy days of summer were over, life moved faster. I took an alternate route home, passed by my old high school before exiting the turnpike.

Niagara Catholic High School was still there with a few more additions. I wondered if the Mercy nuns were still running things. Sister Mary Stella, my favorite, taught English and encouraged me to write for the school newspaper. She was as round as she was tall and wore a more contemporary version of the nun's habit, exposing her short grey hair and round red cheeks. Our meager news staff gathered after her class, beating out the news of the day on sluggish word processors that were barely better than the electric typewriters they replaced. We cut and pasted our printed stories to fit layout boards—shearing off the ends, hopeful the who, what, why, where, when and how were in the lede.

By the time I graduated from college, electronic page design systems and a mouse click had replaced manual cutting and pasting of copy. I laughed at the memories and thought Bob would be overwhelmed at the extra effort it once took to produce the news. During our meeting yesterday, he pulled out his mottled notebook from his back pocket and jotted down a few words, relying on his memory or the record button on his phone to get the info right.

I stopped at DiCamillo's Bakery for takeout pizza and drove downtown. The sun had ended its day as I parked my car in the underground garage. My stomach growled as I took the elevator to the 14th floor. The white pizza was thick with olive oil and fontina cheese. I poured a glass of Chianti to add to my Italian feast and opened my laptop, thinking about Lebeau and the accident that brought him to Milton.

George was too vague about the date he saw Pierre, but I remembered reading that the Lebeau brothers grew up in a small village near Montreal. I searched for stats on Sabres games for the previous season. Their last game was at the end of May. If Guy Lebeau was in an off-season accident, it may have happened at or near the family farm. I sent a text to Matt asking him to research Lebeau's social media accounts and to check the local papers for potential police logs.

Just as I was closing my laptop, my phone rang. Todd. I had not talked to him for a few weeks, not sure if the Lebeau news had caught his attention. He was an avid hockey fan. As much as a divorce and geography kept us apart, invisible threads stitched us together, unraveling so slowly, I thought I might never be free.

"Hi, Ann."

"Hi, Todd."

"Not sure you knew. I'm coming to Buffalo next week for the health care conference at the Hyatt speaking on the ACA and its impact on hospitals."

"I read the program schedule. Are you traveling alone?"

"Do you think I would call you if I wasn't?"

"Never mind," I said, not wanting to talk about his or my love life, especially since I didn't have one. More neutral territory, such as our daughter's escapades, was an easier topic. "Have you talked to Julie?"

"Yes ... well, not exactly. She doesn't talk; she texts. I think she's in Italy somewhere, eating pasta and drinking anything but water."

"She's on a tour of Rome, learning about art and the Renaissance. You're right: she's probably given up water."

"So ... I've been thinking about you lately ... busy time?"

"I've been busy learning about hockey."

"Those stories about Lebeau made the Boston papers; it's hard to believe the family's claims. Care to share any details? Almost forgot—you're the secret keeper, HIPAA and all."

"You got that right. See you next week."

He seemed cheery enough, even seemed to know where his daughter was. Maybe we could be friends; it was the lover part I missed. The last time I saw him was the morning we sold our home to a young couple. We each signed the paperwork without speaking, handed over the keys, and left the attorney's office. My SUV was stuffed with things I hadn't sold, donated, or put into storage for Julie—a box of old photos, a pile of clothes thrown into the back seat, my laptop, Kindle, and a scraggly green plant that defied death so often I had to keep it. Todd had opened the door for me, tears in his eyes.

"Ann, I'm so sorry. I still love you. Please, forgive me?"

I swore I wouldn't let him get to me, yet I sobbed, took deep breaths, could barely speak. "Todd … I'll always love you. I need to move, be on my own. Please don't make it harder."

He held my hand, then closed the car door. As I drove away, I looked back; his watery blue eyes followed me until I turned the corner. He called every day for a few weeks until he slowly let me be. Time was healing the rough edges of our emotions; meeting him again might stir them up.

The conference was paying Todd to talk about the Affordable Care Act and its impact on hospitals and the medical profession. I missed the financial wiz more than I should. Todd and Scott had worked on an outpatient surgical venture just before Scott left Boston. He never quibbled about Todd's exorbitant consulting fees, always called him the health-care guru, just as he did during my interview. When I told Todd I was moving, working for Scott, I sensed a trace of jealousy when he said, "Hmm … always wondered about those long nights you spent working with the CEO." I shook my head at his insolence, told him, "It's a professional relationship, Todd," then threw in, "unlike some of yours."

CHAPTER 20

Milton, Stratton, and Lebeau were missing from the front page the next morning. A reprieve? Dramatic weather changes announced with graphics of a hurricane swirling along Florida's coast, heading north, dominated the news. My relief ended as I checked "Letters to the Editor." The protestors, upset with minimal coverage, had submitted a letter from the organization's national leader. I doubted if he had ever been to Grand Island, New York. He reiterated the group's concern about using animals in research, even lambasted the Milton Center for offering eggs on its patient choice menu. It was pure folderol. I doubted it would deter patients from choosing Milton for their care. The next letter was more concerning.

Secrets abound at the renowned Milton Center. The basement of this pristine place is filled with more than research. They mingle animal and human cells to concoct knee-caps and shoulders by Dr. Frankenstein. Cauldrons of unknown ingredients brew addictive potions to cover the pain inflicted by its famous surgeon—no wonder a young, vigorous athlete met his untimely demise in the grip of fentanyl-laced heroin. The lawsuits have just begun. - David Martín, Esq., Buffalo, NY.

Assuming this Martin guy was a lawyer, why would he jumpstart the legal process with a letter to the editor? This was the first reference in print about the drugs that killed the hockey star; the police had not released this, although they suspected an overdose had caused his heart attack. Neither the Milton Center nor Dr. Stratton had been served notice of a suit. The "pain-inflicted" reference was close to the statement made by Raymond

Lebeau as quoted in Bob's first news story. Scott had suggested the family was hoping for a big payout through malpractice suits, targeting both the hospital and the surgeon. From patient feedback and our data, though, Dr. Stratton's patients were close to pain-free, even after knee replacement surgery. None of these accusations made sense, and the lab reference hinted animal activism went deeper.

It was just past 6 a.m. when Scott called, fuming about the reference to Frankenstein. "Who is this Martin guy? Where did he get all this?"

"I have no idea. Maybe Jen knows or can find out."

"We haven't even been sued—not yet, anyway. I'm not surprised at the lawsuit mention; in fact, I've been expecting something. Jen and our regional legal team can handle it. I doubt they will want us to respond to media once the suits are filed."

"Really, Scott? What the lawyers want and what makes sense may be very different. I think we should keep responding. We can use statements to be sure we are on solid legal footing, but no comments will make us look like we're hiding something. I'll be in around 7; let's get a meeting with Jen. Plus, I need to talk to Lukas. This Frankenstein stuff is too graphic. We need to respond. See you soon."

As I entered the employee parking lot, I spotted Lukas trudging in to work. I often wondered how he never bumped into anyone or anything. Maybe he had hidden antennae in his scruffy beard. His heavy briefcase pulled his shoulders and head down with the weight of its contents. He never looked up. I did not want to distract him in an open area; instead, I emailed him with a request for a meeting, adding "ASAP." I texted Scott to let me into his locked outpost and took the elevator to the sixth floor, stopping by Jen's office, and asking her to join us.

"Hi Ann, this must be about that letter in this morning's paper. I'm sure that Frankenstein reference sent you over the edge."

"That and a few other things. Let's check in with Scott."

Dark clouds drifted past the windows in Scott's office; that east coast storm was getting closer. Scott plunged into his desk chair and gestured for us to sit across from him without saying a word. A good morning greeting seemed inappropriate, so I mentioned the pending storm.

"I hope it's just bad weather we're talking about," Scott said as he turned to Jen. "Who is this David Martin? As far as I know, we haven't been sued, right?"

"No, nothing's come across my desk," Jen said. "I've heard nothing from my attorney colleagues. We expected legal action. As for Mr. Martin, I'm checking. In case you didn't notice, it's early for a lawsuit; the patient only died last week. I did a quick search and found several "David Martin" listings. It could be a fake name or someone who hasn't practiced law in a while—or he might be from a Canadian firm. Not sure."

After a few minutes mulling over the letter's language, I asked Jen and Scott about the lab. "Are we doing anything experimental in our lab?"

Neither Jen nor Scott spoke for a few moments as if they were unwilling to share a secret. Scott broke the silence.

"That depends on your definition," he said. "We're a research facility. Our scientists are working on several grant-funded programs that may sound, well, they might sound unusual. I know you're planning to talk to Lukas. He can give you all the details. Make sure he knows you're on his side."

"Then tell me what you know. I'm not the enemy here."

"Okay, Ann, I'll do my best. Most of the research revolves around stem cells, human and animal. We use human stem cells to regenerate joint cartilage and pig ligaments for repairs like ACLs. It's not that new. Pig valves have been used for many years successfully in heart surgery. I'm sure you already know that."

"Yes, I am aware."

Scott rifled through a stack of files, selecting one labeled "Bio Lab contracts." He pulled out a news clipping from a recent scientific magazine. The article noted the Milton Center Bio Lab was part of an international project with sites in Tokyo, London, Stanford, CA, and other centers to grow human cells in animals, hoping someday these centers could grow human organs for transplantation.

"Ann, look at this. It's amazing science," Scott said. "They've had actual success with rats. It's also unnerving to most non-scientists, religions, and animal activists, so we are fairly secretive, or should I say quiet, about the whole thing. We're years away from anything remotely useable. And, just to be clear, our patients are not part of this study."

Jen had reviewed the contracts and agreements with the bio lab, limiting their role and what they could discuss about the project. "It's difficult to explain. Based on the contract, we are not at liberty to discuss details of the project," she said.

It seemed Mr. Martin had already crossed that secrecy barrier for us, and Bob, the newshound, would be the first to ask about mixing animals with humans. "Well, we need to find a way that won't violate the contract but still allow me to explain what's happening. He'll imply our recently deceased hockey player was injected with animal parts or even worse, his cells are now living in a rat or a cow or something. My God, what are we into?"

Scott looked at me like I was an alien. "Ann, you're overreacting. Let Jen check out this letter writer. She can dig up more about our research contracts and limitations. Let me know when you've met with Lukas. I'm sure you want to respond to your pal, Bob."

"I do. We need to craft a statement for our employees first. They read the news and might wonder about our secret experiments. Only a few employees work in the lab; the rest are taking care of patients, getting quizzed about making Frankenstein monsters in the basement."

CHAPTER 21

To call the bio lab a basement wasn't fair as it was a high-tech, highly secure facility. My thumbprint and eye scan gave me access to the central corridors, well protected from snooping competitors and mischievous reporters. Lukas was waiting at the entrance to take me into his tomb-like office. I felt a little like a groundhog tunneling in for the winter. I supposed it made him feel safe from the vultures like Bob and, perhaps, me. The only light came from computer screens. His hands were sweating, and he kept his head down, avoiding eye contact. He was nervous.

"Lukas, I know you are uncomfortable discussing your work. I also think you are superb at what you do, and everyone I've ever met believes you are an extraordinary scientist."

He looked up, his round face flushed. "Thanks, Ann. I expected you to call or visit. I almost aspirated my toast when I read the letters to the editor. Our work is so extraordinary and far-reaching, but it must be confidential—if not, our competitors will get ahead of us. Or worse, our whole center might risk losing grant funding or being shut down. Our research has made such a positive difference in orthopedics. Who wrote this?"

"I don't know. The editors should check on the senders to verify names and addresses, but I doubt they do. The name David Martin is common, and in a city the size of Buffalo, it would be almost impossible to find him. He signed it "Esquire." It could be a lawyer's tag."

"What should I do?"

"I need to know everything about your research. Scott gave me a cursory review and suggested you could give me more details. Jen already warned me about the contract language. Remember, I'm covered by the same confidentiality agreement you signed."

Muttering to himself, Lukas ruffled through some thick files in his briefcase, pulling out three worn folders marked "Confidential." He handed me a few pages, then clasped his soft hands as he explained the contents.

"These articles cover evidence-based data. We are fortunate to be part of the latest study on interspecies organogenesis. The letter in the paper was right: we are mixing human cells with animal cells—at the microscopic level. In places where they've been successful, they destroy any resulting viable organisms for obvious reasons."

He caught his breath, then continued, "The world isn't ready, nor are the scientists, to evolve the process until they know more. Please understand, we're not making animal people or people animals. This is not a Frankenstein movie."

"Good to know," I said.

He explained the long-term goal of finding new ways to create organs for transplantation: growing livers, hearts, and kidneys from human cells inside animals to be harvested to save lives. People on waiting lists for human organs from donor bodies, or people about to die, wait a long time and rarely make it. The study organizers chose the Milton Center as a site because of its successful work with xenogeneic ligaments for joint repair.

I thanked Lukas, headed back to my office, and began an online search of interspecies organogenesis, trying to dispel my thoughts about alien creatures emerging from test tubes. As logic and evidence set in, I drafted a response to the Martin letter in the form of a statement to send to Bob and other reporters.

The Milton Center is dedicated to advancing orthopedic medicine, much like the major advances in the past few years in cardiac medicine. Our Bio Lab uses FDA approved xenogeneic (animal) ligaments to help repair torn human joints. This process is similar to one used in patients needing new heart valves; you may have a friend or a family member who is alive today thanks to a valve replacement using pig valves. This procedure began over thirty years ago. We are proud of our Bio Lab's successes in probiotics, herbal remedies, and the exciting development of non-opioid pain relievers. While they may be known by other names, the Milton Center Bio Lab prefers we call these lifesavers.

I headed back to Lukas's land for his review.

"Ann, this is great. I love the part about lifesavers. Best to have Scott review and Dr. Milton, too; he's always so worried about grant funding. Most of this innovative research is Dr. Stratton's baby, even though Milt claims to be the principal investigator on all the grant applications. Those two are the oddest couple, always avoiding each other. Stratton's work is brilliant. Good luck. I wish this whole thing would go away."

"Thanks for your help. I'll go find the big boys."

Scott was doodling on a notepad, listening to a long-winded, one-way conversation on his cell phone. When he saw me enter, he told his caller he would get back to him.

"Ann, I was just talking to Dave Brown. He's livid, as you can imagine, and the board members have been calling him. They want a meeting, today if possible. After reading the letters, I think they realize the damage this is creating. Please sit."

I slipped into the chair opposite his desk, sensing his frustration. "I'm not surprised. Look at this statement Lukas approved. I noticed Dr. Milton in Jen's office. I'd like them to approve the statement, too."

After scanning the statement, Scott said, "You've learned a lot since we met this morning. It looks good. I thought you never responded to letters to the editor."

"I'm not using this as a letter. I'm sending it as a statement to Bob and other inquisitive reporters. We could make it a letter format from you— get your name in the news. What do you think?"

"Either way is fine. Should we wait for the board meeting? I'll try to corral them for a lunch today. Can you make it?"

I agreed to come for the lunch meeting and picked up my clippings and laptop. Scott came over and put his arm around my shoulders. "Don't look so glum. I still believe you are the best at this. Thanks."

I didn't flinch at his partial embrace. His warmth was comforting, per-haps more than appropriate. Scott was such a puzzle. I wanted to shake him for the things he did not tell me. Yet, I welcomed his support, physical and emotional.

We needed to move on. Jen reviewed the statement and agreed to come to the lunch meeting.

CHAPTER 22

My phone vibrated as I took the stairs down to my office, my only form of exercise that morning. At the door to the first floor, I listened to Bob's voice message. "Delaney, I hope you read the letters to the editor this morning. Call me."

"Damn," I whispered in the empty stairwell. As I entered my office, I glanced at the plaque on my door, "Ann Delaney, VP of Public Affairs." It was polished metal, denoting an experienced professional, capable of creating positive communication strategies. What happened to that Ann Delaney? The current one served at the pleasure of a sleazy reporter in yesterday's clothes who seemed intent on ruining our reputation and for a CEO who too often left me wondering what else should I know.

My phone pulsed again, this time from a welcome caller, Police Chief Lance Schuller. "Hi, Chief."

"Hi, Ann. I'm sure you saw the letter. We got the lab results late yesterday. I can't figure out how this Martin guy knew the results, but he's right. Lebeau's heart attack resulted from fentanyl-laced heroin. A lot of people had guessed something like this, but it seems Mr. Martin knew. Do you know him?"

"I was about to ask you the same thing. I think the police might be better at tracing this guy. Maybe this Martin guy gave him the drugs or knows who did," I asked.

"Doing your own detective work?"

I laughed. "Yeah, a real Sherlock."

"Don't worry; we're equally puzzled about how Lebeau got the drugs and why his family is so intent on blaming Stratton and the Milton Center. Any lawsuit yet?"

"Not yet. Are you releasing a statement on the drugs to the media?"

"Sgt. Burke is just finishing it up. That reporter from the Buffalo News has already called."

"Let me know when you find something."

"Same goes for you. Thanks, Ann."

Even if I was failing as an investigator, I felt comforted by the chief's kindness and willingness to listen to my rants and occasional mania. The questions were growing, and the answers seemed more and more elusive. I shut the door to my office for a respite from reality when Bob called again.

"Delaney, didn't you get my message? I thought Frankenstein was a nice touch."

"Made me think of you, Bob."

"You're the one hiding monsters."

"I'm in the middle of something. I'll call you back—say 1 p.m.?"

"I bet you're in the middle of something. Talk to you soon."

For as much as the guy bothered me, I needed him to share some of what he knew. He had not mentioned his internal source recently, another concern. That piece of detective work was at a dead end.

During lunch, Jen gave board members an update on potential lawsuits, reassuring them the Milton Center followed all rules and regs for research. There was no basis for a wrongful death suit against the center or Dr. Stratton. Judging by their wrinkled brows and tight lips, the board members' knowledge of Dr. Stratton's covert contract made them squirm. They asked why he'd canceled his recent surgeries. Was it possible he had caused the hockey star's death? Scott reassured them the accusations about the center and even Dr. Stratton were "categorically false." Dave raised his concern about the insider informant. As chairman of the board, he knew the details of the ethics committee reports, but other board members were not briefed on specifics. I was leery he would reveal the confidential HIV/AIDS discussion with Dr. Stratton. Instead, he said, "The exec team is continuing to investigate the possibilities" and that ended the topic.

Each member had a copy of the morning paper. I walked around the room, handing out our statement response. Board member Karen Kowalski, a recently retired school principal, seemed shocked by the details of work being done in the hospital's lab. "The second letter is disturbing," she said. "Made me realize I barely know what happens here. I can't believe we're mixing animal cells and human cells, even for research. Ann's response seems appropriate, doesn't reference this Frankenstein comment. Does her response violate our contracts?"

Jen explained the contract and concluded our statement did not cause a legal problem. David Brown surprised me by saying, "Ann, I want you to know we trust you to do your job, so please send this in your name but add a line, 'The Milton Center Board of Trustees fully supports its CEO Scott Marino and his team of extraordinary scientists and caregivers, dedicated to advancing orthopedic medicine, much like the major advances in the past few years in cardiac medicine.' "I think it makes it a more personal and stronger statement. Do you agree?"

"Absolutely. I'll adjust and send it after this meeting to staff, then to the media. Thanks for your support."

I stopped in security on my way back to the office. Their computer monitors focused on the bedraggled pickets. A few now wore Frankenstein monster masks with new signs, "Beware, monsters inside!" They were a clever lot. I was glad the morning clouds had turned to a downpour. Their message wasn't waterproof.

After distributing the newest statement to employees and printed copies to patients, I sent the statement to Bob and called him back. "Hi, Bob, get my email?"

"Lifesavers, huh? I don't think the Lebeaus think Stratton saved Guy's life. Any lawsuits come in?"

"No." I wasn't about to add more information and waited for Bob to have his say.

"I verified the cause of death from Schuller. What about this Frankenstein reference? Not sure I will use it, though. I guess your response answers that concern. I hear Jake and his friends are wearing masks. Our ace photographer's out there getting some shots since their signs fell apart in the rain."

"Ah ... you're being nice today."

"I'm always nice. So, what's with Stratton? He seems to be missing. I heard he has some kind of illness. You know I was walking around your place yesterday and overheard an interesting conversation between two docs; at least I think they were docs."

Bob was so cavalier about his snooping escapades, I felt like hanging up but pushed a little more. "Trespassing again?"

"Not exactly. I had to use the men's room—public place, right?"

"And where was this men's room?"

"Somewhere on the second floor. It could have been near the medical staff lounge. It's a long hallway, not sure."

I played along. "What did these maybe docs say?"

"Seems either Stratton or one of his patients had AIDS. I heard the name Stratton, then some comments about AIDS and invasive surgery. They were whispering, so I didn't catch it all."

"What a shame. Where's that inside source? Still working with you? For all I know, you made the whole thing up, just to get me to say something."

"I didn't make it up. Stratton's a problem. You'll see."

"I have a piece of advice for you Bob. Don't take skimpy facts and try to make a story. Don't write soap operas. You need to dig deeper. Get your sources on the record if you want to be a great reporter. I'll do my best to help, but you know I'm bound by patient confidentiality; it lasts after death, by the way. And, I can't make Dr. Stratton talk to you. It's his choice."

He hung up. This whole conversation, overheard in a bathroom, had me wondering—with all our security, how did Bob get in and out of here without someone seeing him? I needed to do a little sleuthing and told Alice I'd be back in a few minutes.

Unlike the top floor, public access to other patient floors did not require an ID verification. As the doors opened on the second floor, I looked for security sites. Cameras were located at the elevator door, stairwell door, and every hallway junction. A large "Staff Only" sign hung on the OR door at the north end of the floor, and only a special clearance ID card swipe could open that door. The medical staff lounge was on the opposite side. The entrance to the Intensive Care Unit was in the center of the floor, close to two public bathrooms. If Bob had been ensconced in one of these bathrooms, the gossiping docs had to be closer to the patient unit than the lounge or OR. The closest camera was facing the patient unit and unlikely to capture anyone walking along the far side of the hall.

The whole scenario seemed more and more like a fictional tale Bob created despite the real connection of AIDS and Stratton. I called George to let him know I was on my way and needed to look at some security tapes. He unlocked his office, asked me to take a seat next to him, facing his wall of computer screens.

"Annie, what are we looking for?"

"I'm looking for the elusive Bob McCarthy. He claims he overheard a conversation sometime yesterday between two docs or two people regarding a confidential patient issue. I'm not sure any of it happened, but I need to check it out."

"Maybe we need a restraining order on this guy. Let's look."

George zeroed in on the second-floor camera system and ran through the past 24 hours. As I suspected, the camera nearest the bathrooms was facing the entrance to the patient unit—only shadows were visible of people moving outside the range. No one resembling Bob emerged from the public elevator or the stairwell. The floor also had a secure staff elevator not covered by a camera.

"Could he have accessed the staff elevator?" I asked as George spanned the floor one more time.

"Only if he wore scrubs and waited for some other staff with ID badges to transport a patient. It's called tailgating. Common, too. He'd have to do the same to get out. He's a pain in the ass. I can review tapes from the other floors. He would probably be with a group of people wearing scrubs; might take time. What do you want me to do?"

"Nothing for now. I'm sure you have more important things to do. Thanks for your help."

Dr. Rogers's office was on the second floor, just outside the medical staff lounge. The OR staff were wrapping up scheduled cases for the day and I thought I might bother him again. He was a member of the ethics committee and might have ideas about these "maybe docs" and who might have been chatting in a hallway near a patient area. As I exited the elevator, I saw his long white coat billowing around him as he strode down the long hall. Glad I left my heels at home. I made it just in time not to yell.

"Dr. Rogers, do you have a minute for some advice?"

"Advice? I'm not sure I have any advice left today. I've been in surgery for hours and need to get off my feet. I'll let you into the privacy of the medical staff lounge. This is getting to be a habit, a bad habit. Come on in, let's hear your question."

He sat back in a battered leather chair, looking more weary than usual. I expected to hear him announce a retirement date in a few months or at least give up his post as chief; it was an impossible job to manage your own caseload and the egos of top surgeons who often behaved liked teenagers.

I sat down on a bench across from him, watching as he sank further into his chair. "Thanks, Ian, for giving me some time."

"Get on with it," he said.

"As you know, I've been working with The Buffalo News reporter, a few TV anchors, and several sports broadcasters. Bob McCarthy broke the story; now he calls me once or twice a day. He keeps referring to an inside source, the one that told him about Dr. Stratton being called before the ethics committee."

"If you're asking me who this informer is, I have no idea. We can speculate, but that's all it is. Scott and Dave Brown think it might be someone in a clerical position who may have seen the committee's minutes. Maybe someone in Dr. Stratton's OR team … not sure."

"Whoever this is, he or she is at it again."

After describing Bob's hallway conversation, Dr. Rogers looked away, his weariness replaced by anger. "Ann, I'm not sure how much I can share with you."

"I understand. Scott told me about Stratton's AIDS; he felt it was important for me to know the circumstances of the ethics committee meeting. He authorized Laurie to let me read the minutes."

"Interesting."

I ignored his snide comment. "I'm only trying to find out what Bob knows and prevent him from using misinformation—it could harm the medical center and Stratton. Beneath all his swagger, I believe Bob wants the truth in all of this."

Dr. Rogers stood up, the chair and his knees creaking. "It sounds like you might have a better chance of getting this source issue solved than the rest of us. I know Laurie's team is doing some forensic work. Sorry I'm not much help." He hung up his white coat, stashed his stethoscope in a pocket, and headed toward the door.

"No problem, I'll keep digging. Thanks. I hope you can get home soon. I'd recommend not turning your laptop on. I try it sometimes; only lasts a few hours." He nodded and kept walking.

CHAPTER 23

I stopped at the café for some tea when my phone vibrated. It was Scott. "Hey, Ann, what happened after you sent the statement to Bob?"

"A lot. Are you available to meet?"

"I have my regular meeting with the radiology group. I can delay or cancel. Come up."

Weariness and confusion were dampening my usual enthusiasm. A dose of Scott could help, or not. There were times when he was warm and understanding and other times when I could throw my mug of hot tea in his handsome face. He could be so secretive. He didn't have to talk to the reporters. I worried about every word I said. Did I say too much, sound too defensive, sound weak, sound incapable of doing this job? Most reporters were interested in being fast, getting the minimum, and running with a slim story. Bob was just as interested in speed as he was in a digging deeper than others. The more I talked to him, the more I thought I could push him to reveal his insider track.

When I entered Scott's office, he was leaning back in his leather chair, feet on the desk, watching the rain beat against the window wall, a glass of amber fluid in hand. "Hey, Ann. Come on in. I recommend my brand of tea over whatever you have swirling in that cup."

"Looks good. Thanks."

Rain blurred the sunset as night closed in at the Milton Center. I trashed the tea as Scott poured a hefty measure of scotch into a crystal tumbler, dropped in a cube of ice, and handed me the glass. The liquid heat slid down my throat as I eased into the guest chair and began my review of the day ending with my visit to Dr. Rogers. Scott dropped his feet to the floor, leaning in to listen.

When I ended my monologue, he swirled the liquid in his glass, took a swig, and stood up. "First it was Frankenstein monsters, now it's an AIDS epidemic. Stratton's missing and there's an insider roaming our halls blurting out secrets. When does it end? Even the weather's screwy; we were at the beach last week. That rain out there could be snow any minute. Any forecast on tomorrow's news?"

"They might run a photo of the protesters. Too bad the rain ruined their message boards. The TV stations didn't seem to care about the masked marauders in their grubby blue jeans and dirty sneakers." I said, smiling at the thought.

"So, we shouldn't worry?" he asked, looking for any form of relief.

"Can't promise that. Bob's not sure they'll run their photos, promised me he would quote part of our statement, even hinted he might ignore the Frankenstein message. I think the editors were concerned they hadn't vetted the letter writer. David Martin, Esq. is probably a bogus name. The letter writer might inspire Jake and his activist buddies to create a disturbing visual, keep the media focused on ruining our reputation."

"They've already put dents in it."

He put down his empty glass. "I think I'll blow off this radiology meeting. They drone on and on, complain about not enough staff to meet patient demands. What they really want is more money and less work. How about we get dinner? There's a new tapas place on the Island."

The scotch was working its magic. My resolve to stay strictly professional with the CEO was waning. "Sounds good. I'll meet you over there in, say, 30 minutes. I have emails to check."

I scolded myself on the elevator, then decided I would only have a few appetizers and head home. My phone buzzed. It was a text from Todd. "See you at the Hyatt Thursday—remember?"

I wanted to forget. I texted back. "I remember Todd. See you at the conference."

A cold wind blew the rain sideways and my hair into a tangled mess, pushing against me as I crossed the parking lot. What was I doing, meeting Scott? What if one of the team were at the restaurant? What would I say? "I just happened to be in the neighborhood, thought I might stop in at this remote diner in a torrential rainstorm for a clandestine drink with the charming CEO." Might not work.

The bistro-style eatery was crammed into a new shopping center between a grocery store and a Staples. The signage was subdued, just like the interior lighting. A massive blackboard opposite the bar featured a few dozen cosmopolitan concoctions, wines from California, Australia, and the Niagara region, plus hundreds of beers from around the world. Two hefty guys sat on black wrought iron bar stools, discussing the upcoming Bills game, doing their best to quash the soft music playing in the background. A few high-tops scattered around the black tile floor were empty except for the table at the back where Scott motioned for me to join him. A fireplace flickered in the corner. He stood up, took my hand and guided me to the stool next to him.

"I ordered a cheese plate and two glasses of Cab—red wine's good for your health."

I laughed. "Thanks. Nice place. It's an odd location in a shopping plaza. Not too busy, though. Bad weather for shopping. My hair must be a mess."

"You look pretty good, messed up a bit ..."

We were sitting so close at the tiny table; it was hard to avoid his probing glances. I could see flames from the corner fireplace reflected in his black eyes, looking for something inside me I wasn't sure I wanted revealed. When the wine arrived, his attention drifted to the waiter, the glass, then back to me. I concentrated on the deep red liquid as if it were a fortune teller's crystal ball filled with dire predictions, warning me to be wary. I sipped it slowly, savoring its smoothness, chocolaty undertones—probably the most expensive wine on the menu.

The music, fire, and wine were melting my plans to leave early. I returned Scott's look. He had draped his suit jacket and tie on another stool. His summer tan and shadow of a beard were in stark contrast to his starched white shirt and open collar. He was so quiet. I hesitated to speak. "Scott, what are we doing?"

"I could say we are having a friendly chat."

"We are friends," I said, taking a sip of wine and wondering where this was going.

"Maybe I want to be more than friends," he said, waiting for me to look up. "If this is awkward, let me know. I respect you and your role at the medical center, and if I'm being too forward, just tell me."

I wasn't sure it was the fire that was sizzling. At first, I thought it was just a reaction to my divorce. Scott was magnetic. He had also been a bachelor for the past four years and probably dated lots of women. I had dated a few men but nothing serious. This was different. I wasn't sure how to handle it.

"Scott, you're my boss. I feel like I'd be crossing some red line."

He put my hands in his. "I understand. There have been so many times I've wanted to do this, touch you, take you in my arms, keep you close … and more. You have your own elegance and charm. You're sexy as hell. We've been through so much together. I don't know where that red line is. I've probably crossed it already—or at least my thoughts have."

I withdrew my hands, took another sip of wine, swallowed. We both had tough days ahead, dealing with potential disasters, keeping the board updated, keeping our jobs. We were single adults. It could happen … "Scott, I'm not ready for more."

He sighed, picked up his jacket. "Don't worry. I'm ready when you are. I think it's time to go."

He gave me one of his hugs, a little tighter and longer than before, and whispered, "Be careful driving home."

The drive was treacherous. Rain pelted my windshield as I replayed our conversation. It was almost dreamlike. Was I falling in love, or was I sex-deprived, or both? I needed to get control of this before it affected my job and the rest of my life. Having an affair with the boss was both tantalizing and tormenting. And, in two days my ex-lover husband was about to show up and remind me how falling in love doesn't always have a happy ending. Bob McCarthy seemed the easiest man to deal with.

CHAPTER 24

Julie called just as I stepped into my apartment, temporarily chasing Scott from my thoughts. She prattled on about her stay at a B & B that was once an old Roman ruin in a small village in Provence. "You'd love it here, Mom. They have this incredible wine cellar, olive trees, cobbled streets. We eat these remarkably tangy cheeses and crusty bread. And the wine—it's magnifiqué. The sun shines every day, and we have a pool. The air is so pure."

"Sounds so perfect. I'm glad you're happy, Julie. Have you talked to your dad lately?"

"No. I will … I … I'm still mad at him. I guess I should let it go."

We talked for a few more minutes; I told her to forgive her dad; we both had to move on. Her slower speech suggested she and her friends had been depleting the inventory in the ruin's wine cellar. It was good to hear from her. If only I could fly to France and let someone else be the spokesperson. Leave Todd, Scott, and Frankenstein behind.

After a night of fitful sleep, I turned on Channel 4. The presidential election headlined the morning news, followed by a segment on the Buffalo Bills and a forecast for cooler weather. I turned the sound down, opened my laptop, and scrolled through a list of the top news feeds. About midway down, I saw the headline. "Lebeau death due to overdose" by Bob McCarthy. The story included a quote from police Chief Schuller, confirming the medical examiner's finding of heroin laced with fentanyl, and a new quote from Raymond Lebeau. "As we suspected, my brother was in so much pain after Dr. Stratton's surgery, the special drugs he concocted for

Guy made it worse. My brother died trying to get better. Stratton is incompetent, a coward, and a killer. He and the Milton Center will pay for this."

After dangling death over the doors of the Milton Center, Bob ended his story with part of the statement I had sent from the board of trustees. "We are proud of the work done by our lab in medicine and in probiotics and herbal remedies and the development of non-opioid pain relievers. While some may call them other names, we prefer to call them lifesavers."

My carefully contrived quote sounded so trite stuck at the end of a long story heavy on wrongdoing and light on excuses. Bob did not mention the letter to the editor or use the Frankenstein reference; he also avoided the AIDS hallway conversation. The editors must be squirming. Most people did not read the letters, except for other letter writers, faithful followers, and the persistent ones who had opinions on every topic. For them, the Frankenstein comment was not out of the norm.

I scanned the rest of the news items and found a photo of the protestors in their monster masks with the caption, "Activists continue picketing Milton Center's use of animals in their research lab." It looked like an early Halloween shot. October wasn't far off, and some Islanders had already planted mums and decorated porches with pumpkins. The scraggly group lost the impact of being scary by wearing faded jeans, shabby sneakers, and earbuds connected to pocketed phones. Any comparison to Mary Shelley's grotesque creation stopped at the necks of their rubber skin and fake blood.

I shook my head at the silliness of the scene when my phone vibrated on the countertop. "Good morning, Scott."

"Same to you, Ann. I read Bob's story. Wasn't too bad. He didn't mention AIDS or the letter. What do you think?"

"I still want to know who the is insider feeding Bob info. About last night …"

"Ann, let's move on for now. I have a busy day and the conference tomorrow. Dave Brown and I are meeting with legal counsel. We're trying to contact Stratton. There are too many loose ends in this whole Lebeau mess. The meeting's at 2. You're welcome, of course."

"Sure. See you later." The guy with the warm hands and warmer thoughts the night before seemed suddenly cool and distant.

The sun was shining again even though the temperature was below normal. The tops of the maple trees along the parkway were just turning a rusty red. Fall was my favorite time of year when I'd lived in Boston. Todd, Julie, and I spent weekends hiking in Vermont and New Hampshire, bought apples at roadside stands, stayed at '50s motels, and ate big breakfasts in small diners with checked tablecloths and well-used menus. Not that long ago. Julie was happy now. I was doing my best to make a new life, too.

The entry road to Milton Center was quiet at 7 a.m. After I unlocked my office door, I stepped on a sealed white envelope with bold black letters, "Confidential for Ann Delaney." I thought it might be from Scott. The note was a half sheet of paper folded once. Even though its message was brief, I read it several times. "Stratton didn't kill him."

I held the note by its edges and placed it on my desk. I had enough mysteries to solve in this nasty game of Milton Center Clue. Who would do this? I briefly thought of calling Scott, then decided security was a better choice.

A little out of breath, George walked in a few minutes later. "Annie, what happened?"

"Thanks for coming, George. I'm sorry if I alarmed you. This note was under my office door this morning."

"Did you call the boss?" George asked.

"No, thought you might be better at this. Maybe I'm overreacting."

After reading the note, George assured me he would try to find the offender. Security cameras lined the main hallway on the first floor, and since my office was so close to the main entrance, he thought he would be able to see who put it there. He also said he would call Chief Schuller. Before he left, I took a quick photo of the missive and sent it to Scott with a brief message.

Scott answered with a terse text asking me to let him know what security found. His disinterest bothered me more than it should. I felt relieved when Chief Schuller called.

"Ann, I just spoke to George; he sent me a photo of the note you saw this morning. I'm coming over to review camera recordings. Who was the last one to leave your office last night?"

"I was, about 5 p.m. I had a meeting with Scott and went home after. I didn't come back to my office until this morning around 7."

"Well, that gives us a timeframe. It probably won't take too long. Don't worry."

I roamed around my office, jumping at every little noise, then walked over to security. When I arrived, George and the chief were standing in security's main office while one of the tech guys scrolled through camera recordings. I squeezed in to get a closer look. Around 5:30 a.m., a man dressed in jeans and a dark hooded sweatshirt covering his face came through the main door and turned left. The next camera picked up this same person crossing the hall. He bent down in front of my door, stood up quickly, then passed from view. A few seconds later, the man walked toward the main entrance and exited.

The tech switched to the exterior cameras. It was still dark outside. The guy walked toward the main entrance road and took off the hoodie. His face was clearly visible—he wore a full-face mask of Frankenstein's monster.

"Stop there," George said.

"Oh, my God!" I said.

George nodded for the tech to continue scrolling. The campus cameras lost him after he left the Milton property, walking into the woods. "He could be one of those pickets—a little early in the day for that group." George said. "I'd guess him to be about 5 feet 9, not much taller, wide shoulders. He's probably 25-30, hard to tell. We've seen too many of these masks around here; all the stores sell them. What do you think, Chief?"

"Good assessment, George. This whole Lebeau thing is hard to figure. He died from an overdose. We had decided it was accidental, thought the family's just trying to make money by suing Stratton and the Center. I'm not so sure now."

'Have you talked to Dr. Stratton yet?' George asked.

"We've tried. He's not talking. He has a lawyer, some guy named Dunnington, who isn't any help. The Lebeau family's sticking to their story, blaming Stratton and the Milton Center. This note makes it seem like his death wasn't an accident. It's been a long time since I've worked a murder case."

I took a deep breath. "What happened to the accidental overdose? I guess I wasn't thinking someone killed him ... intentionally. This note has my name on it. Why me?"

The chief moved closer, gently touched my shoulder. "Sorry, Ann," he said, "I can see you're upset. I think you're just the messenger. Whoever sent this thought you would share it with the police or the media. We still can't rule out the pickets either; this whole thing could be part of their plan for stirring up more trouble."

George tried to reassure me. "Annie, I agree with the chief: don't worry, but I wouldn't share this with too many folks—maybe just Scott and Dr. Milton."

I agreed to keep things quiet. Before I left the snug security office, I suggested they keep a lookout for Bob. He might lurk in some dark hallway, looking for this man in a mask or wearing one of his own. I asked George if he or his tech could search through more video.

"I'm not sure we have enough staff on right now to do this. We have two more patients coming in today by helicopter. It'll take time."

I could hear the helicopter blades thumping above us. "No problem," I said. "I'm not even sure this will be helpful. Thanks."

George headed to the helipad as the Milton Center copter landed. Scott needed to know the latest in the Lebeau saga, even though I wasn't sure I was ready to meet with him; the note, the mask, and talk of murder, combined with the remnants of last night's rainy rendezvous, made me shiver.

Scott was in the conference room finishing up a staff meeting. I waited in his empty office, helping myself to coffee, adding cream and sugar for the first time in years. I needed something sweet, something to take the edge off the strong coffee and all the events of the past 12 hours. A patient from the helicopter six floors below me was transferred into the admitting office. Another normal day at the Milton Center.

Scott's aftershave filled the space as he walked toward me, grabbed my hands. "Ann, you're shaking. What happened?"

I let go and leaned against his desk. "Too much coffee … maybe. Tough morning so far. Security was great. The IT tech found the video and traced the guy with the note. He showed up around 5:30 this morning. He knew what he was doing."

"You couldn't see his face?"

"No, he wore a hoodie. Once he was outside, he took if off. He was wearing a Frankenstein mask - just like the pickets."

"Jesus. Do they think he's one of them?"

"Don't really know," I said, feeling tears welling up and trying so hard not to cry. "Chief Schuller thinks someone possibly murdered Lebeau. They're working on it … my name was on …"

Scott asked Mary to delay his next meeting, closed his door. "Ann, I am so sorry about all of this. Maybe if I had been more … I don't know … what can I do?"

"Nothing. I guess this whole thing is even bigger than I thought."

"This is crazy. You're right in the middle," he said as he crossed over to the coffee bar, lifted my face with his hands. His eyes sparkled from the morning sun seeping in his office windows. I put my hands on his.

"Scott, you're right: this is crazy. Thanks for worrying about me. I'm okay."

He cursed his ringing phone.

"It's Lukas. I need to take this," he said, breaking away. I couldn't hear Lukas, but Scott seemed irritated.

Scott pocketed his phone and turned to face me. "Lukas wanted me to know the surveyors will be here tomorrow morning at 8, so I won't be going to the healthcare conference, but you should still go. A day away from this place would be good for you."

"You're probably right. See you this afternoon."

"Almost forgot about that meeting. You're excused if you'd rather not go."

"Excused?" I said, wondering what happened to the man with the warm hands and subtle assurances.

"Sorry. I want you there. It's just … there's a lot going on."

I handed him the half-empty coffee mug and turned to leave. "There is a lot going on, Scott. I'll be there."

CHAPTER 25

The rest of the morning was uneventful. I ate lunch in my office, feeling uncomfortable about being watched. The message still bothered me. I pulled up the next day's conference schedule on my phone. Todd Delaney's talk began at 10 a.m., targeted at finance directors and board members concerned about healthcare costs, a key topic during the election.

Todd was good on his feet, always did a quick review of healthcare, the history of insurance beginning with Teddy Roosevelt's failed attempts to provide medical care for the needy. After all these years and presidential efforts, paying for healthcare continued to get more and more complicated. In the early 1900s, health care choices were limited, mostly palliative and low cost. Current healthcare options included advances in immunology, surgery, and complex bio system interventions. Surgeons could transplant hearts and lungs, insert new joints crafted to individual measurements, and prescribe drugs that could stop or control deadly diseases—all amazing and expensive.

The conference's executive lunch was in the Hyatt's atrium restaurant. I checked the hotel's website: it featured rooms at varying luxury levels, a massive conference center, and a photo of Niagara Falls—as if you could walk out the door and see the vista. That was possible if you could fly—it was 20 miles away—hotel marketing at its best. As a speaker, Todd's bio was online with his photo. The lighting showed off his deep tan, his sandy hair just scraping his collar, and those brilliant blue eyes. He seemed age-less, perfect, and available. After lingering too long on his picture, I shut down my computer and headed to the afternoon meeting.

Dr. Milton and Dave Brown arrived early. Scott came in on time, walked right past them to greet me, "Hey, any more news?"

He yanked the high-backed chair out from under the broad table, caus-ing a ripple down its length. We took turns updating Milt and the board chairman on the latest Lebeau saga just as Lukas slipped in and sat at the far end of the table. Dave asked if this had ever happened before.

"Not since I've been here," I said. "Years ago, when Scott and I were in Boston, a homeless vet suffering from relentless headaches stalked me for a while, trying to get someone to pay attention to him. He wrote *help-me* notes in red crayon. We finally met with him and tried to convince him to see someone in the VA. He refused, jumped out of his seat, and threat-ened to kill us. Someone called 911, and police took him away. The last I heard, he was in a psych unit. It was terrifying."

Scott nodded as I spoke. "Ann's right: it was scary. Some vets are so immersed in killing to survive, some of them can't adjust. I think the guy we're dealing with today is afraid the Lebeau family will get their way and Stratton will lose everything he worked for all these years."

Scott turned to the subject of the meeting and asked Lukas to describe, in layman terms, the work he was doing on the grants with Dr. Stratton. Lukas had drafted a white paper to help the team understand his work and distributed copies to all of us. After we read through the few pages of charts and graphs, he gave a basic explanation, hesitating between points to see if there were questions.

"As you know, Dr. Stratton is a brilliant surgeon and scientist," Lukas said. "He knows more about the science involved in our work than anyone, including me. We worked together three years ago. I have an MD and a doctorate in biomedical engineering, so I am familiar with the terms he uses. We began with our work using xenogeneic graphs—cow tendons and pig ligaments," he said, pausing to look in my direction.

"Ann has done a good job of making our basic research known to the media. When the newest study project about inserting human cells into animal cells debuted, the Salk Institute contacted Stratton and me to apply for a grant, which we received. Due to the nature of the work, we have agreed to keep it confidential. They mesh our study results with those from other centers around the world and will someday announce breakthroughs. Right now, the research is limited, and we destroy any viable cell combinations after creation. Sorry for the long answer."

Scott asked Lukas about the probiotics and his work on non-opioid meds. Lukas blinked a few times and looked through his paperwork as if he had lost his place. He finally mentioned another grant the center had received to participate in human trials of a new non-addictive opioid, one especially useful for patients with a history of addictions to heroin or oxycodone.

"I'm not sure I should say too much more about this. Dr. Stratton and Dr. Milton have had patients in this trial; they've all managed pain after surgery and quickly came off the new drug. As with any trial, the patients receive volumes of information. They agree on a video contract to participate in the trial. They will either receive the new drug or another non-opioid pain reliever—never receiving an opioid like oxy or any others. We encrypt these contracts and store them in the patient's confidential file."

I asked Lukas if one of these patients was Guy Lebeau. He looked at Scott, searching for approval. Scott nodded. "Yes, Mr. Lebeau had received this medication for both his shoulder repair two years ago and for his ACL repair this past June," Lukas said

The room was quiet as we assimilated the information. Scott asked if this drug could be lethal. Lukas said only in extreme volume. The amount prescribed in the trial was not enough to cause a problem; Lebeau had received the drug only during surgery. He had not been prescribed any drugs after surgery, only Dr. Stratton's probiotics.

"Lukas," I asked. "What about the probiotics—are they dangerous? How do you make them?"

If Lukas was antsy before, he now nervously shifted in his chair. "Dr. Stratton is convinced his probiotic formula helps patients heal more effectively from surgery. They are groups of bacteria patients ingest either in a liquid drink like a smoothie, or in yogurt, or a pill. We make them in a capsule form in the lab. The FDA does not consider them to be drugs, so there is little oversight in the market."

Scott looked around the room waiting for questions. After an awkward silence, he tried to put Lukas at ease.

"Lukas, I forget how innovative, cutting edge our lab is," he said. "I wonder why Stratton never mentioned his work at the medical staff report meetings. I'd like to know more about the outcomes. Maybe we should all be using his probiotics."

Milt had been quiet during Lukas's report, indifferent to the conversation until Scott's comment. He pushed his chair back and stood up, splaying his long, slender fingers along the table's edge. "Scott, I am aware of the lab's work. Lukas is a devoted scientist in support of Stratton's research. I am concerned, however, with the time Stratton spends in the lab concocting new versions of what might just be a bogus health benefit. It's too bad he can't stay in the OR where he belongs."

Milt's words and demeanor were completely out of character. Some board members seemed shocked. Scott ignored Milt's outburst and tried to change the subject. "Lukas, thanks for giving us the background. Will any of this work come under scrutiny during the Joint Commission survey tomorrow?"

"I don't think so. We have all the contracts for our research and patient agreements for the drug trial. The bacteria development is in a separate part of the lab—even the staff who work there do not work in the research section. Surveyors read the news, though. I wouldn't be surprised, Scott, if they asked about the Lebeau case."

Dave Brown spoke up. "He's right, Scott. What do you think, Milt? Will the bio lab pass this inspection?"

Still standing, the center's founder seemed to have regained his composure. "Not to worry. We monitor our systems and test equipment on a strict schedule to avoid any variances or inaccurate results. As Scott knows, our research grants documentation is up to date, as are all patient records involved in any of our trials. We should be fine."

Scott pushed his chair away from the table and asked if anyone had questions. The room was silent. "Thanks for coming on short notice. We'll meet again tomorrow after the survey to review their results—my guess is around 4 or 4:30 p.m. See you then."

As I left the room, I noticed Scott asking Milt to meet him in his office.

CHAPTER 26

A thousand conference badges in alphabetical order stretched along narrow tables outside the main ballroom. Two Delaneys rested next to each other, one with a speaker ribbon attached. As I reached to pick up mine, a calloused, suntanned sailor's hand reached past me. "Let me pin you," Todd said.

This was the hand that had caressed me for 25 years, twirled my long hair in his fingers, shushed me when he had things other than talking on his mind. The years had added more depth, more charm, and intrigue. I loved his freckles, his unruly, blond-streaked hair, his blue eyes tinged with Irish gold. All he needed was a chunky Aran sweater to make him irresistible. And that smile. I couldn't help but smile back.

"Hi, Todd."

His nimble fingers clipped the name tag onto the collar of my suit then he moved his hands to my shoulders. I took a few steps back, trying to avoid an emotional embrace. His eyes never left my face.

"You look terrific, Ann. I'm so glad you're here, just like the first time we met. Remember the conference in Boston, long days and nights, as I remember."

I took another step back. "Okay, Todd. There were some great times and some not-so-great times. You should get going. I'll be in the audience. Same old jokes?"

He laughed, pressed his hand to my shoulder then sneaked a kiss on my cheek. "You know I still love you," he said. I wasn't ready for his easy closeness. I wanted to slap him and hug him at the same time. After gently pushing his arm away, I suggested he move on.

"Todd, please ... you should go."

He laughed again, moved toward the double doors, turning around. "We're still on for lunch, right?"

"Yeah. I'll meet you there after the session."

Fresh doses of perfume and aftershave mingled in an aromatic cloud at the back of the room. The coffee bar was inundated with pushy professionals acting like it was the last call for food or drink on a long voyage. I got a cup of coffee without spilling it and found a seat midway in the crush of healthcare executive humanity. It was ironic that Todd's talk focused on saving healthcare dollars when everyone in this room had spent over a thousand precious patient dollars per person to mingle with colleagues, eat sticky pastries, and be on the lookout for the next beneficial contact. Everyone handed out business cards.

Todd was at his best when injecting just enough witticisms alongside some healthcare dollar realities. Mr. Charm walked around the stage in front of three massive flat screens with simple graphics, cartoons, and pictures, starting with his favorite of Teddy R., the Rough Rider. He used some YouTube videos showing the presidential candidates proclaiming the righteousness of their healthcare agendas, promising to cover everyone and cut costs. "Ladies and gentlemen, how will they do this?" Todd asked. The room buzzed, until a disgruntled executive in the back said,

"They have no fucking idea how to do this."

The room roared at this crude but timely comment as Todd made a slick comeback: "You've got that right; they're not going to do this, we are."

His last slide was a photo of a very familiar baby. The caption said, "Health ... not care."

"The only way to really cut costs is to focus on health from the time we're born," he said. "If we don't get sick, we don't spend money. It's not easy. We have to do it the hard way: eat right, exercise, get involved in our community, laugh and love. Or, you can call me." His signature logo appeared on all screens with his web address at the bottom. The room exploded in applause.

Todd hung around for 20 minutes, handing out his business cards, shaking hands, patting backs. I swore the sun followed him inside the dark auditorium. I left to freshen up before lunch and checked my phone. Scott had sent a message, noting the survey team had arrived, and all looked good so far. He asked if I could make the summary meeting at 4 p.m. I agreed to be there.

Todd was late for our noon lunch, so I ordered a Niagara white wine and took in the city's view sprinkled in sunshine. The top-floor atrium restaurant looked out at the Peace Bridge spanning the edge of Lake Erie where the Niagara River formed. When I was in high school, our debate team made frequent trips along the river, passing this famous bridge, to competitions in downtown Buffalo. Debating was the perfect outlet for news junkies; it taught me to be well prepared, to look at both sides of an issue, not knowing what we would argue until we stood on the debate stage. I had lots of practice from debating my dad at an early age.

The news of the day always charged his batteries. After a long day of welding and a stop at the corner bar for his usual shot and a beer, he would pick up that day's Niagara Falls Gazette, peruse it, then begin his commentary, puffing out the newsprint between page turns. I could still see him sitting there. His dark blue work clothes were covered in tiny holes from stray welding sparks and the occasional hot ash from his unfiltered cigarettes. I loved the smoky smell of him and his ruddy cheeks flush from hard work and hard liquor.

I took role seriously as my dad's sounding board. He analyzed the deeds and disasters of governments, local and national, and cursed the culprits he found in the fine, serif typeset pages of the Gazette. A Purple Heart vet who had served in his beloved Patton's 3rd Army and oral assaulter of Dwight D. Eisenhower, my father always found something wrong that needed fixing. My mother ignored both of us, hustling pots and pans to get dinner done, her soft, cotton skirts swaying as she moved. Looking back, I think she was delighted that I was finally old enough to take her place, as an audience of one, to absorb my dad's daily rant on the state of the nation. Her calm acquiescence on all topics was a valuable lesson in the art of listening and marriage survival, or so I thought.

Todd slipped into the seat across from me. "What are you thinking?"

"Oh, just remembering my dad, the debate team. I loved those competitions; it felt good to be in control, convincing an audience I was right."

"You have skills in the argument arena."

116

"Thanks. Not sure you meant that as a compliment."

"Sure I did. Did you order yet?"

"Just the wine so far. I'll have a Cobb salad."

We ordered lunch and let the sun soak us in its warmth. I could smell the faint odor of chlorine from the hotel's indoor pool a floor below. How many times had we stayed at high-rise hotels just like this one, visiting towns and cities on our vacation routes, making sure they had pools for Julie? She loved to swim. I even thought she might be an Olympian one day. Maybe she was swimming somewhere this very moment.

"Todd, I almost forgot. Julie called yesterday. She's moved on from Italy. She's in Provence now having a great time with friends and discovering the joys of perfect weather, French food and fruit of the vine. She's staying at a Roman ruin hotel with a pool."

"My little fish. Good to hear. She seldom calls me. Guess she's a mommy's girl."

Todd knew Julie was still upset with him since discovering his infidelity. He came to Julie's graduation and asked for her forgiveness. She thanked him coolly. It would take a while. I, meanwhile, would not let his past interfere in the present or my future. Despite his behavior, I had to admit, I still loved this guy, always would, but I couldn't trust him. He played with the truth like a house of cards; no matter how carefully he added levels, it eventually collapsed.

"Ann, you may not want to hear this, but I really miss you. I've been a fool. I've hurt the two most beautiful women in my life—you and Julie. When you moved away, it broke my heart."

My heart felt like it was burning up then trying to heal. My new life was built on escaping this man I had loved most of my adult life. I should have stayed in the office, hiding. I gulped the last of my wine before responding.

"Todd, you're the one breaking things. I don't want to do this again. We've argued enough for a lifetime. Can't we be friends? I think Julie just needs more time and some growing up to forgive and forget. I can't trust you. How many women were there?"

"Ann ..."

"Never mind. One was enough."

He was silent; his usual method of coping. I let him brood, watched the sun cast a bright light on the rake's face, revealing deeper creases around his eyes, thinner hair with streaks of grey. It had only been one year, but worry mixed with time had done a number on both of us. I had packed all my emotions and belongings in my dusty old SUV and moved away. I had a new car, a new job, a new apartment, and a new life, yet I wallowed in deep feelings of love and loss.

"Todd, I'm sorry. We both need to let go of the past. Let's remember the good times and move on."

"Sure, let's talk about healthcare. Something neutral, huh?"

"You were your usual magnetic self out there—charmed them all. Still using Julie's baby photo. Love that shot."

"I love it, too. Not sure she'd be happy I keep using it."

Even if she wasn't the boy he'd wanted, his love for Julie seemed to grow year by year. I knew he missed her as much or more than he missed me. He managed a fleeting smile and changed the subject.

"How are Scott and commander-in-chief Ben Milton coping with their reimbursement issues?"

"I've only been there a few months, but I'd say the Milton Center is thriving. Patient volume is at an all-time high, patient complaints are low, and our Facebook comments are, at least were, strong. I'm not sure what this media circus around the Buffalo Sabres goalie will do to our ratings."

"I doubt it will change patient perception, but things could get tight. Scott asked me to come to a finance committee meeting to talk about costs and ways to improve revenue. We haven't set a date yet. As I recall, he left Boston after the bombing."

Todd's after-the-bombing comment made me think of how we define our lives—after 9/11, after Oswald shot Kennedy, after wars, after births, after deaths … after divorce.

"Scott's … we're in the middle of a challenging time. Animal activists are parading around the entrance road complaining about our research lab and even our menu items. And then there's the hockey star."

"I've been following some of it."

"One of the local reporters is hot on this story, so it's a day-by-day news flash. I shouldn't be discussing this."

"I lived with you long enough to know you won't violate all the secret HIPAA stuff."

Twenty-five years was a long time. I didn't want to relive it, even if some memories were special, only to end up at the same place. "I hope we can still be friends, Todd, but I'm needed at the center, one of those secret meetings."

He laughed. "Okay, I get it. No more questions. I miss you. Call me sometime. I'll let you know when I come back to meet Scott. If Julie calls again, tell her I love her—lots."

I wanted to say, 'Love you, too,' but the words caught in my throat. I swallowed. "Thanks for lunch. It was good to see you again."

He smiled, moved to another table in the restaurant. A stunning blonde got up to give him a hug and congrats on his earlier performance. I tamped down my jealous sensors enough to remember he was free to do what he wanted—and so was I.

CHAPTER 27

Lab techs, floor nurses, and housekeepers jostled for seats nearest the back and closest to the refreshments in the first-floor auditorium as everyone waited for the summary report. Milt and the exec team ambled in and joined Scott in the front row with a few board members, each checking the time on their phones, impatient for the surveyors to arrive. The low hum of casual conversations subsided when the side door opened, and the three-member team entered the room. Board Chairman Dave Brown welcomed the trio with an investor's grin and escorted them to a broad table equipped with microphones and bottled water. Once they had paperwork sorted and their laptops opened, the lead surveyor, Carlos Mendez, MD, began the summary. He thanked the staff for their assistance and commended bio lab Director Lukas King for his meticulous management.

"We survey labs throughout the country, and all of us are impressed with Dr. King's work here. Bio labs, such as Milton's, are rare, and for those that exist, scrutiny is rigorous."

Mendez listed the areas of focus—animal research, contracts, and patient trials—noting documentation was missing in one record, but after a search, the team found the information. A random sampling of contracts showed all were followed to the letter. The use of the bio lab to develop probiotics was not covered by Joint Commission standards and was out of scope on their visit.

Dr. King suppressed a smile for the compliments then thanked Dr. Mendez for his thorough review. A few staff members standing in the back of the room moved closer to the buffet table when Dr. Rogers stood.

"Dr. Mendez," he said, "thank you for your kind words about our lab. Dr. James Stratton developed our probiotic formulation. Unfortunately, he was not available today. Is there another governing body that might regulate this area of science?"

Dr. Mendez seemed surprised by the question. "Based on the formulation and the specific ingredients, the FDA could get involved depending on the intended use of a probiotic, whether as a drug or a dietary supplement; regulatory requirements differ. It is my understanding the formulations developed in your lab are dietary supplements, and the Milton Center has already notified the FDA of the product's safety. Notification is the only requirement, and you have met that."

Dr. Rogers thanked the surveyors for their explanation. Scott's grip tightened on the paper report, his eyes burrowing into Ian's cranky face. Even from a distance, I could sense Scott's unease. Why had Ian needlessly mentioned Dr. Stratton's name in a roomful of people already questioning his role in Lebeau's death?

Brown asked the surveyors about their encounters with animal activists. Dr. Mendez responded that he was not an expert in this field. "The news stories we've read recently point fingers in many directions. We have found nothing to support the accusations regarding your bio lab, and you may quote us on that. In other parts of the country where animal activists push their agenda, time and anti-activists usually resolve the issue. We recommend patience. I hope our visit has helped."

The threesome packed up their laptops, shook hands with the execs and lab techs then left to head to the next hospital. Attendees devoured the finger foods and pastries before moving on to other commitments. Scott walked over to where I was standing.

"Ann, can we meet in your office for a few minutes?"

Alice was just shutting down her computer as we walked in. She had been in the summary meeting. "Hi Scott, great comments, don't you think, especially about finding the lab compliant with the commission's standards?"

We both agreed as she left for the day. The light was dim in my office. I moved to turn on the floor lamp on near my worktable, when Scott took my hand. "We have enough light."

I kept my hand in his. "Scott, what are you doing?"

"Just holding your hand. I know I said I would take it slow. So, let's talk about the meeting. Ian surprised the hell out of me. Why would he bring up Stratton?"

I let go of his hand and leaned against my desk covered in notebooks and old newspapers. "I have no idea. It was so out of character for him. He's grumpy. Every time I ask him a question, he acts like I'm Godzilla. I'm glad Bob McCarthy wasn't in the meeting."

"Ann, think about it. There were a lot of staff there. I know they came for the food; we never said this meeting was confidential. I think Ian's words will get out."

Scott forged a trail from my desk to the door and back several times, calming down, thinking. "Ann, I have concerns about Ian that may or may not have something to do with this Stratton mess. I haven't mentioned this to anyone, not even Dave Brown." Scott sat down, barely touching the edge of his chair.

"What kinds of concerns?" I said, sliding into the opposite chair.

"Lukas King came to me a few months ago to let me know Ian had been asking him questions about our grants and how many patients were in the trials. Lukas told him to talk to Stratton. None of it made sense. It's all mysterious."

After listening to Scott and thinking about the insider comments Bob mentioned in his stories, docs talking about AIDS, I saw the pieces coming together. "Scott, do you think Ian's the insider?"

"That's nuts. I know he's prickly and needs to retire, but I can't believe he'd jeopardize the center."

"Then who is it?"

Scott slumped back and shook his head. "I don't know."

The stillness in the room was irritating. The only sounds were the low whine of the elevator and the scraping of Scott's hand across his chin. Maybe I could get Bob to give a little on his unnamed source. "I'll give Bob a call. I have to let him know about the lab surveyors and their good news. I'll push him for a name."

Scott looked up, then smiled. "It is good news, isn't it? How was the conference? Did you see Todd?"

"Todd did his usual mesmerizing act making healthcare financing problems seem easy to solve—if you hire him, of course. We had lunch, talked about Julie. He said you asked him to come to a meeting."

"Yeah, we haven't set the date. Knows his stuff. We talk once in a while. Hope that's okay with you?"

I shrugged like it didn't matter. "Not sure you can trust him. We both need to move on. He was pretty cozy with a little blonde from another table; she gave him a big hug as I left."

"Whew. Is that jealousy I see in those beautiful green eyes? So, what does moving on look like to you?"

"I'm still trying to figure that out," I said, as I scrolled through my text messages.

"How about dinner, drinks?"

I thought he knew I wasn't ready for a new romance. "Not tonight," I said. "It looks like Bob is after something. Left me two messages in the last 30 minutes. I'll take a raincheck."

"Sure, see you tomorrow," he said, looking like a boy that struck out in a Little League game. I wanted to put my arms around his neck and feel the stubble on his checks, let him wrap his arms around me, walk out hand-in-hand to the next place in our relationship. No. It was still too soon.

CHAPTER 28

Bob answered my call on the first ring as if he knew I would call at just that moment. I even looked out my window to see if he was prowling about.

"Delaney, thanks for calling me back. I understand you had a survey team from Chicago checking out the lab today."

I thought I heard a baby crying in the background; I could not imagine Bob had a child or was married to anyone. "Hey, is that a baby I hear?"

"Sorry, had to stop at my house to pick up a few things."

"Don't be sorry. I love babies. Is it yours?"

"Yeah, it's mine and my partner's—none of your business."

I should have let it go, but I was too curious. "I guess not. Funny how we never talk about our families, always focused on our jobs. Is this baby a boy or a girl?"

"It's a baby. Really, Del, let it go." Wow, I had touched a nerve.

"No problem. Oh, by the way, I have a beautiful daughter; her name's Julie," I said, hoping he'd open up a bit.

"Your personal life is not my concern. Let's talk about the survey. I heard Dr. Stratton's name came up. So, what's the scoop?"

"That didn't take long. Were you lurking in the hallway, wearing scrubs, trying to fit in?"

"I wouldn't do that. Just heard a rumor; I wasn't even near the hospital."

I believed he wasn't at the hospital as I could still hear the not-girl or not-boy baby in the background. "Good to know. I'm pleased to report the Joint Commission survey team spent the day in our lab reviewing research records, contracts, and physical spaces. I wrote down the lead surveyor Dr. Carlos Mendez's comments, just for you, Bob. He said, 'We have found nothing to support recent accusations regarding the lab.' He also thanked the staff for their assistance and commended Lab Director Lukas King for meticulous management, noting, 'We survey labs throughout the country, and all of us are very impressed with Dr. King's work here. Labs, such as Milton's, are rare and for those that exist, scrutiny is stringent.' I'll send you a statement."

"What about Stratton?"

"There was a question from one of the staff regarding the survey, approval process for probiotics. Our probiotic team is chaired by Dr. Stratton, therefore the connection. The surveyors said that since Milton Center's probiotic formulations are used as dietary supplements and do not require FDA inspection, although the formula is reviewed for safety and reported to the FDA—that's all that's required."

"Where is the famous Dr. Stratton?"

"I don't know. I've never met him. What do you know about the good doctor?"

"Hey, I'm the one asking the questions."

"You know Bob, I've been trying to give you accurate and timely information. I can't tamper with patient privacy. The only one who can speak for Dr. Stratton is the man himself. You seem to know a lot more than I do. I'm not sure your source is reliable. He or she could give you false information. How gullible are you?"

"Hey, my source is deep within the organization. You'd be surprised."

"Do you trust this person's motives? Why does this person have a problem with Dr. Stratton? Is it a disgruntled tech, a clerical staffer? Are you pushing housekeepers to spy for you?"

My prodding worked when he reacted without thinking. "Hell no, it's a physician. Yeah, a real doctor; in fact, one of your esteemed surgeons."

"I am surprised, Bob, and deeply troubled. Are you willing to stake your career on this person's slanted point of view?"

"It's not slanted. I've already said too much. Send me that statement." He hung up. I had touched a nerve, exposed something human in this cranky reporter, father, and partner to someone.

Bob was probably regretting our conversation and debating whether to let his source know about the revelation he'd made to me. Could Ian Rogers be the insider? It made little sense, but then none of this did. I texted the head of surgery to see if he was in his office and had a few minutes to talk. He was just finishing a case. He said he would come to my office as soon as it was over.

It was just past 6 p.m. I could have been dining with the boss, drinking deep red elixirs, exploring a tantalizing romance; if Todd could do it, so could I. Instead, I was in an empty office waiting for a tired surgeon. I dropped a K-cup of vanilla chai tea in my brew machine as Ian arrived. His white coat seemed to have wings as he flew into my office and sat down across from my desk, refusing my invitation for coffee.

He looked as rumpled as ever, with grey whiskers growing in to match his rough brush cut, making him even more prickly. "So, what's so important?"

"Thanks for coming, Ian. I'm running out of people to talk to about this Lebeau news story. I noticed you were in the summary meeting with the Joint Commission and asked about Dr. Stratton's probiotics."

"Is that what you want to talk about?"

"Not really. I wanted to talk about The News reporter, Bob McCarthy. I had a long conversation with him, asked about his inside source. He finally told me his source was a real doctor, an esteemed surgeon at Milton. I'm just trying to get your reaction. Do you have any idea who this might be?"

He said nothing at first, rubbing his rough beard, looking at a blank wall. I almost thought he would explode with some rant about my ineptitude. When he spoke, though, I could barely hear him.

"Ann, we have 40 surgeons on staff, all experts in orthopedics. Stratton can be abrasive and pushy—and he's convinced he's the best in his field, so at any time any one of the other 39 surgeons could be pissed enough with Stratton's supremacy antics to talk to this reporter. I can't single anyone out. Stratton's making it worse by not showing up, hiding out. Frankly, I would be relieved if he resigned, left Milton, and did his expert mayhem some other place. Please don't quote me."

"Of course not, I was just trying to understand, decide what to do next. I'm sure Bob's running something tomorrow morning. He's not about to let this whole Lebeau story fade. Thanks for your time. Dr. Stratton sounds like a real prick."

"He's a smart prick. Goodnight, Ann."

It was late. I stopped by the hospital café for takeout—a bowl of chicken chili and a crusty roll. I crossed the North Bridge, took the river road home as remnants of the sun fell in the sky. I could still see Scott's disappointed look when I declined his suggestion for another dinner, or whatever comes next. At least I had the guts to decline the invitation. But why was I so down?

Seeing Todd after more than a year apart had stirred some emotions I thought were stored away like the unopened boxes in my apartment. I often wondered if I had discovered his blatant infidelity, instead of Julie, could I have forgiven him? He had convinced me years before when I carried the guilt of miscarriages that he had sought solace in the arms of another woman. I thought that excuse had expired when Julie was born, and he made a solemn promise of "never again." "Never" didn't last too long. Todd begged for forgiveness a final time from two women—his wife and grown daughter. His excuses were shallow. I asked him to move out. And he did. Julie and I packed up his shoes, socks, suits, sweaters, and everything Todd Delaney, covered them with our tears, then dropped the goods at his hotel with the divorce papers on top. His surprise was profound. My anguish almost overwhelming. We hugged each other, still crying and clinging with slippery arms to the love we thought would always bind us. We let go. It was over. I thought I was hardened to the bitterness of our divorce, but his early morning kiss on the cheek had me wondering.

I went to bed early, was up before the sun once again. Bob's story accurately covered the lab's survey results, yet he or the editors had construed the comments about Stratton into a misleading headline, "Investigators questioned about Stratton."

The medical staff headshot of Stratton ran in the story along with another photo of the hockey star's funeral procession.

One more day with Milton on Page 1. If I had written the headline, it would have been, "Surveyors commend Milton lab, find no cause for accusations." They added enough background to make this latest distortion front-page news. It was the first time Stratton's photo had run with one of the accusatory stories. He was being found guilty and convicted of murder, inch by column inch.

CHAPTER 29

I turned off my phone and vented my frustration during an early hour run through the park. The cool misty morning was the perfect stage to clear my head for the day, resolve my issues with Mr. Ex and get serious about Scott's advances. Todd missed me—or said he did. I missed him, too. The separation was still raw. I enjoyed our downtown lunch at yesterday's conference; too bad blondie appeared. Why should I be jealous? I wanted the divorce. I couldn't forgive Todd for using our home and our bedroom for an afternoon quickie. I needed to pack both Todd and my shifting emotions into one of my storage boxes, filled with broken vows and shattered dreams.

I stepped up my pace, sweat mixing with mist, my heart beating as my thoughts shifted to Scott. We had been close before. Even though neither of us had said anything, I'd always felt drawn to him. During our nights and days together in the ER bombing incident, he often had his arm around my shoulders; the whole experience was so emotional on many levels. As the drama abated, we went back to being boss and employee, married to others.

All of that had changed. Accepting this job put me back in his seductive aura. What would my staff, all the staff, think? I wasn't even sure Scott was truthful about the inner workings of the center—about Stratton, Milt, or Ian. Why was he consulting with Todd?

I slowed to a walk when my phone buzzed with a voice mail message. Scott? Bob? I peeked at the screen. The call had come from an unknown number, and the caller left a 10-second message.

As the sun crept up between the trees, I crossed River Road to my apartment building, entered the elevator, and listened to the message. "Ms. Delaney, this is James Stratton. Call me as soon as possible."

I rushed to my apartment, poured a mug of coffee, found a notebook, and tapped the call icon.

"Ms. Delaney, thanks for returning my call. I wasn't sure what time you came in."

"I was in the park running when you called. I'll be in my office in about an hour. How can I help you? Oh, please call me Ann."

I sipped the coffee as he spoke. "Yes, Ann. These fucking news stories need to stop. Not only do they think I murdered Guy Lebeau, but now someone thinks I'm mixing poisonous potions in the lab. Where the hell are they getting all this? They're goddamned supplements, nothing else … not remotely dangerous. In fact, they're amazing compounds, helping people, like Guy, heal with remarkable speed. I assure you I had nothing to do with Guy's death. What lunatic asked that question about probiotics?"

"The luna … questioner was Dr. Rogers."

"Ian? He's an over-the-hill pain in the ass."

"He only asked if the surveyors included the probiotic lab in their survey. It wasn't really negative, although the way the reporter used it, I agree, it sounded like something diabolical was happening in our research lab."

I scribbled "diabolical???" in my notebook, took another sip of coffee, not sure what he might say in response.

"What can you do about this? You're the media whip around here."

I felt more like a media wimp, seeking wisdom from the room's stark walls and my half-empty mug. "Dr. Stratton, the reporter is repeating what the family told him. And, to make it worse, a hospital insider is leaking incomplete facts. As long as reporters have people talking and a sensational story, they're not about to let up. I'm open to any ideas you have; maybe we can come up with another way to get the truth out."

"My attorney is specific: I shouldn't talk to reporters."

"I agree. You should not talk directly to the media. Let me think of a way to get your message out. Do you have any idea who this insider is?"

"It's probably one of those incompetent security guards."

"The reporter told me it's one of Milton's surgeons."

"What? That's fucking insane." I could almost feel his spittle hit the phone.

"Dr. Stratton, I don't think he's making it up. In fact, he let it slip out. He might regret it."

I could almost hear him seething. "Listen, Ann, I may not get along with some of these so-called orthopedic experts on our medical staff. Milt and his right-hand man, Rogers, can't tell a surgeon from a butcher. How about our dear Dr. Lukas King: he was a surgeon before he took over the lab—a failed surgeon. He's a good scientist, though. It's hard to believe he'd harm his big, beautiful lab by blabbing to the media."

The coffee was too cold to drink, and I was running out of media advice. "Before you get too involved in this guessing game, I'll try squeezing the reporter again."

"This shit has to stop. Why can't the detectives do their damn jobs? I read the results of the lab were conclusive; it was heroin laced with fentanyl. I had nothing to do with this."

"I don't think they suspect you, but they haven't completed their investigation yet."

"Guy was a fucking great goalie. Why would I kill him? He trusted me. I have a video talking with Guy about his surgery. I thought we might use it to market my probiotics."

A video? Maybe I could be a media whip after all. "Dr. Stratton, have you mentioned this video to your attorney?"

"I almost forgot about it until now."

"Why was Guy's surgery—his accident—so secretive? He was out front about his shoulder surgery two years ago."

"Sorry Ann, not sure what I can reveal—damn HIPAA."

"I understand. Can we meet in person?" I asked, not sure he'd agree.

"I need to pick up paperwork on Monday. I'll meet you in my office at 6 a.m. Maybe you can run on over."

I laughed. "I'll be there. Thanks."

I was a few minutes late for the 8 a.m. morning exec team meeting. The Stratton/Lebeau update was first on the agenda. Furious with Bob and The News for running the morning's slanted story, Scott was spewing some choice expletives as he trudged around the room, making everyone uncomfortable.

"Ann, I can't believe editors of this Buffalo rag let this distortion run. It sounds like Stratton is being investigated for wrongdoing. He makes supplements, for God's sake. What do we do to turn this around? We need a correction."

Everyone turned in my direction as if I had the secret to solving the problem at my fingertips.

"Scott, running a correction accomplishes little, gives the story another day, and few people read corrections. The editors have to take responsibility. This story has ripped whatever ethics The News had into shreds. I'll call the editor this morning to set up a meeting. I have some news that will get them to hold off for a few days, maybe turn the story around."

"What do you have?" Scott and everyone in the room turned to face me.

"Scott, I need to meet with you, in private, to discuss recent developments. I hope the team understands the sensitivity of this information."

No one nodded. The HR director spoke up to remind me a thousand employees were anxious for good news and wondering what I was doing. The meeting ended with a conversation about how to reward the lab staff for the commendations from the survey team. They settled on a cake and ice cream event at 2 p.m., despite the expected outcry from the dietary director's effort to foster a sugar-free environment. The VP for HR was adept at knowing what employees wanted versus what employees needed. I wished a little sugar could solve my concerns.

Scott escorted me back to his office, closed the door and asked me to take a seat. "Ann, every time I read these stories, I cringe. I feel so powerless at the hands of this nosy, disgusting guy. And, I hate to say this, but people, some people, aren't sure you are up to this job."

I caught my breath, stepped away, then turned to face him. "Do some of these people include you?"

"No, no," he said, shaking his head. "I know you're doing your best. Let's talk about this news of yours."

"Let's first talk about who thinks I'm not up to this job?"

Scott backed away, almost reluctant to speak. "Fine. If you must know, Milt is concerned about the reputation of this center, and Ian Rogers is just angry, grumpy, and hates all surgeons; not a good thing when he's their leader. Dave Brown is one of your supporters. It's good to know the board's on your side."

"Anyone else?"

"That's it." Scott said, sitting down in the opposite chair. Did he agree with Dave Brown or was he doing the board's bidding?

"Thanks for the resounding affirmation of my qualifications."

He sighed and changed the subject. "What's this new information?"

I filled Scott in on my conversation with Dr. Stratton, about the video with Guy Lebeau and his willingness to talk even though he was equally angry about the news story.

"If I can get Stratton to let me look at the video, I might piece together something we can use without violating patient confidentiality. I think he's looking for someone who isn't judgmental like you or the rest of his colleagues. I'm sensing there's tension between the surgeons and the CEO around here."

"Perceptive, aren't you? No matter where I've worked, when normally sane people are confined in sterile environments, holding life and the potential for death in their hands for hours and hours, they get irritable, paranoid, or worse. The clock is always ticking. It's no wonder it gets to some people. At least most of our cases at Milton are pre-scheduled. Emergency cases are rare."

Scott knew he was ranting, looking for answers, even salvation.

"Speaking of emergencies, do you know why Guy Lebeau was admitted in June? He told everyone about his shoulder surgery here a few years ago; his Facebook posts covered the whole process from beginning to end. He probably boosted Stratton's career just by being his patient. Then, he has another surgery, never talked about it."

Scott inched closer to the edge of his seat. "All I know is he came in the second time and used an alias. He had an ACL repair, went home with probiotic therapy. I think the only one who knows what happened is Stratton and the family. They kept it quiet. I suspect they didn't want to alarm the coaches or team about his ability to play the next season. He had a right to privacy. We need to keep it that way."

"I know, I know, even after death. Maybe Stratton can give me something we can use. We're meeting Monday at 6 a.m. in his office. I suggest we keep this between us. I'd be willing to bet Milt will stop by to get an update. Let's not jeopardize our chance at setting things right."

Scott's admin knocked to let him know his next appointment was waiting. "Thanks, Mary, we're almost done."

He moved closer and lowered his voice. "I'm sorry. I've been on edge. I know you can handle this. Not much more we can do until Monday. How about a break from all of this? There's a wine festival this weekend in Niagara on the Lake. It's beautiful this time of year."

Who is this guy? One minute he's charging around his office complaining; the next, he's dreaming up a romantic getaway. As on most weekends, I had no plans. A visit to Niagara on the Lake was enticing, just like the man waiting for my answer. I hesitated.

"Come on. It will be fun."

"Okay, Scott. As long as we keep it light—nothing serious, right?"

"Don't worry, I can pick you up tomorrow around 11 a.m. We should be there in time for a light lunch."

I thanked him for the invite and headed back to my office to do some ranting of my own at the editor of The News.

CHAPTER 30

John Rodham, a.k.a. "Big John," had run The Buffalo News for the past 30 years. He'd been my first boss when I was an intern. He looked old when I first met him; now he was old but he hadn't changed. His bushy grey hair puffed out in clumps around his high forehead. Moist blue eyes were always bloodshot from squinting at type all day and sipping whiskey most nights. In the early days, a cigarette dangled from his mustache-covered mouth. I was afraid of him once, not sure how I felt now. I admired the man. News was his business even as the world of print journalism was headed to the remember-when-we-had-newspapers era.

Today's daily was old news by the time it rolled off the presses, especially with 24-hour news outlets. Even print systems tried to keep pace with breaking alerts on their websites and through Twitter feeds. Making money was the problem. The loss of classified and display ads to slick social media sites ended the usefulness of ink by the barrel.

I called at noon, knowing Big John ate lunch at his desk and read his competitors' versions of the same events. TV news and cable stations appeared on monitors on his desk.

"Hi Ann, how've you been. Heard you were back working at Milton—what's it been, 20 years?"

"A little more, John."

"Hmm ... time goes by. What can I do for you?"

"I'm sure you're aware of Bob McCarthy's stories on Guy Lebeau and the Milton Center."

"I've read them."

I almost laughed out loud at his droll comment. "John, I'd like to meet with you if you can spare the time to discuss the accusations Bob's making and distorting. I know how you value the truth."

"We're going down the truth road. Of course, I value the truth. We haven't heard a word from your CEO, Scott something. Seems like he's hiding the truth. How about we meet with him?"

"I might make that happen, but first I'd like to talk to you. You can invite Bob or not. Scott Marino and the board have asked me to serve as spokesperson. I hope you can respect the role I have, listen to our side of this story. We're bound by patient confidentiality. You understand. Do you have time on Monday? I can bring a box lunch over around noon."

"I think you're wasting your time, but lunch sounds good. I bet you're still as perky as ever. You know I never turn down an invitation that involves food. See you then."

Perky? I had not heard that descriptive in a long time, nor have I felt perky. At least he agreed to meet. One step at a time. I understood why he wanted to meet with Scott. A meeting on our terms with Big John and Scott might work. Legal would need to set parameters since they believed a lawsuit was pending. Legal roadblocks often impeded telling the full, real story.

No matter what Stratton told me or showed me, I wasn't sure I could use any of it. Even if I could get around HIPAA rules, the Lebeau family might react, even add new lawsuits to the one already pending. I would be the instigator. My ally on the board, Dave Brown, might rescind his trust in me. Milt and Rogers and even the exec group would tell Scott, 'We told you so.' I put my head in my hands and sat at my desk wondering if I could get things turned around. If Stratton did nothing, then someone else did. The guy died, and it didn't look like he intentionally, or even accidentally, took his own life.

I grabbed all my notes and news releases and laid them out on my desk. So many unanswered questions. Who was this insider? Did Stratton have anything to do with Lebeau's pain or death? How did the fentanyl-laced heroin get into the probiotic capsules? What were the police doing? Who left the note under my door?

On my way home, I drove along Pine Avenue, stopped at Como's restaurant for a container of sauce to mix with some linguine—something I used to do when I lived across the street from this Italian eatery. The smell of warm oregano, tomatoes, and garlic in a cardboard container was enough to make me salivate. Just like tonight, I used to go home, throw pasta into boiling water until it was al dente, mix with the sauce, add fresh Italian bread and a salad. It was my favorite meal then and now. I added a bulbous glass of Chianti. The evening news covered the national election campaigns and the cooler-than-normal September weather. No mention of Milton or Stratton or anything health related. A few days away from the news, plus a road trip to Niagara on the Lake might soothe the growing tension that filled my last few days.

CHAPTER 31

Scott eased a gleaming, silver BMW roadster through the portico out-side the entrance to my apartment building. The sun was out; the top was down and he was grinning like a college kid taking his dad's treasured auto on a joy ride. I had to laugh. I thought the weather was too cool for the open-air ride. I also knew it was useless to complain. Part of me felt the same thrill of abandon he seemed to radiate. After mulling over what to wear for longer than usual, I had decided on a pale, flowery summer dress with a draped neckline and soft ruffles along the hem. It was the kind of pay-attention-to-me feminine purchase I had relegated to the back of my closet in hopes of a date with an eligible man.

Scott exuded eligibility. I watched him strut around the silver car and shivered as he rubbed his hand across the back of my dress, guiding me into his chariot.

"Good morning, Ann. You look so ... good. Are you ready for this?"

"Thanks." I said, not sure what "this" meant. "I'm ready."

I pulled a protective sweater from my tote, bundled up, and slid onto the chilly leather seats. Scott seemed oblivious to the cool morning air. The sleeves on his black shirt were rolled up to his elbows revealing tan, muscular arms covered in a film of fine black hair. The blue stone in his University of Buffalo ring reflected the sun as he turned the leather-cov-ered wheel. Traffic on the Rainbow bridge was heavy, so we drove along the Robert Moses Parkway to Lewiston, showed the serious border patrol agent our passports, and crossed into Canada on the Lewiston/Queenston Bridge, high above the Niagara River. From there, it was a short trip along the parkway to visit a place I had not been to since I was a child,

Queenston's Floral Clock. I checked the time, like everyone else when we drove in. Perfect. It looked the same, after all these years. The massive clock's flowerbeds were exquisitely manicured. I marveled at the intricate plantings. We parked nearby, waited for the Westminster chimes that marked the quarter hour to peal, checked the time once more, smiled at our silliness, then drove on to our destination, past local wineries and farmer stands ripe with baskets of peaches and apples.

Scott found a parking space at the far end of the festival grounds. He raised the roof, locked the doors, and looked back as we walked away to make sure his macho sports car was safe. It wasn't quite noon, a bit early to begin wine tasting. Our first stop was the Estate Winery, where we sampled their famous peach wine, followed by a crisp Chardonnay. We watched young couples walk in step, arms wrapped around lithe bodies, eyes only on each other, new parents with strollers in tow, and craggy farmers hawking their wares. Scott held up a plastic tasting glass. "To today, Ann. Let's not worry too much about tomorrow or Monday or any day after that."

I returned his salute. "To today, Scott."

We strolled through the downtown of this quaint lakeshore town, filled with shops, eateries, and wine sampling stops. The sunshine followed us, turning a cool day into a warm memory. We stopped to admire the crafts of local artisans and listened to vintners extoll the virtues of fine wine, doing our best to sniff hints of oak, citrus, cranberry, and cinnamon. We bought two garish souvenir wine festival glasses before settling on the perfect place for a quiet lunch, a small French bistro; its lush window boxes were bursting with coral geraniums and sweet potato vines, so abundant they puddled on the sidewalk below.

"Looks good. I'm ready for some food to go with all this wine," Scott said, his dark eyes searching mine.

I took his hand as we crossed the threshold into the dimly lit restaurant, transporting us to Provence, far away from Grand Island, Milton, Stratton, and Bob. I missed dining out. The joy of being with someone close, sharing quiet moments, smiling, and laughing. It felt good. I tried to ignore Scott the CEO and relax with Scott the man. No matter where he was, pacing a board room or tasting wine in the sun, he always looked like he belonged.

138

I felt like Julie on this beautiful day, carefree and single. The slim, aloof Maître D' guided us to a table in the corner by the front window. Scott ordered our meal in a delightful mix of English and French, "We'll have the fromage plate, salade Niçoise, and a bottle of Côtes du Rhône rosé. Thanks … er … Merci."

"Sounds good. Have you ever been to Provence?" I asked.

"Many years ago, after college. Just like Julie, we roamed Europe, slept on benches, in barns, fell in and out of love, and discovered wine. We stopped in small villages, tasted samples at local markets, and watched the sun melt into fields of sunflowers. It's a beautiful place. I'd love to go back. Would you … sometime?"

"Hmm. Let's just enjoy our lunch. Nice thought, though."

Ceiling fans whirred above us. Streaks of bright sun broke through the weathered awning outside our window, turning our faces into changing masks of shade and light. We lingered over our meal, savored the creamy, pungent cheeses, picked at the salad, sipped the smooth rosé, shared a crème brûlée, soaked in the sounds, the scenes, and the peace.

"Scott, this was such a good idea." He took my hand, looked pensive, as if he wasn't sure what to say or how to say it.

"Ann, I know you need time. And, yes, I know I'm your boss. I have to tell you, I wish I wasn't. I want more of this, being with you … laughing, enjoying simple pleasures. I'm not good at being alone. I wander around that big house looking for something that isn't there."

I caressed his hand, fingered his blue and gold ring, not sure what to say. "Scott, I understand. It's new for me, too. I miss so many things … my daughter, my friends, and my old job. At times I wish you were not my boss, but you are. Can we just enjoy today?"

His eyes glistened as he gave me a reassuring smile, "Yes … and more to come."

I laughed. "We'll see."

After sipping the last of the rosé, we sat back in our bentwood seats watching passersby. Scott moved closer, draped his arm around the back of my chair, his hand caressing the sleeve of my dress. The sexual tension crackled like static between us. I stifled a moan as an elderly woman at the next table winked at me. Did she think we were lovers? Her silent question left me wondering what it would be like.

Scott pushed back his chair and held mine as I gathered my festival treasures. We took our time strolling back through the wine festival's exhibits. I gave Scott the wine glasses to carry after I bought a bottle of ice wine and a commemorative corkscrew with the festival's logo and date. I held on to them like prized possessions while he fondled my shoulder and smiled. As we approached the parking area, I noticed a tall man in a baseball cap walking toward us, the sun at his back. He moved closer. The shadows disappeared from his face. I gasped.

"Scott, I think that's Dr. Milton. He's coming right at us."

"You're right. Don't worry; I'll talk to him."

Milt walked up to us with a Cheshire grin. "What a pleasant surprise, our little spokesperson and her boss," Milt said. "Lovely day for a—"

"Hello, Milt," Scott interrupted, taking my hand in his. "It is lovely. Ann and I were enjoying an afternoon away from the medical center. Seems like you are, too."

"I can see that. Have you been sampling the fruit of the vine?"

"It's a wine festival," Scott said. "You should try the Estate Winery. Their ice wine will appeal to you. I know you're a connoisseur."

Milt shifted his gaze toward me. "Ann, I see you're prepared to continue sampling, nice corkscrew."

"It is nice, isn't it?" I said, unable to think of a more appropriate comeback. "I hope you enjoy the festival, Dr. Milton. We're just leaving."

Milt tipped the brim of his Milton Center cap and moved on. Scott squeezed my hand tighter and laughed. "I think Milt's jealous. Bet he wishes he was holding hands with a beautiful woman carrying a bottle of wine."

"Scott, I don't trust him. He'll probably blab something to the board about an inappropriate relationship. You know—boss, employee, alcohol—who knows."

"Stop worrying. Nothing will happen. We don't even have a relationship, not yet, anyway. I think you handled him well."

Scott's car was where we left it. He put the top back down though it was even cooler. The wind blew my hair into tangles and Scott's into errant ringlets. We drove along the parkways in silence, enjoying the remnants of the day. He dropped me off where it began, at my front door. I stuffed the souvenir glasses, ice wine, and opener in my tote bag, and thought about inviting him in. No. It was too soon.

"Do you need help to carry all that?" he asked with a hopeful grin.

"No, I'm good. Thanks, Scott. It was fun. Loved it all."

He looked as if he might ask again. Instead, he nodded and left.

CHAPTER 32

I spent the rest of the weekend humming French tunes and sampling the wine we purchased on our trip across the border. Scott's hints at forming "a relationship" had me wishing the dark-haired man with the olive skin and shadowy black beard was not my boss. I set my alarm on Sunday night to wake me at 5 a.m. and, for once, slept soundly until it rang. The only news was about the weather. A cold front had crept in overnight, coating western New York's lower valleys and open fields with a swath of thin ice. An early and unwelcome reminder of seasonal change.

I pushed my summer dress to the back of the closet and chose a conservative suit and a bright shirt for my first meeting with the esteemed Dr. Stratton, hoping to appear confident and intelligent. It was barely light as I entered the medical center and climbed the back stairs to the second floor. The hallway to his office was deserted; the only sounds were my huffing as I tried to slow my steps and my nerves. His office was dark when I arrived a few minutes before the appointed time. A young security officer passed by and asked if I was lost. No, I had an appointment. He smiled and kept moving down the long, empty hall. I paced, checked my phone to see if I had any messages or emails. Nothing. By 6:20, I thought enough time had gone by to send the good doctor a text. No response.

As I got up to leave, the intercom sounded an announcement, "Red alert. Red alert." At the same time, my phone lit up with multiple messages, "Red alert, red alert, report to Command." Scott sent a separate message. "Urgent, meet me in Admitting."

I ran down the stairwell to the first floor, down a dark hall to admitting. I could see the blades of the center's helicopter whirling outside the entrance. Security officers were setting up a perimeter from the helipad to the admitting office. First shift employees were arriving as the third shift remained in the lobby, waiting for instruction.

Scott spotted me coming down the hall and rushed over, grabbing my arm and pulling me into one of the empty exam rooms. He was out of breath, talking too fast, barely making sense.

"Ann, there's been an accident on the South Bridge ... oil tanker ... exploded. We don't know how many cars or how many people. We're sending our helicopter to pick up injured." He caught a breath and continued. "The Island's ambulances are on scene. We're monitoring their radios, checking TV reports ... set up ham radio operators. The flames ... black smoke ... from the sixth floor you can see it ... unbelievable ... the injuries will be awful."

"Scott, slow down. Are they coming here? We don't have an ER. Can we handle this?"

He scraped a hand through his thick hair and shook his head. "I don't know. We have to try. We'll triage, set up a transfer system to Kenmore and Memorial. We drill for this every six months, but I never thought this would happen here. We're canceling all scheduled surgical cases today until we know more."

"My text message says to report to command. Where is it?"

"It's the Smith Conference Room. You haven't been here long enough to go through a drill. We both need to get up there. I just wanted to check on our readiness down here."

Scott detoured into the security office, put his hand on George's shoulder. "Call in extra people or recruit staff in administrative offices—whatever you need, do it." George's friendly smile had changed into a grimace.

As we entered the nearby elevator, Scott turned his flushed face toward me, "I keep thinking about the Boston bombing. God, I hope this isn't as bad as I imagine."

I couldn't believe I was so calm. As we exited the elevator, Scott followed me into an alcove away from the conference room. "Scott, this isn't Boston. We'll deal with it ... one day, one patient at a time. Once we have an update, I'll need to get a statement out and talk to the media. George has already set up a perimeter to keep visitors and press out of the path to patient care."

"Thanks. I'm sure you'll do a good job. Let's go."

My phone was dancing with text pings and voice mail messages from Channel 4 reporter April Monroe, the Channel 7 editor, Big John, Bob, and a reporter friend from the New York Times who covered metro Buffalo. I needed more information before I checked in with them.

The conference room felt like the morning frost had settled inside. The only bright light came from the flat screen at the end of the room, projecting Channel 4's coverage at the accident scene. Scott rushed in and turned up the sound. The fire roared. People screamed and ran from the blazing oil truck as it spewed flames in every direction. A soot-smeared EMT hugged a small boy wearing a cowboy hat in his arms. A crying woman and a small girl dressed in pink tights and a blood-spattered white tee clung to each other as they followed the EMT and the little boy into an ambulance.

April Monroe surveyed the damage. Her normally perfect hair was disheveled, her voice cracked, her eyes were filled with tears as she described the scene. The news team had traveled through Kenmore and Tonawanda to Niagara Falls and over the Island's North Bridge to get to the accident. All lanes on the Southbound Bridge were closed. Traffic backups, during the busiest commuting time, covered the Island's main road. Grand Island police seemed overwhelmed trying to keep bystanders away from the melee.

She gave a rundown of the accident from preliminary reports. "Although unconfirmed, we understand an SUV was crossing the bridge, and slid on some black ice. It had been unusually cool overnight. No one was prepared." The camera zoomed in on the slick pavement, broken glass, and mangled vehicles before returning to April.

"According to the driver of one car that made it over the bridge, the SUV skidded near the Island side of the bridge, a sports car hit the SUV, and an oil tanker lost traction trying to avoid the small car and smashed into it. Four cars directly behind the oil tanker crashed into each other just as the tanker exploded."

April paused her report as the camera panned the wreckage. "The fire chief told us the oil tanker driver died instantly. Survivors are being transported to the Milton Center for triage and transfer to other hospitals. After this broadcast, we will move to Milton for more information. This is April Monroe, Channel 4 News."

Scott opened the command center manual stored on a crisis cart and tore out assignment sheets. He handed them to the team assembling in the conference room. Most of the executives were standing at the room's windows, watching plumes of black smoke billowing from the bridge. Scott asked Meredith Sloan, vice president of nursing, to determine bed capacity and supplies. He also had her select triage personnel, giving preference to nurses with ER or critical care experience. The vice president of operations set up communications with a medical flight company then called in the plant operations team to support the makeshift ER.

I grabbed a laptop from the storage unit in the conference room and set up a communications system, assigning Matt and Alice to cordon off a media area outside the main entrance. They turned a small first-floor conference room with an exterior door into a press staging area for media to use during the crisis. I typed up a status report with the date and time, knowing it would change quickly. My first call was to April at TV 4.

"Ann, thanks for getting back. We're on our way over. Tell me what you know."

"April, I only know what you've been broadcasting. What a horrible accident."

"I've seen things I wished I didn't. How are you guys treating this?"

"As you know, we're not an ER, but we are a hospital with nurses and doctors and labs. We plan to triage all the patients who come here by car or by flight. Buffalo Memorial is sending their helicopter here to help with patient transport. We've set up our admitting office as a temporary ER, and we have great caregivers with emergency medicine background. Anything orthopedic could be treated here. For now, we're just waiting. You might get here before the patients."

"Got it. See you soon."

I called the other TV and print reporters and gave them the same information, put up a summary on our Facebook page and Twitter feed. Big John reminded me of our meeting at noon. "We'll do it another time," he said. "Keep us informed on this accident. We need to keep our website updated, and we'll need a more in-depth story for tomorrow's paper."

As if on cue, Bob sent a text. "I'm here at the main entrance. I can't get in. John wants something ASAP."

"See you when I can," I texted back, knowing he would not be happy with the curt reply. I sent all employees an email highlighting our triage status and asked them to stand by for more information. HR was still working on a staffing plan and waiting for the first victims to arrive.

The fire chief at the scene called the command center with an update. Scott muted the TV and put the call on speaker. "Hey, Scott; tough morning."

"Yeah. What do you have?"

"So far, one deceased—the oil truck driver. Our rescue team is bringing him to your triage, and his wife will be there soon. The SUV had a mom and two young kids, boy and girl. I'm guessing ages about 2 and 4. Mom's shook up, might have minor injuries, may need a social worker if you have one. The little boy, the 2-year-old with the cowboy hat, has a broken arm and his sister looks okay … just some small cuts from breaking glass."

"We might be able to take care of the broken arm," Scott said. "We'll have a social worker meet them in triage. What's next?"

"The guy driving the sports car is in tough shape. He was caught between the SUV and the flaming tanker, looks about 50. He has severe burns, and his right arm is … it's bad. He's in your helicopter. The driver of the Toyota, the first car to hit the tanker, is a young woman, maybe 25; the male passenger is about the same age. They're heading your way."

Scott scanned the sullen faces in the room. Despite their accumulated years of medical training and hands-on care, the chief's descriptions left them wondering how they would cope with this tragedy about to cross their threshold. No one spoke. After a few moments of silence, the chief's voice filled the room.

"Scott, are you still there?"

"Sorry. Please continue."

"Right now, we have one dead, 10 adults and two children injured. We'll try to get IDs for the unconscious victims from what's left of their cars. The others are alert and talking."

Scott thanked the chief and looked at the numbers he had written on a chalkboard. "Looks like two or three critical cases. Depending on other injuries, maybe we can treat the little guy. Get Ian Rogers down there. He can decide."

Scott flipped through the command center manual threading his way across the room to a corner designated for the nursing head and her support team. "Meredith, you used to work in a trauma center. What do you need?"

I barely knew the head of nursing but could recognize her anywhere. Tall and confident with a maturity and experience that demanded respect, her usually neat mane of blond hair was slipping out of its tight bun forming ringlets around her face. "Scott, we've got this," she said. "First, we need to get these to admitting. We have four rooms with stretchers, and we can open the staff lounge for another treatment room and the inpatient waiting area for two more. The area directly behind admitting could turn into the triage area. We'll need some more stretchers. I'll call housekeeping and get things moving."

He smiled briefly and thanked Meredith for taking control of patient care, crossed the room, and hovered over me. "Ann, once we verify the chief's numbers, get that out to the media. Identifying patients will be next. Can you get some of your team to help with that?"

"Most of them are in by now."

Dr. Milton rushed in, searching for Scott. "What the hell? We're not an ER, Scott."

Scott's face reddened. After thumbing erratically through the command center manual, he tore out the "Chief of Medicine" section and thrust it into Milt's bony hands.

"We are now, Milt. How are our blood supplies?"

"Blood? We've got plenty of blood … for orthopedic surgery. That is what we do here. Not sure we can or should treat anything else."

Milt looked at the startled team members, then walked closer to the windows. Black smoke was still swirling around the accident scene in the distance. "Looks like we don't have a choice," he said. "I haven't worked emergency for years. I guess it's like riding a bicycle."

"Yeah, maybe," Scott said, not quite convinced.

CHAPTER 33

I headed down to the makeshift ER. Staff crowded around the nurses' station, checking assignments, moving stretchers, IV poles, and portable monitors. The transporters, usually young EMTs, were adept at moving patients in and out of tight spaces. The nurses, docs, and techs wore drab scrubs and anxious looks; their faces reflecting a range of ages and a world of nations: they came from China, India, Slovakia, Ireland, the Philippines, even Buffalo.

The doors flew open, the mom and kids arrived first. Meredith, a mother herself, clutched the young mother who seemed to need the support.

"We just got back from the airport," the mom said, "their dad had an early flight. I can't believe it. I never saw the ice; it happened so fast."

The registrar took her name, address, kids' names, and insurance information. She printed off a copy for me. I tucked it in a folder that was sure to expand.

Just as the young family moved into the triage area, a brisk wind from the helicopter landing blew through the entry doors. The EMTs rushed in. Their tall patient was covered in a cooling blanket, groaning in agony. The right side of his face was burned, the skin peeling away, looking like raw meat. The pain must have been unbearable. The burns on his arms were so deep that EMTs had to insert the IV in his leg. I swallowed and walked back to be out of the way. The man had thick grey hair, and his body took up most of the stretcher. His shoes were undamaged, even the one on the badly burned leg.

They registered him as John Doe. The newly formed triage team lifted him onto a stretcher in the treatment room. He screamed in pain. I cringed. The PA ordered morphine, injected it into the IV bag, and waited for it to begin its numbing magic before removing his clothes and beginning the process of debriding the dead skin.

The ambulances carrying the driver and passenger from the Toyota backed up to the entrance doors. Nurses from the surgical floor were waiting; each of them had worked in an ER in a major medical center and knew what to expect. Yet, they gasped when they saw the victims. The young woman's blond hair was singed around the left side, her face red and blistered; the burns traveled down her left side as if someone had aimed a blow torch at her from head to toe. Her right side was untouched. She had pearls around her neck with smaller gold hearts in her pierced ears. She wore jeans and a T-shirt, her right foot still in a black flat, her left shoe missing. Her breathing was labored. Dr. Milton took one look, ordered pain meds, and said he would return to do a more thorough exam. I doubted she would make it much longer.

Her male passenger had burns on the right side of his face; he must have been talking to her when they hit the tanker. His left side seemed untouched by fire but his arm looked broken, maybe from the impact of the air bag. He awoke when they shifted him from the ambulance gurney to the treatment room stretcher and bellowed in pain. "What happened? Where am I ... where's Susan?"

One nurse tried to calm him down. "You're in the hospital; you've been in an accident. We'll take care of you. What's your name?"

"My face is burning. Please stop the burning ..."

"What's your name, son?"

"Joe, Joe Davidson. There was an explosion, fire ... Oh, God, where's Susan?"

"Joe, we're giving you some medicine to help with the pain. In a few minutes you will feel better. Susan is here, too. We're taking care of her."

"I'm burning ... something's wrong with my arm ... please" As the meds took hold, his hands slowly unclenched, and he let his head rest on a pillow.

Meredith picked up his left hand to get his attention. "Joe, what is Susan's last name? Do you know?"

Joe grimaced as he turned to face her. "She's my wife; her name's Davidson ... is she .... burnt too? Oh, God. We just got married. We drove all night for our honeymoon ... Niagara Falls."

Still holding his hand, Meredith paused before responding, tears filling her eyes. "Joe, we're checking out her injuries. We gave her some pain medication too. Try to relax. We're going to X-ray your arm. Looks like it might be broken. Where does your family live?"

"Charleston. We grew up together. Got married Saturday ... on our honeymoon," he said, struggling to talk.

I could hear the bridegroom's southern drawl in his raspy voice before he drifted off. I had added more IDs to my folder. So far, we had identified the mom and kids and the driver and passenger of the Toyota. Victims from the other three cars were being treated in the newly named triage area. Their injuries were less severe: they would be transferred by ambulance to Kenmore Hospital. The patient in Treatment Room 1 was still a John Doe.

Scott had left the command center and was milling around the improvised ER. I wasn't surprised to see him. Staff nodded as he walked by, thanking the surgical nurses and techs who volunteered to stay past their regular shifts. Two housekeepers accepted his offer to move office furniture into a storeroom so the team could set up monitors and IV pumps. He brought coffee to the paramedics and pilots. Worried family and friends were arriving. Scott called one of the social workers to set up a family center in a meeting room next to the café and stopped by security to verify staffing with George.

I checked in with the team to see how Mr. Doe was doing. While I knew drugs could kill, they were miraculous at taking pain away. Despite his horrific injuries, John Doe had relaxed enough to let the team remove the cooling blanket and the rest of his clothes. His bowels had let go, feces mixed in with blood and raw bone. They cleaned him up without flinching; years of training and hands-on experience had kicked in. They had a job to do and did it. Inch by inch, they cleaned him up. When they had done as much as possible, they gently moved him to get a better look at some of his other injuries and determined he had crushed a vertebra. His neck was already in a brace. I heard a PA talking, "Hey, this guy's had trauma before—he has an old scar along his left leg, might have a rod in his femur. He's one unlucky son of a bitch."

Dr. Milton was giving Scott and me an update on other patient injuries when he heard the PA describe John Doe's prior injury. He crossed the hall, entered Treatment Room 1, looked at the patient, and yelled, "Where's the helicopter pilot who brought him in?"

Scott went into the supply room where the pilots and ambulance crew had gathered, found the pilot, and asked him to come with him. Dr. Milton shouted at the pilot, who was close enough to hear a whisper.

"Was this guy driving an Audi?"

The helicopter pilot was surprised by the question. "Yeah, it looked like it was a red Audi—it was black when we found him, no ID we could find, even the license plate was destroyed."

Milton turned to Scott and me, looking like someone had just slapped him. "Oh my God," he said, "This is Jim. Jim Stratton. Dr. Jim Stratton."

Dr. Milton's normally reserved veneer vanished as he struggled with the realization that his partner was writhing in pain. "Jim drives a red Audi. He was injured in medical school; that rod was inserted after a horrific skiing accident. I don't understand. He told me he was staying away from here until this Lebeau thing was over. Why was he on the bridge so early?"

He sat down on a metal folding chair outside the room entrance, shaking his head and repeating, "I don't understand."

I had never met Dr. Stratton, envisioned him as a strong, virile, confident surgeon. His headshot photo captured a handsome chiseled jaw, deep blue eyes, and steel-grey hair that looked like it needed a trim. Not like this man, almost burned beyond recognition. He was coming to meet me. It was his idea.

I walked over to Dr. Milton, almost choking on my words. "Dr. Milton, Dr. Stratton … he was coming here to meet me."

He lifted his head and shouted in anger. "What! You! You'd be the last person he'd want to meet. Why would he do that? None of this makes sense. What did he want from you?"

I moved a few steps back, still struck by the implication of what he was saying.

"The news stories upset him," I said, "especially Friday's story about the investigation. He wanted to talk, to see what I could do to turn this all around. I was supposed to meet him this morning at 6 a.m. at his office. I waited and waited and tried to call him, and then I heard the red alert. I've never even met him … I feel awful."

Scott sensed my anguish, moved closer, and touched my arm. "Ann, it's not your fault. This whole Lebeau nightmare keeps getting worse. Right now, we need to take care of Jim. What are his chances, Milt?"

Dr. Milton stood up, scanned the unit to see if he was needed anywhere else, rapped his thin fingers around his stethoscope, and moved in to examine his old friend and colleague. Scott and I moved away from the emotional scene. Even the nurses came out of the room and closed the door. It was 10 a.m. and only four hours since the early morning ice altered the lives of families, friends, and caregivers. Scott suggested we take a break.

"Ann, let's get a cup of coffee. We have to make sense out of some of this, put out a statement, send staff an update. I'm sure your friends in the media are eager for sordid details."

The skin on the back of Scott's neck was getting redder as he left the ER. It wasn't the heat; he was angry.

"I might not say sordid," I said, "but they are eager for details and maneuvering their trucks and vans outside our entrance. We still have some time. Let's get coffee in my office."

CHAPTER 34

As soon as my office door closed, Scott came up from behind and wrapped me in an embrace. It seemed right ... and wrong. I accepted the comfort without pulling away. He needed it as much as I did. As he let go, I turned around. He looked angry and sad at the same time.

"What a nightmare. I thought when I took this job as CEO, the lack of an ER was a blessing. I can't believe John Doe is Jim Stratton. I'm not even sure he's going to make it. His burns look unbearable."

He was close to tears. I asked him to sit, not knowing what to say. I felt such a deep sense of guilt mixed with sorrow. I didn't even know the man in Treatment Room 1. Underneath his scorched skin and shallow breaths was a mystery, a man caught in the drama of another's death now facing his own.

"I don't know what to think, Scott. It was his idea to meet. He was upset about the story on the lab. Bob and that damn editor knew what they were doing. A simple question turned into an accusation. For now, we need to focus on these accident victims—all of them," I said, making coffee and thinking out loud. "I can release the patient count, ages, sexes, and status without using names. At some point, it will come out fact that Dr. Stratton is a patient, no matter how hard we try to keep it confidential. Milt screamed his name. Lots of people heard it."

Scott looked at me, then shook his head. "We should ask Milt if Stratton has a family. We need to let them know first."

I nodded and agreed to release limited information until we reached family members. "That young bride's in terrible shape, and her husband's

153

frantic. I hope we can get them some support. I'll check with the police chief to see if his department has located any relatives."

I wasn't sure Scott was listening. His head was down, those dark eyes focused on his mug of coffee, looking for miracles. "Scott, we need to get back to command and call Dave Brown. He can notify the board."

He gulped the rest of the coffee and told me to call him if I needed anything. He turned toward the elevator as I went out to face the media. Alice and Matt had set up the conference room. Coffee, fruit, and yogurt cups were lined up on the table against the wall. I wasn't sure I could even stomach something as simple as yogurt. I opened the exterior door and encountered an army of handheld devices—mics, phones, cameras, and lights held by demanding journalists.

"Ann, how many patients? Any deceased? Names? Are you keeping these patients? This center is not an ER, so who's caring for the injured?"

I took a deep breath and spat out what I could.

"Good morning, for those I have not met, I'm Ann Delaney, VP of Public Affairs for the Milton Center. We have all experienced a tragic event this morning. Our hearts and prayers go out to all the victims and their families. We have one fatality, the tanker driver: he died at the accident scene, and the fire chief is trying to find his relatives. Our condolences go out to his family and friends, and we thank our firefighters who valiantly tried to save him. We set up a temporary morgue in an outpatient treatment area where he rests for now."

I looked up from my notes, cameras clicking, lighting techs maneuvering for better shots. Reporters scratched notes, and smartphones recorded my words.

"The remaining victims of the crash brought here this morning are in our admitting office, our temporary ER. We have cancelled all scheduled surgeries today and recruited some of our staff, who have years of experience in critical care and emergency medicine, to staff up this unit. We have received 10 adults—six women, four men, and two children—a 2-year-old boy and a 4-year-old girl. As I mentioned, one patient is deceased. One male adult and one female adult are in critical condition; another male and two females are in serious condition; and the remaining patients are in fair condition."

I paused, letting the statistics sink in. Then I tried to reassure the reporters that the Milton Center was performing at a high level.

"We are fortunate to have Dr. Ian Rogers and Dr. Benjamin Milton supervising patient triage. Both physicians have had extensive experience in emergency medicine, especially orthopedic trauma and served in the military caring for injured troops. We expect to transfer the patients suffering burns to Buffalo Memorial; their helicopter and ambulances are en route. We are still determining the extent of injuries. Although we have some identities, we will not release them pending notification of family."

April Monroe, the TV reporter, moved forward from the mass of faces and asked, "Ann, how long will that take?"

"April, as soon as we know, I'll let you know."

Another reporter asked why we did not send patients to other hospitals.

"I appreciate your concerns," I said. "The Grand Island Fire & Rescue team decided transport at the scene. The Milton Center was the closest medical facility, and our lab has the largest blood bank in western New York. We also drill for emergencies twice a year as a requirement for our accreditation."

Bob pushed his way through the crowd, "Hey, Delaney, I heard one patient is a doctor. Can you confirm?"

"We are not releasing names until we have attempted to contact family members. I will hold another press conference around 2 p.m. If you have specific questions, please give them to Alice or Matt. Thank you for your patience."

A few reporters yelled my name and tried to get me to turn around. I had nothing more to say. Bob's question irritated me more than usual. How did he get this stuff? I walked down the hall toward admitting and stopped in security to check if an officer could play back video from earlier in the morning. George saw me enter.

"Annie, what can I do for you?"

"George, I know how busy you are. Thanks for doing such a great job. I think my reporter friend Bob McCarthy must have come through admitting. Can I look at the video from this morning?"

"I'll set you up. I'm sure you can do it yourself."

The security office had an array of monitors displaying black and white video with muffled sound from multiple cameras inside the medical center and throughout the parking lots. It was a simple process to zoom in and out or change locations with the click of a mouse. I clicked the backward arrow on the time indicator and stopped at 6 a.m., hit play, and watched the entire morning unfold once more.

The first admitting clerk arrived a little after 6, holding a cardboard cup of coffee and a stack of folders. She arranged them in time order and turned on her computer as the phone rang. She picked up the receiver phone, listened to the caller, dropped the phone, then ran from her post toward the ambulance entrance. The helicopter lights were flashing and moving out of view. Transporters, housekeepers, and security officers rushed to the doors forming a pack of anxious bystanders. The next minute, Scott ran across the screen, grabbing George's arm.

The first patients, the mom and her kids, arrived at 7:10, the little girl clutching her mother's hand, as unfamiliar faces carried her brother to a treatment room. Two firefighters came in next; one went back to check on the ambulance team, the second man walked to the supply room at the back of the triage area, followed by a man in a dark coat and khaki pants.

The helicopter landed. Two attendants in scrubs rushed in with the tanker driver, a mass of charcoaled skin. His face was so burned it was hard to distinguish a mouth, eyes, or nose. Dr. Rogers met him at the door, shaking his head. He directed the attendants to a room in the unfinished spa, out of the camera's range. Dr. Stratton arrived next, covered in a fire blanket. He was rushed to Treatment Room 1. Ambulances were lining up at the door. Curious onlookers were off in the distance. The honeymooners came in next: Susan unconscious and Joe writhing in pain. I wasn't sure I could watch any more suffering.

I moved the camera to the inside again and saw the man in khaki pants checking a chart or reading something and taking notes. He kept his head down most of the time but lifted it briefly; it was Bob.

I fast-forwarded the video to 10 a.m. when Scott and I were outside Stratton's treatment room talking to Dr. Milton. Bob was tucked in an alcove. An hour later, he followed the firefighters as they left through the unit's double doors.

The on-screen cursor pulsed, waiting for my next move. I turned off the system, turned on my phone and called Bob. He answered with a crackling cough trying to say my name.

"Del ..."

"I hope you know trespassing's a crime."

"What are you talking about?"

"We have a video of your morning visit to admitting. I'm sure your editor will pat you on the back for being so clever. You know, I can write a news story. Let's see, 'Local reporter invades privacy of patients in the most tragic circumstances.' What do you think? Maybe April Monroe could do a standup in front of the hospital."

"I'm just doing my job."

"I'm sick of you sneaking around here. I'd bet if we look at more video, we'll find you all over the place. I'm sure we have enough to get a restraining order. If you violate that, you go to jail. Now that's a real news story."

"Okay, okay. Let's talk about this. I know Stratton's in bad shape. I need this story," he said, trying to muffle another bout of coughs."

"Bob, listen, you need to keep that quiet until I announce it. Tell your editor or I'll call him. In case you didn't know, Big John and I go back a long way. After we get through this crisis, I plan to sit down with him and get some things straight. And, I think those cigars are killing you."

He coughed again and hung up.

Scott was walking into the triage area. I could see Dr. Milton heading his way. I restored the camera system to the current time and joined them in a small staff lounge. In a shaky voice, Milt described Stratton's injuries.

"Jim has extensive burns. We sent him for a CT scan. From what I can tell, his chances of survival are less than 20 percent, and he has a flexion-distraction fracture, a broken back." Milt stopped talking, looked at Scott then at me. "He's in bad shape. Controlling his pain is all we can do now."

"Milt, can you fix his back?" Scott asked.

"All the surgeons here could fix his back; that's the least of his problems," Milt said. "Jim should be at a burn center. NY Presbyterian's the best; they could set up a temporary burn unit at Milton, fly in a team. Either way, we need to decide in the next few hours. He's at risk of a massive infection. I don't think he'd survive the transfer flight; the pain would be excruciating."

As Milt talked, he seemed to come apart. The sweat on his narrow face was causing his skinny glasses to slide off his nose. He kept pushing them up, rubbing his scalp with his bony fingers. More than upset, he seemed on the verge of collapsing. I motioned for Scott to come with me and let Milt sit with his friend. The newlyweds were my next concern.

CHAPTER 35

As I verified patient names and conditions at the main desk, I stopped scratching notes and looked up at the drama unfolding around me. The bright silk shirt, pencil skirt, and stilettos I had worn to impress Dr. Stratton were sorely out of place in the mass of pale scrubs and rubber-soled shoes. Yet, I needed to be here. The admitting cubicles offered the flimsiest privacy and barely enough room for the crash carts, IV poles, patients, and caregivers. Hastily numbered signs identified the rooms.

Meredith was the only nurse in Treatment Room 2—Susan's room. She had turned the petite bride's bed so her scorched left side was partially hidden from the room's entrance. Susan's silky blonde hair was carefully positioned around her heart-shaped face, gently stroking the right side of her pale cheek. The only sounds were Susan's agonal breaths. Her lungs were struggling to overcome the trauma. She didn't have many breaths left.

Once the pain meds set in, Joe Davidson woke up and pleaded to see his wife. His nurse suggested he rest. He ignored her. "What room is she in? Please, tell me."

"Come with me," she said.

I wasn't sure if Susan could hear or if she was already making her way to a spiritual life. I watched Joe hobble in. He was about to walk to her left when Meredith guided him to his bride's right side. She helped him sit down.

"Hi Joe, I'm Meredith, Susan's nurse. She's a beautiful bride. I'm sure she loves you dearly." She paused, not sure how much to say about the severity of Susan's injuries. "Joe, the explosion hurt Susan's lungs. She's having trouble breathing."

Meredith leaned in closer, not sure Joe was listening. "I'm so sorry Joe; there's not much we can do. We'll keep her pain-free. She's close to dying. I thought you'd want to know."

He looked up at Meredith. "Die? We're on our honeymoon ..."

Ignoring his pain, Joe picked up Susan's right hand, a young woman's hand, no age marks, no visible veins, recently manicured nails painted a soft pink. He stroked her arm and gently caressed her neck. "The pearls were her grandmother's ... why did I let her drive?"

He broke down. Meredith left them alone, then nodded to me as she passed—tears in her eyes, tears in mine. How fragile we all are, I thought. Every bride and groom should live happily ever after.

Police Chief Schuller slipped into the triage area, removed his cap, and placed a folder on the desk next to me. "Ann, it was my day off today. I had to help.

His deep blue eyes searched my face, noticed my tears. "How're you doing?"

"Not the best day, is it? I was going to call you. We need to find some relatives —"

"Already on it." We moved into an empty room as he handed me the folder with the names of the groom's and bride's parents.

"I called Joe's dad, then I spoke to his mom." He gulped down his emotion as he filled me in on the difficult conversations and their plans to meet with Susan's parents. "They're flying in as soon as possible," he said, scanning the crowded unit.

I followed his gaze. Nurses scurried in and out of treatment rooms after triaging pain levels and noting vitals behind masks of worry. The lights were dim in Susan's' room. Joe was still holding her hand and weeping between words of love and hope. He'd need a lot of support to get through this.

Sadness swirled around us. Neither the chief nor I spoke. As he guided me past Treatment Room 2, barely touching my shoulder, he whispered. "I have to get back to the scene; call me if you need me."

The admitting office's digital clock added minutes to hours in a noise-less rhythm, neither fast nor slow, just another heart beating out time. It was almost 2 p.m. I wasn't sure I should acknowledge Dr. Stratton as a patient to the press. HIPAA allowed hospitals to relax the regulations in emergencies to help find family members in a crisis. Except for the truck driver identified at the scene, the police had not released the names of the other victims, waiting until our social workers had time to contact families. We were still trying to find Dr. Stratton's sister but denying he was injured would only make the Milton Center look like we were hiding something.

I updated my statement to note two of the victims were on their honeymoon, married yesterday in a small town just north of Charleston, SC. Their families were notified and expected to arrive in a few hours. I confirmed Dr. Stratton as one of the accident victims who was critical and verified the conditions of the other victims: three were treated and released, four others were being stabilized for transfer to Kenmore Mercy Hospital via helicopter. A young woman and her daughter were also released; her 2-year-old son was in fair condition and was being transported to Buffalo's Women & Children's Hospital.

Our temporary communication center was empty as I passed through. Coffee cups and crumbs covered the conference table; a cable TV station was on mute in the background with closed-captioned comments running across a video showing the crash. The scene alternated between current conditions and the immediate aftermath of the accident. A blazing fire covered the bridge; its black smoke coiled around helicopters trying to land. A team of medics pushed through a crowd of people rushing from the carnage to pick up a small boy in a cowboy hat. I went out to meet the press.

Microphones from Buffalo's Channel 5, Channel 4, CNN, Fox News, and local radio stations were already standing at attention as I walked onto the makeshift platform. News vans and their satellite dishes were parked at odd angles behind a ragtag group of reporters, who were mostly young with a few news veterans mingled in the group. Photojournalists held heavy cameras with powerful lenses that made me cringe at my rushed makeup and hairstyling. My eyes were probably swollen and red. April looked perfectly coiffed, and her makeup was fresh—she had used her break in news coverage to be camera-ready. I spent it crying with young honeymooners on their last day together. I took a breath and stepped up to the lectern.

"Thank you for your patience today. This has been a difficult day for all of us. Once again, on behalf of the Milton Center, we offer our condolences to the family of the tanker driver, and our hearts and prayers are with the other victims. I understand the police have released his name. Please check in with their public information officer for more details. Our patient count remains the same as I reported this morning."

I confirmed Dr. Stratton as among the injured and the added information about the honeymooners. Several reporters called my name, trying to get their questions and my answers first. I called on April.

"Ann, can you give us more information on the injuries suffered by this young couple?"

"Their condition is critical. They both suffered burns from the explosion and may have other orthopedic or internal injuries."

"Are they going to make it? Can we talk to them?"

"Not at this time."

Bob thrust his hand up, yelling. "What about Stratton? Will he make it?

"My answer is the same as the previous patients. He's listed in critical condition."

Bob continued, "Why is he still here, and why are the honeymooners still here? This is an orthopedic hospital, not a trauma center. Why aren't you airlifting them out of here?"

I wanted to yell back some expletives but maintained a fragile composure to answer his questions. "Bob, transfers are being arranged. Some of the patients are not yet stable enough for travel by helicopter or ambulance. Our medical team is consulting in real-time with burn specialists from NY Presbyterian via our telemedicine system. In addition, our medical staff currently managing this crisis have had training in emergency medicine and critical care."

Bob once again raised his hand and shouted. "You're not a doc, Delaney. I think we should get an actual doctor out here to talk to us."

"Thanks for reminding me, Bob. I am not a doctor. I am bringing you as much information as I can in the current situation. As soon as one of our physicians is able to take a break, I will set up another news conference. I suggest you get more information on the accident and state of the bridges until then. Thank you for coming. We will keep our communication center open and provide written updates as the need occurs."

CHAPTER 36

As cameras and phones clicked images of the Milton Center sign, I returned to the conference room. Fresh coffee and a clean room awaited me. I was sure Alice had something to do with it. She was one of those stealthy assistants who knew the right moves and who to call to get things done. I never thanked her enough or even asked her more about her life outside my chaos. She often asked me about Julie, sorted through my calls, and made my life run smoothly. I noticed her questioning look, small squints, and tight lips a few times when Scott rolled in. The closed door probably had her wondering. She never said a word.

The snugness of my office beckoned me to stay away from the anxiety brewing in the ER and shirk my responsibility to protect Milton's reputation. Bob was right. It was time for Dr. Milton to stand up for this center he created.

I called admitting to see if Milt was still there. After a fruitless search, the receptionist suggested I try his lab office. An antiseptic smell and cool air greeted me as soon as the elevator opened on the lower level. Its maze of labs, designed with crisscrossing corridors, were tinted blue-grey from subtle lighting. Lukas was in his dim office, bent over monitors emitting colorful graphs, small-point type, and erratic squiggles. I startled him.

"Ann, I wasn't expecting you."

"Sorry, Lukas, I'm trying to find Dr. Milton. Have you seen him?"

"No, but if he's here, I can show you where he might be."

He closed out the programs until his monitors were wallpapered with a photo of a kayak tucked into a cove surrounded by a rocky shoreline. "Where is that?" I asked.

With reddening cheeks and the hint of a smile, he said, "It's an island off the coast of Maine ... his office is this way." He motioned for me to follow him, abruptly ending our conversation about his personal life. For all I knew, he had a family hidden in the wilderness.

At the opposite end of the research lab was a plain, closed, unmarked door. Lukas knocked. "Milt, are you there?"

"What is it?" Milt asked in a sharp voice.

"Ann Delaney is with me." I could hear the screech of his chair moving around his office floor, followed by heavy footsteps as he opened the door.

"Why are you here?"

I swallowed a mouthful of the cold, perfectly hydrated lab air and stepped in front of Lukas. "Do you have a minute to talk about Dr. Stratton and the emergency patients?"

Despite the coolness, sweat beaded on Milt's forehead. "Come in."

All the lights were off in the cramped, windowless room except for a row of gleaming monitors, each emitting the tag line of the Milton Center in an endless run across mid-screens—Innovation is standard ... patient care is exceptional.

A high-tech microscope sat on a table next to his desk, dark and still for the moment. He turned on a small desk lamp, removed a stack of folders from a stiff plastic chair, and gestured for me to sit, his spindly fingers shaking. He sunk into his black desk chair, rolled it around to face me, and sighed.

"So, what is it?"

My voice was as shaky as his fingers. "Um ... sorry to intrude. I know you've known Dr. Stratton a long time, and I need ..." I ran out of words, feeling awkward in this tiny room with this complex man so close our knees almost touched.

He didn't respond, so I filled in the blank space, talking too fast, "I met with a group of reporters, and some of their questions were about the ability of the Milton Center to care for these patients, especially the critical ones like Dr. Stratton." I caught my breath and kept going. "I thought it might be a good time for you to talk to the media about our capabilities, your medical background, how decisions on transfer are made. They reminded me I'm not a doctor. Anyway, here I am. Would you consider doing this? We could wait till tomorrow morning or … just let me know?"

Milt had been staring at the tile pattern in the floor the entire time I spoke, twisting his college ring around his finger. When he looked up, his eyes were moist and his skin paler than usual. His words were whispers.

"Ann, I need to confess."

"Confess?" I asked, not sure I heard him right.

"I'm not talking to your reporters. Saving lives isn't my specialty. I fix bones. Everything here is pre-scheduled. I once did an ER rotation in a trauma center in New York City. It was a horror show—rapes, gunshot wounds. I learned a lot, never slept, couldn't wait to leave at the end of my stint. When I finished my ortho residency in Buffalo, I followed in my father's footsteps, and here I am."

He peered at the wall behind my head where his past seemed to reside. "I played the piano. I liked calm and order, loved research. This lab is my safe place, discovering new things, playing the stock market, too. The money and fame built this place." He turned to look at his computers. "Like it says, exceptional care."

He paused before turning to face me. "It's all true. I'm proud of what we do here in a smug way, I guess. This emergency was so unexpected. We drill for it, but it's not the same. We're giving cursory care, and those reporters are right: we're not an ER; we're improvising."

"But we're a hospital, a great hospital," I said, trying to bolster his confidence.

"Ann, you're right. We are a hospital, maybe even great, but not an ER. The problem is making decisions. Some were easy. The little boy has tough injuries, but he'll be fine. Transporting him to Children's made sense, like the others with less-severe injuries. The honeymooners. She won't make it. Joe will survive, but he may not want to live. And Jim …"

Milt clasped his bony hands as he reminisced. "I met Jim Stratton in San Francisco during our fellowship program. We spent weekdays perfecting arthroscopic procedures and weekends grinding down the steepest slopes of the Rockies. It might have been the best time of our lives until the accident. It was icier than usual, and I begged off the last run. Not Jim. He was fearless, even convinced his fiancé it was worth the risk. They lost control. I watched them airlift my broken friend off of the mountain, wondering if he'd make it. His fiancé died that day."

Milt looked back at the computer screens. "We use the word innovation because of Jim. That tragedy shattered Jim's relationships with everyone and everything except his drive to be the best specialist in his field. And, he is. His skills as a surgeon are far beyond mine. Even his research is extraordinary. Now he's lying on a stretcher in agony once again. I don't know if he'll make it this time. I need to apologize."

This ramble was getting more and more uncomfortable. I wasn't sure what he wanted to apologize for, something from his past, I guessed.

"Dr. Milton, I understand how dreadful this is for you. Human tragedy is always front-page; even Dr. Stratton knew how that can change a life. When I talked to him on Friday, he said he had something to tell me related to the hockey player's surgery. The news story about the lab investigation really upset him."

Milt turned away, put his elbows on the desk and his head in his hands.

"Dr. Milton, are you okay?"

His voice was barely audible. "Those stories in The News, that reporter, Bob, referred to a reliable source a few times. It was me. I'm the source. When I looked at Jim struggling to breathe, I wished it'd been me in that accident."

I was shocked. The Milton name was everywhere I looked—running across the gleaming monitors, the coffee mug on Milt's desk, the Milton Center ballpoint pen I held in my hand, and, in stark black letters on his white doctor's coat.

"Dr. Milton, why?"

He shook his head. "I'm not even sure I know. I've been rich, famous. It didn't matter. I envied Jim's skills and outcomes. We were in the same practice. My patient volumes were going down while his were soaring."

He stopped to catch his breath while I looked incredulous.

"Dr. Milton —"

"Ann, I need to get this out." His confession spilled out of him. When he found out the patient was Guy Lebeau, he called the reporter, distorted the ethics committee review to make Jim look unethical, trying to tarnish his sterling image. He didn't tell Bob who he was, but I knew how easily Bob had traced the phone number and within seconds he'd identified Benjamin Milton.

Milt added, "I thought I saw that reporter near the medical staff lounge, coming out of the bathroom wearing scrubs. He probably overheard me talking with another surgeon about a patient that had AIDS. I've been worried about reading that in the news. Guess you stopped him."

I wondered how such a brilliant surgeon could be outsmarted by a sleazy reporter. I should be irate, yet I felt sorry for this wilting man.

"Ann, I never realized how tricky the media were. Bob could recognize my voice. I can't talk to him."

Moments passed while neither of us spoke. The room was too small to hold the fullness of his repentance. He took off his glasses to wipe his red eyes and slumped before me. When he spoke his voice was muted, pleading.

"Ann, can we keep this confidential?"

"Um … considering, I'll try." I could maintain a confidence but if Bob threatened to reveal Milt's identity, should I deny it?

"Dr. Milton, I'll do my best to manage Bob. I agree you should not meet with the media. What if I ask Dr. Rogers? He can be gruff, but he's been doing his best to take care of our patients today."

"Sure, you can ask him. Please don't discuss our meeting," he said.

"I won't, but Scott should know."

"Sure. Scott's good at keeping secrets. Thanks for understanding."

"I'm not sure I do understand. Can I get you anything: some light, something to eat, drink?"

He laughed. "No. I'll be up in a few minutes."

His trembling hand reached up, grasped my fingers momentarily then let go. Without another word, he turned back to his computer screens. I closed the door quietly as I left him alone in his gloomy confessional.

CHAPTER 37

The subdued lighting seemed to mimic my mood as I snaked back through the hallways. Lukas looked up when I passed his research haven, but he didn't say a word. I was sure he sensed something was wrong—or would be. Dr. Milton's burden was mine now. I once thought doctors were experts at detachment, able to separate the brutality of injury or disease from their daily lives. During my early years in healthcare, I discovered doctors had hearts and feelings. As I was leaving our hospital cafeteria in a previous job, a family doctor in practice for 30 years, passed me in the hall. I had met him a few times. He had a quick wit and loved to tease me. On that morning, his head was down, and he was crying. I asked him if he was all right.

He shook his head. "I just lost a patient," he said. "She had cancer. We both knew it would take her someday ... today, it did." He shuffled down the hall and left me to wonder how he and other docs dealt with the loss of patients they could not heal.

The earlier chaos in our admitting office-turned-ER had settled into a tense but organized system. Registration had updated its list of patients. Two more of the patients in serious condition had been stabilized and transferred to Memorial. The families of the honeymooners, recently arrived, were gathered around the tiny bride. Joe ignored everyone, held his new wife's hand, telling her she would be all right. His parents held each other, watched the monitors pulsing an erratic heart rate, listened to her labored breaths. Meredith motioned for me to join her in the staff lounge.

"Ann, Susan doesn't have much longer. Joe won't let us take care of him. He's in so much pain. I've asked the social worker to call a priest—

they're Catholic. I think they can give Last Rites or whatever it's called. We've booked the family into our Inn, but I'm not sure they'll leave Susan's room. Reporters are walking around admitting. That guy Bob's out there. I really don't want this family to deal with them."

"Thanks for the heads up. I know security's busy, but they need to take charge of this. I'll talk to George and send a reminder to the media covering this tragedy."

As Meredith went back to the Davidson family, I noticed Scott talking to Ian Rogers at the end of the treatment area. "Scott, Dr. Rogers, can I have a word with both of you?"

Ian rolled his eyes at me. "What is it, Ann? We're trying to decide on who gets transferred and who stays—important work."

I ignored his look of disgust and verbal slap. "Dr. Rogers, the media are getting edgy and want more information. They want to talk to a doctor—someone doing important work—about our capabilities and why some patients have not been transferred, especially Dr. Stratton and our honeymoon couple."

Scott jumped in before Ian erupted. "Ann, the media are not our priority. We're straining our staff, and we need to get this temporary ER back to its original purpose. I doubt Milt will talk to you, either. He's probably worried about losing revenue with so many cases canceled today."

What happened to the compassionate CEO who, just minutes ago, was pushing stretchers around and bringing coffee to staff?

"Sorry to bother you two. I just left Dr. Milton. He's upset and not willing to talk to a reporter. I thought, Dr. Rogers, you might meet with the press."

The hairs on his prickly head seemed to stand up. "No damn way. Can't you see I'm busy?" Rogers said.

"Yes," I sighed. "I can see that." I hesitated to say more, but I needed something to give the media. "We don't have to do it right now. In fact, we can probably do it tomorrow morning. By then —"

"By then, we will have a dead bride, one of our doctors in jeopardy, and angry patients and families because someone they loved is not coming home."

I could feel my face getting hotter as he spat out his anger. I turned to Scott, waiting for an intervention, some words of support. Instead, he said, "Ann, the media are not —"

I raised my hand for him to stop. "Scott, when you're done, I need a few minutes."

"Sure, why don't you come up to my office in half an hour."

I left the disgruntled men and sent a text to my list of reporters reminding them to stay away from any entrance except for the designated media center. As I entered my office, Alice greeted me with a rash of phone call requests and asked me if we would keep the communication center open or close it for the night. Without a physician to go into details about the medical decisions, it seemed a waste of time. I could update them on the number of patients and conditions in an email or just post it on our Facebook page. I had not looked at it since yesterday and opened the site.

Most of the posts were heartfelt, offering prayers for the patients, especially the honeymooners. Only one comment was piercing in its anger. "Milton Center is no ER ... tragedies mount as incompetents care for burn victims." It was from "marybeth." Instead of responding, I posted an update with our thoughts and prayers for the patients and their families.

It was almost 8 p.m. I told Alice and the team to head out, thanked them for being there all day, and said I would text them with updates. Scott was trudging around his office, scrolling through his phone as I entered.

"Who the hell is marybeth?"

"Ignore it," I said, moving across the room, watching his red-faced anger slowly dissipate as he dropped to the arm of the sofa.

"I can't, Ann. We can't. Our reputation is taking one hit after another. We've turned our whole hospital inside out to make an ER, stabilized all these patients, and brought in a burn team—at great expense. First it was Lebeau, and now this. What will happen when that little bride dies? We really need to get on top of this."

Scott was exhausted. Neither of us had much to eat and too much coffee. He was probably replaying the same scenes I had witnessed: patients moaning in pain, the little boy being carried in on his mother's arms, Joe bent over his bride, and Dr. Stratton's torched skin. Scott slumped deep into the sofa cushion.

"Ann, please, sit down. What should we do?"

"Scott, we'll get through this. I need to talk to the Davidsons and Brays, Joe and Susan's parents, before she passes. We have very little time. They need to know that after they leave here that the media will haunt them. They'll need a spokesperson when they get home, a niece or nephew maybe. I can do it for now if they approve. Joe still needs care."

I suggested we find a trauma center in Joe's hometown area, somewhere in South Carolina, and have social work arrange transport for Susan's remains. Her parents could leave by a back door, maybe in the receiving area. I jotted a reminder in my reporter's notebook to check in with Meredith, call George about adding back-door security, and meet with the parents.

Scott squeezed my hand as I wrote. "Ann, I can't believe you can be so logical. Are you sure you want to do this spokesperson role for the family?"

"If they agree. Susan's the same age as Julie; what a tragedy. I don't even know this young woman, never heard her voice or heard her laugh. I'll do my best."

He sighed, tears rimming his bloodshot eyes. "I don't know why I'm so emotional."

"We're all emotional, but we have jobs to do," I said, then suggested he meet with George and the operations team while I sat down with the family. "I'll fill you in later about my talk with Milt."

CHAPTER 38

I gathered my notebook and as much courage as I could, then walked back to Treatment Room 2. The scene had not changed since I had looked in earlier. Meredith agreed that it was time to help the family prepare for the inevitable. Before leaving, the social worker told me she wasn't sure the families were ready to begin the process. I knocked on the door frame, pushed back the soft plaid cubicle curtain, and entered Susan's room. Joe didn't move.

"Good evening, I'm sorry to intrude at such a difficult time. I'm Ann Delaney, VP of public affairs for the Milton Center."

The parents looked up, their eyes filled with tears, faces mottled. Joe Sr. spoke, "Yes, we saw you on the news this afternoon ... talking about the accident victims. What can we do for you?"

"I'd like to talk to you for a few minutes. We can use the staff office down the hall." They looked reluctant. I assured them it would only be a few minutes, knowing the short walk would feel like a long way from the dying bride.

Both mothers sank into the room's loveseat. Each dad perched on the edges of adjacent chairs, too upset to lean back.

"Thanks. I can't imagine the emotions you are all feeling. The joy of a wedding and —"

Susan's mom let out a horrible cry then muffled her mouth with her free hand. "I can't believe it. They were just saying their vows."

I sat in a chair closest to Susan's mom. No one spoke. As I moved toward the door to dim the lights in the too-bright room, both dads looked ready to jump up to fight a nameless foe or do anything but sit still. The moms were sobbing. The media would crush them, hound them and ignore their despair.

"As you know, I'm the hospital spokesperson and all too familiar with overzealous journalists. This accident is already a national news story. We'll do our best to escort you from our hospital when the time comes to avoid reporters and their cameras. If you approve, I will be glad to serve as your spokesperson while you're here. Once you leave, you'll need help."

I suggested they consider a close family member to deal with the media. The longer they avoided them, the more difficult it would be. "I'd like you to tell me about Susan and Joe—their story."

The families seemed to relax for the first time. I had coffee and sandwiches brought in; some drank the coffee, but the sandwiches stayed untouched. Joe Jr. was a carbon copy of his dad—tall, thin, same dusty brown hair, amber eyes. His mom was fair-skinned and so still, almost in a daze, as her eyes wandered around the room looking for miracles. Susan's mom, Johanna, had the same blonde hair as her daughter. She tightened her grip on a coffee mug, took a sip, then looked at her husband. He took the mug from her hands and said, "You can do this; tell her about Susan and Joe."

They held hands as she spoke. "Susan's ... she's old-fashioned. Sometimes I think she was born in another time. Since she was a little girl, she would open my cedar chest, pull out my wedding gown, slip it over her head, and dance around my bedroom, saying, 'Mom, can I wear this when I get married?'

Johanna closed her eyes, paused for a moment, then continued. "She didn't even know Joe then, but she knew what she wanted. She always said, 'I will marry a man just like daddy.'"

Susan's dad sank deeper into his seat, gulping air. Johanna looked at her husband, grabbed a tissue from a box on a side table, and wiped her eyes. "She sure loved Joe. I know he loved her ... it was ... magical. Before she walked down the aisle, I gave her my mother's pearls," she said, inadvertently caressing her neck. "I can still feel her skin under my fingers. Oh, God."

Johanna broke down, sobbing uncontrollably. No one said a word for a long time, then, in a hoarse voice, Joe spoke. "I thought ... we thought they were too young to get married—but we were young when we married." He looked at his wife. She smiled while the Brays just nodded. "Joey is, was so happy; he just graduated, got a new job, a new car. They wanted kids."

His voice faded. I remembered the joy I felt on my wedding day and the feeling that Todd and I would never part. What happened to us? I pushed my feelings behind a flimsy facade and offered my advice to the grieving parents.

"Thank you for sharing. You'll need all your strength and friendship to get through this. Our social workers will help you with logistics—travel. My job is to work with the media. I'd like to describe Susan and Joe not so much as victims but as newlyweds with hopes and dreams and a family that cares deeply about both of them. I will only refer to them as the bride and groom even though the names of the accident victims have been released by the police.

"Didn't you tell us not to talk to the media?" Joe's dad said.

"I did. For now, I will be your surrogate; you will approve everything I say. I have a friend in public relations at one of Trident's hospitals in Charleston. I can call her. We're trying to arrange for Joe's transport to their trauma center and Susan's. I'll need your contact info."

Joe's dad answered for the group. "Can you send us that person's name, how some of this will work? May we stay here a few minutes?"

"Of course, I will let Susan's nurse, Meredith, know where you are." I left them slumped over in the dimly lit room.

Meredith came out of Susan's room as soon as she saw me. "Ann, we're losing her. Her pulse is very weak. Joe's in tough shape. I think their parents need to come back soon."

I walked back to the staff lounge, and they all looked up, hopeful and afraid. They followed me to Treatment Room 2. I moved away and watched the monitor's faint heartbeat. Johanna held her daughter's hand and told her she loved her. When the heartbeats stopped, Joe's dad put his big, rough hand on his son's shoulders and told him, "She's gone, Joe, she's gone." The young groom screamed, "NO! NO!" until his voice gave out and his head dropped to his bride's chest.

I thought of the movie scenes that made me cry even though I knew the actors were only playing a role for an hour on a Sunday afternoon. Tears streamed down my cheeks. Meredith touched my shoulder. "Come on, Ann," she said, "we'll leave them alone."

Dr. Rogers and the Davidsons wheeled Joe into the adjacent room. His sobs racked his injured body until pain meds set in, and sleep gave him a respite. Johanna and her husband stayed behind and talked to the social worker about the next steps for their daughter's lifeless body.

Meredith suggested we take a break in her makeshift office that was, until a day earlier, a medical closet. She stopped on the way to pick up two bottles of water and rolled out some exam room stools from behind a supply cabinet.

"Thanks, Meredith," I said, sipping the water. "How will they ever get through this?"

"Time." She took off her glasses and wiped her eyes. "Lots of time."

We leaned back against the pale green walls; our feet braced on the floor as the stool wheels squeaked with the sightless shift in our weight. The room's air filter blew a cool breeze over our faces, drying our tear-stained cheeks. The welcome respite ended with a knock on the door.

A young social worker with a sparse goatee peered in, looking from one of us to the other. "Meredith?" he asked, which made me smile. I was the one in heels and a black skirt. Meredith's scrubs should have been a clue.

"You found me," Meredith said, standing to greet him.

"Sorry to interrupt, but my supervisor wanted you to know the Bray family is leaving."

Reading from a thick chart, he reviewed detailed plans to airlift Susan from the center's helipad to a funeral home in their Charleston neighborhood, noting the Davidsons were staying with their son until he was stable and ready to travel.

I could hear the helicopter revving up outside. We pushed the stools back behind the cabinet and closed the door to the med closet. I stopped at the nurses' station as Meredith went into the bride's room. EMTs covered Susan in white sheets and lifted her onto a narrow gurney. Her mom and dad held hands as they watched, wordless and stunned. Meredith picked up the bride's pearls from the bed stand and handed them to Johanna as they made their way to the helipad. They hugged, squeezed hands, and said goodbye. The night sky was clear with brilliant stars. A full moon would follow them home.

CHAPTER 39

The digital clock high on the admitting wall kept its steady beat ... 21:28, 21:29, 21:30. A day longer than most. I walked back to my office to write up Susan and Joe's story. I wept while I wrote it, doing my best to capture the mix of tenderness and tragedy, then sent it to the parents for approval.

It was just past 10 p.m. when my office door opened. I thought it might be George or one of his security officers checking on me. It was Scott. His face was almost blackened by his stubbly beard; his eyes looked distant. His tie was crumpled in his hand. I smelled the faint odor of Scotch and all over sorrow. "Hey, I thought you left for the day," I said, moving to the front of my desk.

"I'm on my way. Knew you'd be here. I think it's time for you to quit whatever you're doing and get out of here."

"I'm going. I needed to finish a press update, a love story actually, so Susan's mom and Joe's dad could review it."

He looked quizzical. "A love story?"

"I met with the parents of the honeymooners and asked them about their son and daughter."

"Don't know how you did that," he said, shaking his head.

"We're being criticized because we are not an ER. Neither Milt nor Dr. Rogers will speak to the press. I couldn't send out a news release with cold hard numbers and curt status reports. The young couple needed more. I added their family's gratitude. Let me know what you think."

Scott pulled a chair from under my small conference table and picked up the two-pager; it was longer than my usual statements. He was close to weeping when he finished reading. "Ann, this is so sad and wonderful at the same time. The pearls, the magic, and marriage ... makes me remember my own wedding." In a softer voice, he recalled happier days.

"Maria and I were young, maybe too young, when we got married. When our kids were little, we laughed, played, and had some great times. Then something broke or got lost. Our careers got ahead of us, at least mine did. I was never home. Maria spent her days at the country club. The kids were grown up and gone before I knew it. We lost the joy in being together—or maybe we never tried hard enough to keep it."

I never felt so drawn to this complicated man or so vulnerable. I eased into a chair close to him. "I've been thinking the same thing. Todd and I were that happy couple, too ... once. I kept looking at Joe and Susan suffering only days after the happiest moment of their lives. I thought about my beautiful Julie and Todd. I guess I will always love him in some way. Then I thought about you." I hesitated to say more until his smoldering eyes questioned my meaning. "Maybe we can create something special of our own," I said. "I'm willing to explore."

Scott grabbed my hands and pulled me closer, enveloping me in his arms. "Oh, Ann." His rough skin touched my cheek, his lips touched mine. The kiss was tender and soft, then more intense. We both wanted more until I pulled away.

"Scott. We're exhausted and too emotional. I need to go home and rest; you do, too. Let's wait a few days — "

"Wait? Jesus, Ann, I have wanted to do that for so long. I get it. I am exhausted." He sighed and moved toward the door. "What about Saturday? It's a few days away. Drinks, dinner?"

I smiled for the first time in a long day. "It's a date. Let's hope nothing else happens."

As I was locking up, I checked a text from Johanna. She was okay with my statement. Joe's dad sent a separate text, "Fine with me, thanks."

I looked up at the bright moon, the stars, thought about the helicopter flying south with Susan and her parents. The evening air was cool once again; the thruway and North Bridge were nearly empty after the chaos of traffic earlier in the day. I took the parkway to follow the river and listen to its steady pulse as it battered the rocky shore, fighting to survive ... like the bride, the groom and Jim Stratton.

Channel 4's late news repeated the bridge accident scene, a clip from my press conference, an interview with the owner of the oil tanker, and the driver's distraught wife. She was shocked by the death of her husband, by the media pushing microphones in her face. They could be merciless, trying to beat the competition, regardless of who was hurt.

It was midnight when I checked my remaining emails, a dozen from local and national news operations. I sent them a group response. "We will hold another press conference tomorrow at 9 a.m. Until then, I have no further updates."

I preferred an earlier press conference to accommodate the night reporters, but I needed time in the morning to visit the Davidsons and check on Stratton's condition. His critical status had not changed before I left; I was more focused on the honeymooners and their tragic story. I hadn't even discussed Dr. Milton's confession with Scott. I wasn't sure it was important anymore or if Stratton would even survive.

Mystery surrounded this man I'd never met. He had to know more, a lot more, about the hockey star, what had happened, and who had killed him. The bridge accident moved all other news stories to inside pages; even Lebeau's death was missing from the headlines, TV alerts, and news feeds. The election coverage had evaporated, at least for now. How quickly news changed.

I remember sitting in the newsroom at The Buffalo Evening News, clicking away at my computer trying to vitalize the boring details of a city council meeting, when the editor flew in, red-faced and shouting commands. "Ann, stop what you're doing. I need everyone on this breaking story—a crew team capsized this morning. At least one student may have died. Get over to the college campus and the lake. This is front page. I need it now."

The photographers rushed to the lake while the rest of us interviewed students, college officials, and tried to find members of the crew team who'd survived. One of photographers got into the boathouse where a few of the young men huddled, waiting for rides to campus. Others were still in the water, looking for their classmates. When the photographer looked up, he saw the tall, drenched rowers dragging a young man out of the water to shore. He took pictures of everything, telling me later how the men had cried. The tragedy of it all would have torn him up if it had not been for the lens between him and the dead man. I was sure he still relived that moment often. As his photos came into the newsroom, the editor laid them out in the paste-up platform. The original front page was scraped, filled instead by our stories of student heroes, fortunate students whose lives were saved, the tragic loss of a talented young man from upstate New York, and the grief of the crew team coach. For all the words we wrote that day, nothing told the story as well as the photo of a young man being dragged out of the lake.

The editor took the photo out of the layout, put it back, and paced. He finally signed off on putting the photo on the front page. That editor was Big John. For all his bluster, I respected him for running the photo. He took a lot of heat, even years later. The emotional impact was stunning, some thought unnecessary. Big John taught me to find the emotion in the story, not to shy away, look through a lens if you have to, but get the real story even if it made you cry.

CHAPTER 40

The sun seemed brighter than usual, rising in the distance as I crossed the North Bridge. Traffic was lighter today. Commuters were avoiding the shortcut to Buffalo after yesterday's accident while contractors repaired the damage to the bridge. Although it was still early, pickets and signs were absent at the Milton Center. Alice was walking ahead of me in the parking lot and turned around smiling when she heard my heels clacking on the pavement.

"I thought that was you. Same shoes as yesterday. Did you work all night?

"Nah, I left around midnight. Are you coming into the office?"

"Not yet. I need to stop in admitting. We need to prepare for another press conference. I won't be long."

Meredith was at the nurses' station, viewing a patient list on the registrar's computer screen. Her thick blonde hair was tied into a loose bun. She brushed a few stray strands away from her face as she turned to me. "Hey, did you get any sleep?"

"I should ask you the same. How are we doing?"

"Let's get some coffee."

I followed Meredith to a refreshment station at the rear of the unit. The smells, sounds and chaos of the day before had softened overnight as if the admitting space had let out a deep breath and relaxed. We filled card-board cups from a freshly brewed pot of coffee, moved to an empty room, and took seats in patient-guest chairs.

"How's Joe?" I asked.

She swiped through patient charts on her tablet and read through recent notes before answering. "He's on some heavy meds. Slept for a few hours, according to the night shift. The transport helicopter is prepping for his trip to Trident—should be taking off soon. His parents had coffee and some toast about an hour ago. We packed them a lunch and snacks and arranged for a rental car to get them home. They'll have a long road ahead of them."

We blew on our hot coffees in the quiet room, waiting for them to cool and remembering the tragedies that brought us together only a day ago. "I suppose the road trip will give them some time to think. I've worked in hospitals a long time, but it's still hard seeing people suffer. How's Dr. Stratton doing?"

"About the same, came to a few times. Milt was here most of the night. We can't keep Stratton here," she said, perusing the empty rooms nearby and nodding to the housekeeping staff. "We'll need to admit him or trans-fer him to a burn center. The rest of the patients have been discharged or transferred."

The admitting/ER was ready to return to its normal function with pa-tients arriving for scheduled surgery after noon.

"That's good news, Meredith. I'm doing another press conference at 9 a.m. It'll be an update about our honeymooners and a brief status on the other patients. I'll use some of the comments from Johanna and Joe, Sr. Do you think I could talk with Dr. Stratton?"

"Not sure. I'll call you."

"Thanks."

Alice was reading my press statement when I walked into my office, dabbing a tissue on her eyes. "Ann, this is so sad. What will happen to the moms and dads and Joe? How awful. It must have been hard to meet with them."

"It was hard and good, if you know what I mean. I couldn't just say Susan died and Joe went back home with his parents. I needed to know more about them."

"You did a great job. Are you ready for another round of media? Dietary's coming back in about 20 minutes with coffee, pastries, the usual."

"I'm ready. You're the best. Thanks, Alice."

My office was dark. The window shades were still down. I could feel Scott's presence. I touched my lips, remembered his kiss. I was tired and emotional, and I hungered for more. Thank God I moved away. What was I doing? Had I agreed to a Saturday date? I could always back out.

As I lifted the shades, sunlight spread across my desk over a small stack of news releases ready for distribution. The headers were in bold type: "A love story emerges from the bridge tragedy." I wondered if I'd put too much emphasis on love in the statement. Were my feelings for Scott surfacing in news releases?

I straightened the skirt of my pale grey suit, shook my head, picked up the news releases, and headed out the door. The haphazardness of yesterday's early meeting was gone. The TV vans lined up evenly, reporters talking back and forth. I sensed they were eager for more than numbers and data. The helicopter lifted off in the background as I went to the lectern. When the whirling blades faded, I began.

"Good morning. I noticed you looking at the helicopter taking off. The bridegroom is heading off in that med flight to a trauma center in South Carolina. His parents have been here all night with him and are on their way home, too. I'm sad to report his bride of only a few days passed away late last night." I swallowed my emotions and tried to speak clearly, knowing every word was being recorded.

"We arranged air transport last night for the deceased and her parents to take them to their hometown for funeral services and burial. Before I read this news release, I hope you will be considerate of the family's feelings. They're devastated and need time to heal. Please give them that time."

I read the statement slowly. "This is a love story ..." No one spoke for a while. Although I did not reveal the names of the honeymooners, the reporters would refer to them as Joe and Susan. My efforts at confidentiality had already evaporated. April Monroe asked if I had contact information for Susan's parents. I told her the family might ask a relative to serve as their spokesperson. For the time being, I would do my best to assist the family. I was sure the national media networks and cable already knew where they lived, had talked to neighbors, gone to their high schools, colleges and talked to folks in town. They were probably camped outside their houses. Even the best spokesperson could not stop the invasion.

Bob raised his hand from the back of the throng. "Is Dr. Stratton still here?"

"Yes, he's here. His condition is still critical. I'll let you know if that changes."

Alice distributed the statements. "Thank you for your patience. Please help yourselves to our breakfast buffet."

Bob was already on the move, slinking toward the north wing of the medical center. I was about to call security when Alice rushed over. "Ann, Dr. Milton's in your office. He looks terrible. I've never seen him like this."

"I'll be right in. Oh, one more thing. Please call security, I think I saw Bob McCarthy heading toward admitting."

As I walked in, Milt started to stand but seemed to lack the strength to get up. I brought a tray of coffee and egg sandwiches. His eyes were bloodshot. His were hands shaky.

"Dr. Milton, please have something to eat. You're no good for anyone if you pass out."

He nodded, accepted a sandwich, and drank some juice. "I feel like I'm falling apart. Did you mention our talk to Scott or anyone else yet?"

"No. I've been busy. I forgot about it until driving in this morning. I know how important this is, but my priorities keep changing. How is Dr. Stratton?"

"That's why I'm here. He's a real fighter. He's been in and out of consciousness. Keeping him hydrated and his airway open are our top priorities. He should probably be in a burn treatment center. We can take care of his shattered vertebrae after his skin heals; the chance of infection is extremely high, and the pain ..."

"I can't imagine."

"He's heavily medicated but conscious. I told him about my indiscretion, my jealousy issues. All he said was, 'Shit.' He didn't even seem angry. Maybe he knew, or he's so drugged he's not rational."

He took another drink, nibbled at the sandwich.

"Jim's adamant about not leaving. Told me to send in the burn specialists, like they would just pick up and stop by. He knows the head of the burn team at Presbyterian, a guy named Blake. They worked together on the development of porcine graphs. Jim's an expert on everything pigs. I called his pal, and, would you believe it, they're coming today."

"What are his chances? Yesterday you told me it was 20, 30 percent, maybe worse."

"Jim's just mean enough to make it. I don't really know. He has third- and fourth-degree burns on his right arm and hand; deep ones, charred muscle and bone. We may need to amputate his arm, or at a minimum, his hand. I think he used it to cover his eyes and face in the explosion. He has bad patches on his forehead and hairline, but the rest of his face is untouched. If he survives, he will never do surgery again, at least not right-handed."

"I hate to even ask — do you think I could talk to him?"

"He's an angry guy right now. I'll ask him later after the New York team determines treatment options. They should be here soon."

We heard the helicopter coming in and walked outside to the landing pad. The media trucks and news leeches were gone. Four people jumped out, wearing scrubs, each carrying satchels filled with antibacterial salves, dressings, and packages of skin. When I turned, Milt was already on his way to greet them, his white coat rippling in the helicopter's wake. I stayed back and watched. As the shadow of the helicopter lifted off the pad, Scott walked out to join Milt.

CHAPTER 41

"Hey, got a minute?" I asked, as I knocked on Laurie's open door. Her short black hair was perfectly coiffed, and her lipstick matched scarlet nails that danced lightly over an ergonomic keyboard. There was nothing out of place except me, frazzled, tired, and needy.

"Ann, come on in. You look like you could use a rest. I watched you on Channel 4's roundup last night. What an awful accident—the honeymooners, Dr. Stratton, and that little boy. I don't know how you do it."

I sat across from her desk as she closed the door. "Not sure I always know what I'm doing, either. I met with the honeymooners' parents last night."

Laurie moved around her desk to sit next to me. "I can't imagine how they'll get through this. I'm sure the family appreciates your sensitivity."

"Thanks, I hope so."

Laurie opened a small refrigerator in the corner and pulled out two bottles of lime-flavored sparkling water. I accepted the fizzy drink, and we laughed when the tiny bubbles made me sneeze; it was a welcome break from sad love stories, confessions, and a churning romance with the boss. I just needed a friend, a friend who could help solve a murder.

Laurie seemed to understand my need for friendship and changed the subject. "How's Stratton doing?" she asked. "I've been in my office since 6 this morning working on a report for the quality committee. I'm kind of out of touch."

"He's alive, for now. If he lives, he'll never perform surgery again. I just spoke to Milt about his chances. His right arm took the brunt of the fire blast from the explosion. He has third- and fourth-degree burns, but doesn't want to transfer to a burn center."

"He's a stubborn SOB."

"So, I've heard." I took a few more sips of the seltzer water, trying to organize my thoughts before resuming our conversation. "He was on his way to meet with me yesterday morning to talk about last Friday's news story; the one about investigating his lab work. It was a convoluted piece of news, ginned up by The News reporter, Bob McCarthy. Stratton called me right after it came out—told me all the accusations about causing Lebeau's death were false, 'fucking false' as he put it."

Laurie laughed. "Sounds like him."

I hesitated to discuss more of Stratton's rant, but I needed Laurie's help to maneuver around HIPAA barriers because IT reported to her. I wasn't sure how willing she would be to leave her black and white world of rules and regs to slide into my world of grey possibilities.

"Stratton has recorded conversations with Guy Lebeau and has more information he wanted to share with me. That's why he was on the bridge. He was coming to see me," I said, not realizing how emotional I sounded in this room of calm and order. I couldn't seem to keep it together. "I don't know what to do."

"Is he conscious? Can he talk?"

I took another swig of bubbly water. "Milt said he's in and out and swears a lot. He's in terrible pain and told Milt to bring in the burn team from NY Presbyterian. They agreed to come. The helicopter that just took off brought in four surgeons. Dr. Stratton apparently worked with their head doc on skin grafts."

Laurie got up and walked over to her office window as the helicopter headed south. She watched for a few seconds then turned toward me. "Ann, about the recording. These are patient records … protected patient records. Stratton and whoever he assigns as caregivers are the only ones who can access the files. I'm sure a password is needed to open them. What information do you think he wants to share?"

When she mentioned assigned caregivers, I wondered how I could become "assigned." Not a nurse, not a doctor, not a tech, but a PR person was caught in the middle of this drama. "He said it was something I needed to know. Hopefully, he can talk with me today or tomorrow."

"Good luck."

"Right now, I'm more worried about Dr. Milton." She arched one eyebrow as if she wasn't sure what I said. "Remember our conversation about The News reporter's inside source, the one who revealed Stratton's ethics committee review?"

"We didn't come to any conclusions, as I recall. It could have been an admin assistant, someone with access to the file."

I shook my head as I answered. "It wasn't an admin, Laurie; it was Dr. Milton."

"What!" The normally calm, in control doctor looked as though I'd punched her.

"Laurie, he confessed. He thought he did it anonymously using his cell phone. That's no problem for a reporter as tricky as Bob to figure out who was calling."

"Why would he do that?" she asked, still looking surprised.

"Stratton's accident really upset Milt. He envied Stratton's fame, his amazing skills and new surgical techniques. He was mostly jealous of his research, Milt's bailiwick. He and other surgeons scoffed at Stratton's use of pig ligaments, animal parts, and then his probiotics. Milt admitted the outcomes were better than expected: they turned his detractors and grant funders into supporters."

"I'll admit I was one of those docs who questioned Stratton's work."

I wanted to say something about doctors being smart in most spheres— in medicine, science, and math, but clueless about a reporter's shenanigans. I decided it wasn't appropriate.

"He thought he could topple the superstar," I said, "it all backfired. Not sure how this will turn out. His colleague may be dying. I doubt he realized he was jeopardizing the reputation of his own medical center."

Laurie sat down next to me again. "What are you going to do?"

"Not sure. Might not do anything. Bob never used Milt's name as the source. Milt seemed repentant. What's your take?"

She shook her head, got up, and moved behind her desk, holding onto the back of her chair, red nails shining. "It's a lot to think about. I like numbers and data. Confessions and subterfuge are a little outside my expertise. Scott needs to know; maybe he can help you. I suppose the board wants an update; have you sent them your media statements?"

"Not the most recent one. I've been too embedded in all this subter-fuge, as you put it. I'll stop in to see Scott and have his admin update the board." I tossed the empty water bottle in the recycling bin and thanked her for listening.

CHAPTER 42

It was close to noon as I entered the executive suite. Scott's assistant Mary told me he was working on hospital financial projections but would welcome an interruption. Although I couldn't be sure, I thought I noticed a slight wink and nod. "I'm sure he won't mind seeing you," she said. "Let me check."

She dialed his extension to let him know I was there and smiled. "He'll be right out."

Scott opened the door after a few minutes and asked me to come in. With a loosened tie, rolled up sleeves, and a missing suit jacket, he looked out of place in his own office yet oddly endearing. He held a pair of reading glasses and stuffed them in his shirt pocket as if I didn't know he needed them to read. He rolled his eyes and tilted his head back toward his desk when I heard a rather forced cough from someone behind him.

I squelched my original desire for an embrace when Scott moved away to reveal his gangly boss, looking irritated and uncomfortable in one of the leather guest chairs. Milt was rifling through some ledger sheets with one hand and fidgeting with the stethoscope around his neck that seemed to be choking him. Scott's desk was covered with file folders and half-eaten trays of food.

After a few moments of silence, Scott spoke up. "Ann, I'm glad you're here. We needed a break," he said, guiding me to the empty chair next to Milt. "Would you like something to eat or some coffee?"

"I think I've had enough coffee for a lifetime. It's been a tough 24 hours."

Scott sat in his executive desk chair, swiveling back and forth as Milt kept reading. "We've been trying to make sense of the last few days. Dave Brown's coming in for a board update."

"If there's anything I can do to help, let me know."

I was beginning to wonder if Milt even knew I was sitting next to him. To break the awkward silence, I asked him about the burn team.

"How's Dr. Stratton? I noticed the helicopter crew leaving."

He tugged the stethoscope off his neck and tossed it on the coffee table. "Ah, yes. Dr. Stratton. The New York team's in the OR prepping—not sure they can save him or anything else around here," he said, spreading his lanky fingers across the stack of files and papers. After a pause, he continued his rant. "As Scott, our exemplary CEO, pointed out to me before your arrival, the board's not going to cheer when they see how much this ER debacle costs. Then add these new revenue projections without Jim's caseload no matter how much PR we spin out there."

Whew. I wasn't sure Milt was attacking me, Scott, or the inert file folders. His stiff white coat seemed to deflate around him. What happened to the abject confessor who hours before had come to my office for solace and assurances? Scott sighed, shook his head, pushed his chair back against the wall, and walked over.

"Milt, I know you're upset about Jim and all this media attention. Go check on your patient. I'll update the board. They'll understand. These are only blips in revenue. We'll be fine."

"Fine? The board's worried Scott. Did you do the right thing? We're not a real trauma center," Milt said, looking at Scott, then me. "What do you think, Ann?"

The man who hardly knew I existed suddenly wanted my opinion. I was proud of our efforts to care for the accident victims and reminded Scott and Milt about my earlier press conference. "My message was clear—our staff members are highly qualified and acted appropriately. I also said we used the Milton Center helicopter to transport several victims to other medical centers, saving time and reducing trauma. Maybe that will quash some of their concerns."

"Yeah, too bad no one's paying for those flying ambulances." He stood up, stuffed the irritating stethoscope into his pocket, and walked out. A whoosh of dankness left with him.

Scott moved into Milt's vacated seat, leaned in, and pushed a strand of hair off my forehead. "Ann, I'm sorry you had to witness Milt's melt-down—he hasn't slept, and he's worried about too many things. Dave should be here soon, and I need to finish this damn report. Is there something you need, or can we meet later this afternoon?"

I thought about revealing Milt's confession, but it could wait. I stood up, moved toward the door. "No problem, call me when you have more time." As I turned to leave, Jennifer, our in-house counsel, approached us with a sheaf of papers in her right hand and an angry grimace.

"Ann, Scott. This is the wrongful death lawsuit from the Lebeau family, accusing the Milton Center of employing James Stratton, MD, who, it says, 'tampered with his probiotic pills developed in the Center's lab, lacing them with fentanyl to control the hockey star's pain after botched surgery.' We've been expecting it but not the amount—it's a $100 million lawsuit."

Scott grabbed the papers from Jen's hands. "This is ridiculous," he said. "Stratton may be mean, but why would he do that? He's not doing so well, either. Does Milt need to know?"

"We could keep it quiet for a while," Jen said. "Word will get out. I expect Lebeau's lawyer will be calling a press conference. You'd better get ready; the bad news keeps coming."

"Thanks, Jen," I said. "Please send me a scan of the lawsuit. I need to call Chief Schuller, for an update about their investigation." I left the sixth floor distracted by a hefty lawsuit, our erratic founder, and an anxious CEO.

CHAPTER 43

The Grand Island Police Department's call center forwarded my request to talk with the police chief, letting me know he was at a meeting. About 30 minutes later, he called back. "Ann, how are you?"

"I think I'd like to slow down, thanks. Doesn't look like that will be anytime soon."

"Is this about the accident or the Lebeau case?"

"As awful as the accident was, we're facing another crisis of sorts. The Lebeau family filed its lawsuit, delivered this morning, suing the medical center and its employee, Dr. James Stratton, for wrongful death. They claim Stratton laced his probiotic capsules with fentanyl to reduce Lebeau's pain caused by botched surgery. It's a $100 million lawsuit."

"Lot of money," the chief said. "Top goalies make millions a year, so I guess I'm not too surprised. I'm on my way back from a meeting with the Williamsville police about the Lebeau case. We're on to something important. I can stop by if you have time."

"I hope it's good news. I'm open most of the afternoon."

I looked forward to his visit despite my smoldering feelings for Scott. The chief had a way of making me feel better. Alice lived in his neighborhood and was quite vocal about the attributes of this charming man who had lost his wife to ovarian cancer five years ago. After her death, Alice and her female neighbors kept the chief and his young son Michael supplied with casseroles, pastries and kindness. Whenever he showed up at my office, Alice jumped in to deliver coffee and ask about his son, who was the same age as her son Jeff.

I heard the screech of her desk chair as she stood up to welcome the chief. Her voice was warm, and he returned her welcome with "Good to see you, Alice. Thanks for that great apple pie. Michael's waiting for hockey season to get going. I'm sure you've seen the boys tearing up the roadways, playing street hockey." She laughed and agreed. I walked in to greet him.

"Hi Ann, if you're ever in the mood for cakes or cookies, let me know. Alice and my other neighbors seem to think I need sweetening up."

"I doubt that's the reason. Thanks for coming by."

Maybe it was the uniform or his solid build that exuded self-confidence, strength, and power. I would hate to be a wrongdoer in his presence. His gleaming leather boots and shoulder holster crunched as he sat down in my office chair that was almost too small to hold him. He accepted my offer of coffee and leaned back, challenging the chair's flimsy frame.

"Good to see you, Chief. What's up?"

"Ann, please call me Lance. I think 'Chief' is fine for my officers to use, way too stuffy for friends and colleagues."

I smiled at the thought of being his friend, picked up my cup of tea, and blew the steamy brew to cool it down. "So, Lance, what's the news?"

"The last time we talked, I told you we were aware the fentanyl-laced heroin that killed Lebeau came from ingesting capsules containing probiotics. We believed they were the ones provided by Dr. Stratton. The medical examiner discovered some undigested capsules during the autopsy. Williamsville police searched his home and bedroom but found no trace of the original capsules, no pill bottles—nothing. People in pain or contemplating suicide are not that neat."

"So, what does that prove?"

He flipped through a small pad to reference his notes. I noticed his handwriting was neat and truncated, unlike my notebooks filled with erratic whorls and annotations along the edges. He was both handsome and efficient. No wonder Alice swooned in his presence.

"We're still working on proof but we're getting closer. The Williamsville detectives brought in another forensics team and searched the hockey player's home again. They found a few capsules in Lebeau's bed, stuck between the frame and mattress. They brought the pills back to the lab, determined they were tampered with and refilled. And, they found some partial prints—they're running them now. They also traced the source of the narcotic to some dealers in South Buffalo they've been monitoring for a few months. Lots of lowlife scuttling in and out of that area."

"So, where does that leave Stratton?"

"Not sure. We're searching through massive amounts of recordings to see if we can spot Stratton at a game or near the player's home. And we haven't found Lebeau near the medical center since the day of his surgery. We also doubt Lebeau intentionally overdosed; it looks like someone wanted him out of the picture."

"Lance, that's good news ... for the Medical Center. Are you going public with this?"

"Not yet. It's too early. What I've told you is confidential. We don't want anyone to know we found these capsules. If we're lucky, we may get some prints—even DNA."

"Can I let Scott know?"

"Let's keep this between us for now. I trust you to understand the fragile nature of this investigation."

I sipped the still hot tea and wondered why he didn't trust Scott. "I'll do as you say. We'll continue to claim our innocence. I'm hoping to talk with Dr. Stratton. He was coming to meet me the morning of the accident to give me some background on his communication with Lebeau. It may be HIPAA-protected. What will you say to the media if they call about the lawsuit?"

"That's easy, Ann. 'This is an ongoing investigation.' That's about all I can say."

"How long will it take?"

He shifted his weight in the narrow chair. "We can only say we don't know. I can't discuss the capsules or the fact we've traced the fentanyl pushers. I'm hoping we can get the results of the lab work in the next day or two. Most of the buyers in this illegal trade know how to be invisible. Not everyone's in our ID database, either. We'll work all the angles."

His mention of working the angles made me think of Bob McCarthy. "Be on the lookout for that reporter from The Buffalo News. I'm close to requesting a restraining order. We have him on tape dressed in scrubs, tailgating in employee-only elevators. We also saw him milling around in the ER with the accident victims. I don't trust him."

"We'll watch out for him. Let me know if you get that order. We'll have to enforce it, or maybe George and his team will be enough. Keep me in the loop if you hear anything from Stratton?"

"The same for you. We appreciate your personal attention. For a quiet island, things have been crazy."

He stood up to the sound of crunching leather and a chair sighing in relief. We shook hands as he headed out and said goodbye to Alice, who was probably beaming.

Scott called to let me know he was available to meet. I headed to the elevator when I saw my nemesis come through the main entrance. "Bob, what are you doing here?"

"Hey, I'm in a public area. I have a right to be here, just like Chief Schuller. Interesting visitor. Anything you want to tell me about the hockey star's death?"

"Nothing's changed since the last time we talked. The Milton Center's not at fault for the death of Mr. Lebeau."

"Really, how about the $100 million lawsuit? I suspect that's something new."

"Sounds like you're the one with new information. Do you have a copy of the lawsuit?"

"Not yet, but I will. Mr. Lebeau's attorney just sent us a heads up; it's being delivered today."

"Aren't you full of news? I'll let you know if we have anything to add to my statement. I doubt it, though. In case you didn't hear me before - we're not at fault for the death of Mr. Lebeau."

I turned toward the bank of elevators, hoping he'd go away. He ignored my affront.

"So, what did the good lawman have to say?"

"Ask him. I suggest you turn around and leave the way you came in. My warning about a restraining order is still there. According to security, they had to escort you out of a staff-only area this morning after the news conference; seems you were lost again in a hallway near the admitting area."

"It's a big hospital and easy to get lost. I'll talk to you later." He shuffled off toward the main entrance with his messy notebook stuffed in his back pocket.

He was so arrogant and sneaky, and even though I understood his instincts to get the gritty details and break the story, I felt like breaking his neck. I needed some fresh air and texted Scott to let him know I'd call him later.

CHAPTER 44

I switched my heels for a pair of flats I'd stashed under my desk, grabbed a sweater, and headed outside. Shade trees and flower gardens lined a narrow, cobbled walkway behind the helipad. Generous families had donated benches along the path that ended in a circular labyrinth, designed to slow rushed lives, relieve stress, and calm worries. The sky was a soft blue with wispy clouds covering the afternoon sun. Once vibrant hydrangeas had turned a dusty grey, the plants tinged with rusted edges from the recent cold snap. Even though I loved autumn's crisp days, they changed rapidly, leaving leaves and flowers to curl and crumble.

As I walked, I noticed a trail of weeds and grass tamped down by heavy boots and shoes, heading toward the Leone property. A soggy placard was caught in the tall grass; its faint letters spelled out, "Milton Kills."

Claire Leone was working her way down the path, picking up discarded signs, tossing them into a black trash bag. She had wide, serviceable shoes with frayed laces, a pale, moon-shaped face, and a mass of fluffy grey hair. She noticed me approaching and turned away. I wasn't sure she was shy, angry, or just afraid to speak.

"Good morning, Claire. I'm Ann Delaney; we haven't met yet." She seemed a bit stunned that I spoke. Yet, she turned to face me.

"Oh, I know who you are. You're the one on TV and in the paper … PR person, right?"

"Yeah, that's me. Beautiful morning."

"That depends."

"Are you alright?"

196

She clenched the damp sign, shoved it in the trash bag, and stepped closer. She looked like she needed a warm sweater or a hug.

"I'm not … it's this animal rights mess. Jake is so hard to deal with. You know we really don't believe in this. We grew up raising animals, naming our cows, loving our dogs. It was a hard life but good. Now, we can't do any of that."

"Why not?" I asked, moving along the path with her.

"Because of your big hospital. No one seems to give a damn about us."

I wasn't sure what comfort I could offer. "Claire, I understand why you're upset about the land loss. When I look out the windows from the top floor, I can see your house. Our Medical Center throws a big shadow and blocks your view of the sunset. I'm so sorry; I wish it were different."

Claire looked up at the imposing building then back to her ramshackle home. Her voice cracked. "I appreciate that more than you know. This is really about our son. Activism is like a religion to him. He lives in Seattle, doesn't even come home. Calls all the time. He's in tight with lots of crazies, smokes marijuana, tells people what not to do. I love him, but we can't keep this up. I'm tired; Jake and I are both tired. We have to let go and enjoy what's left of our lives on our remaining land."

"Are you planning to continue the picketing?"

Claire bent over to pick up another soaked sign. "No. No more. I'm done. Jake's had it, too, although he won't admit it. Jake will go for days without talking then fume over the smallest things. Your hospital is one of the biggest things. I love him deeply and wish I could take his mind off what other people eat for breakfast. He actually eats eggs himself … Oh, please don't say anything."

I placed my hand on her soft shoulder rounded from the weight of an erratic husband and domineering son. "Don't worry, Claire. I'm good at keeping secrets. This may sound silly, but have you thought of getting Jake another dog? It could take his mind off other things."

I picked up a remnant of another tattered sign caught in some brambles. "I need to get back in. Call me someday, and we can have lunch. I'm so glad we met." I said, shaking her hand with both of mine.

"Thanks, Ann. I look forward to it. The dog's not a bad idea—we used to have a black lab. A good boy; we called him Blackie—not too original, was it? Loved the guy. He lived to be 15, passed away around the same time our son moved out. It was a double tragedy. I'll think about it," she said, smiling for the first time.

I tried to knock the mess from my shoes before walking into the lobby and right into Scott. "Where've you been? In the mud?"

"I took a break. Were you worried?"

"Yes, no ... it doesn't matter. Let's get a coffee and sit out on the café patio. The weather's warmed up."

We found a table near some shrubs at the edge of the patio, deserted after the lunch crowd had gone back to work. Scott was back in his CEO trappings, wearing a sport coat and a knotted tie. He waited for me to sit before pulling out a chair for himself. "I got the feeling this morning you had something more to say."

I lowered my voice in case errant eavesdroppers were about. "It's Milt; he told me something yesterday I didn't mention. We were so involved in the honeymooner talk and other things."

"Hmm. I remember: the other things," he said, with a silly grin that made me want to stall even more. "Scott, this is serious. I've found Bob's insider source —it's Milt."

Scott seemed as shocked as Laurie. He listened as I explained the jealousy motive, the guilt Milt felt with Stratton close to death, shaking his head as if I'd made it up.

"Damn, this is nuts, Ann. Milt hired me. His mission was my mission. His dreams were my dreams. We talked for hours and days about creating a unique center for advanced orthopedic medicine," he said, gesturing at the surrounding buildings. "He's so fixated on money. Does he really hate Stratton that much?"

I sat back as a cloud covered the sun. "Scott, I don't know. Milt confessed to Dr. Stratton, who apparently forgave him. It's the screwiest thing. I don't think Bob will reveal Milt's identity; his unethical tricks have given us some leverage if we need to use it."

"How's that?"

"Bob has ignored all our trespassing warnings, stolen some Milton scrubs, and he's shown up in staff-only areas more than once."

"You're sure about Bob?" he asked, looking for the reporter's shadow in the empty chairs and glass doorway.

"Let me worry about Bob," I said. "He's squeezed all he can out of Milt. His new target is this lawsuit."

"A hundred million dollars' worth. This'll be another negative news story. How much more can we handle?"

The wind swirled maple leaves around the slate terrace and over our glass-topped table, floating over our mugs. I tapped a few words into my cell phone notebook. "We'll stress these are allegations only, with absolutely no proof. I hope they leave the images of Dr. Stratton's accident off the front page."

Scott sat up at the mention of Dr. Stratton. "Ann, I almost forgot why I wanted to talk to you," he said as he scrolled through his phone messages. "Meredith sent me a text. The burn team transferred Stratton to the ICU. He's in tough shape."

"I hope they don't intubate him. I need to talk to him."

"You might still have time," Scott said.

I kicked the mud off on my shoes before getting up.

"Ann, what's with the mud? Where were you?"

The patio was still empty. Some landscapers were off in the distance blowing leaves away from recently planted mums. I moved my chair closer to Scott to overcome the noise. I described the path, the wet signs, and the good news about the pickets, adding Claire's story of a lost son and a lost farm.

Scott leaned forward, put his hands near mine on the glass tabletop. In a whisper, he said, "Ann, you seem so sad … we've been through a lot lately."

I swallowed my emotions and wrapped my hands around my empty coffee cup, acutely aware of how our patio meeting might look to other employees. What was I thinking when I agreed to date this man, the CEO and my boss? I could still cancel. For the moment, I suggested we go back inside.

Scott didn't seem phased by being out in the open. I even thought he was enjoying my edginess. "Ann, I know what you're thinking: this is too public, right? Let's go. Saturday can't come soon enough."

I looked around to see if anyone was near enough to hear him. Empty tables were our only neighbors. My phone was filling up with reporter texts. "The lawsuit must have hit the airwaves."

"Will you do another press conference?"

I shook my head. "Don't think so. It would only give this whole lawsuit too much credence. I'll send something brief."

"Whatever you say. Glad you talked to Claire. Tough stuff; at least the picketing is over."

"Yeah, she's got a lot to deal with. See you later."

I went back to my office, posted a reminder note to check in with Claire if she doesn't call in a few days, then wrote up a brief statement regarding the lawsuit and hit "send." I wished I could add something about the police investigation, then remembered another promise made to the kind, charming chief of police.

CHAPTER 45

Bob McCarthy followed Scott and me to dinner, listened to our conversation, came back to my apartment, slipped between the sheets with us, and laughed louder and louder until everyone we knew was in the dark room, whispering. I woke up sweating.

Bob wasn't there, nor was Scott. Sleep was elusive the rest of the night. I rose before the sun and the news broke, headed to the park's footpath. It was cool and misty; the only sounds were the cawing of a trio of seagulls. Spirits haunted me around every bend. I could see Milt's arched fingers, bowed head, glasses slipping down his nose, then Stratton's scorched skin, followed by Scott smiling, grabbing my hand, asking me to trust him. Bob was gone. I knew he'd return.

I left the ghosts outside my door, caught my breath, called Meredith to check on Stratton. "Hi Meredith, hope it's not too early to call. How's Dr. Stratton?"

"He's still with us, spitting out verbal venom. He refused transfer. The burn team eased some of his pain, not much else they could do. Doesn't look good. I suppose you want to talk to him."

"I do. Is there a good time?"

"Bring your earmuffs—he can be loud."

Even though my ID badge gave me access to the Intensive Care Unit, I picked up the wall phone in the waiting room to let the charge nurse know I was there to see Dr. Stratton. She buzzed the locked door and told me he was in Room 4.

The ICU was physically and emotionally removed from the hustle of the main hospital. The lights were dim and sounds muted. Each room had large windows covered in translucent shades revealing softened images of trees, birds, sky, and drifting clouds. Metal-framed sliding glass doors enclosed fragile patients. Beating hearts and breathing lungs left imprints on high-tech equipment, emitting the sounds of life tucked under crisp white sheets and thin hospital blankets.

One of the intensivists, Ray Amara, stopped me as I walked past the nurses' station, his voice at low volume. "Hey Ann, saw you on the morning news. So sad about the young bride and groom." I'd only met this young doctor once before at a new doc reception. He was born in the Philippines, board-certified in internal and pulmonary medicine, and a rising superstar at Milton or any hospital he chose. He was one of the few bachelors on staff, so my female friends went out of their way to cross paths with this specialist. I was surprised he knew my name.

"Good morning, Dr. Amara. I can't imagine how the families of the honeymooners will get through this. Time heals, so they say."

"Sometimes. Hope you're ready for the good doctor," he said with a smirky smile. "He's a bit grumpy."

"I won't be long. Thanks for the warning."

From the hall, Room 4 looked serene. Dr. Stratton's right arm and right leg were wrapped in thick white bandages. An IV was running into his left leg; his feet were covered in booties. A spray of angry black pockmarks across his forehead distorted his pale skin. I knocked. He turned and slowly gestured with his left hand, grimacing in pain.

"Good morning, Dr. Stratton. I'm Ann Delaney. How are you feeling?"

His voice was gravelly from sedation. "Like shit."

I wasn't sure if he knew who I was or could hear me. I moved a little closer. "I'm Ann, Ann Delaney."

"I know who you are … I was coming to see you … that tanker blew up … could have died … everyone would be happy if I did."

"I don't think so," I said, shaking my head. "You're an amazing surgeon … famous."

He spat out. "Are you an imbecile? You can't even control the press. What the hell can you do now?"

I gulped, found my thin voice. "If you let me ask you a few questions, maybe we can get answers," I said, searching for a more confident tone. "Believe it or not, I think we have a good chance to change the storyline."

"Ask your questions. I'm not going anywhere," he said, clenching his teeth.

"Thanks. When we talked a few days ago, you were upset about the news story after the surveyors' visit. The reporter twisted a positive result into something negative, calling it an investigation into the lab."

"Hmm…"

"That's not what happened. Dr. Rogers asked about the survey process for the probiotics. They said it wasn't in their purview but noted the lab had followed the FDA regulations."

"Busy bugger; that's just like Milt. He hates me. Confessed …"

"He told me about calling the reporter, about the ethics. He's been very upset since your accident. I think he really cares."

Stratton looked puzzled when I told him Milt cared about him. "What do you want?"

I shifted in my straight-backed chair, referred to my scattered notes, ready to listen or leave quickly. "When we talked, you mentioned a video recording of your conversations with Guy Lebeau that might explain a few things. Can you tell me more?"

"Video …" His eyes strayed from me as he looked at something in the distance that seemed to be dragging his thoughts to a place far away. I wasn't sure he would say more.

"Dr. Stratton, what's on the video?"

He turned, moaning. "Marketing ploy …"

"Did Guy Lebeau agree to the promotional stuff?"

"Yeah. Never used this one. Three years ago. Amazing job. No pain. Great goalie … was…"

He paused again, took some deep breaths. "Jesus … Are you done yet?"

"I have a few more questions."

"Hurry up."

"Can you tell me about Guy Lebeau's second surgery this year—June, right?"

"Desperate … called me at home," he said looking at his bandaged hands. "Didn't explain. Gave him phony name. Sent chopper to Montreal…"

"Can you tell me more about the accident?"

He shifted in the sheets. I could see blotches of blood and ointment when he moved, thought I might need to leave. He wasn't done; the drugs must have kicked in.

"Met him in admitting. John Doe or something. Guy said he'd been playing street hockey. He lied. His ACL ripped; there were slashes across his face."

He continued his story, looking out the covered window. "Guy's knee was in bad shape from a hard blow with a hockey stick. God-dammed brother. Look at the video," he shouted.

"Is this privileged information?"

His face was turning red, spit collected in the corner of his lips. "Fucking HIPAA ... know what that means?"

"I do." Despite his invective, I needed more. "Who hurt him? Do you think I could look at it?"

"I didn't hurt Lebeau. I helped him."

I was furiously taking notes with underlined question marks. "Do you think one of his brothers has something to do with Guy's death?"

"Video ..."

I thought about my next request and wasn't sure I should ask. "Can you give me the password to access the video file?"

For the first time I saw tears in his angry blue eyes. "angela84... supposed to get married." He moaned. "Milton ... secrets ..."

Stratton closed his eyes and turned away. His crankiness and mean exterior couldn't hide the sadness that never abated. I left him in the sterile room, monitors beeping life and death in a duel, not sure which would win.

CHAPTER 46

I was in the middle of a swamp where no matter how I moved, I sank into secrets: Chief Schuller and the investigation; the lawsuit; Stratton's revelations; potential HIPAA violations; and Milt's erratic behavior. If I told Scott this litany of things, I'd drag him into the quandary with me. I sent Jen a text and headed to her office on the sixth floor. She met me at her door.

"Ann, you're looking a little ragged. I was just about to head out for a staff meeting. Is this about the lawsuit?"

"It is in a way. It's about Guy Lebeau."

I reviewed my meeting with the Stratton and the existence of the video including a few of his aptly placed blasphemies. She winced when I asked if I could look at the video then pulled me into her office and closed the door. We sat down facing each other. The atmosphere seemed a bit chilly. I wasn't sure I was welcome.

"Ann, this is tricky. Seems like you're single-handedly trying to solve a crime. Not sure you or I should get involved. Information in the patient record can't be disclosed, even if the patient is deceased. A court could order a search warrant, then we'd be required to release only the relevant parts of Lebeau's records."

"Who asks the court to issue the warrant?" I said.

"The investigating police. Do you know what they're looking for?"

"Some way to implicate or exonerate Stratton and the Milton Center. I know they want to talk to him."

"You do? What else do you know?"

"The police chief mentioned he'd like to meet with Stratton, but I wasn't sure he could. Stratton's in tough shape. Although ..."

Jen leaned in a little closer when I hesitated. "Yes?"

"Stratton gave me his password," I said, not sure she would give me access to the video or just tell me to leave.

Jen rubbed her forehead, in the cool, neat room, considering options. She absently scrolled through some messages on her cell phone, then looked up at me. "Ann, I'm really a little uneasy about this. The video contract is confidential, although we can use it for potential marketing after the patient's recovered. You know I'm not a fan of those carefully edited patient stories but since marketing's one of your roles, you might be able to look at the video."

Jen kept checking the time on her phone as if she wanted to leave for a vital meeting or just end our conversation. I wasn't sure Stratton wanted me or anyone to view the video—or did he?

"What if we watch it together, even get Laurie involved?" I asked.

She was quiet for a moment, checked her watch again then lowered her voice. "If there's anything incriminating, we may need to involve more people like Stratton's lawyer and the police. Let's wait and see. It may be nothing. How about tomorrow afternoon?"

My anxiety waned with her suggestion. "Thanks, Jen. I really appreciate your help."

We walked out of her office together. She continued down the hall as I veered off to administration to see if Scott was around. Mary smiled and said, "He's meeting with Dr. Green." It was her way of letting me know he was off playing golf.

Great. My world was in turmoil while the CEO whacked a white ball across a path of short green grass. I couldn't blame him. The last few days were tough; the sights and sounds of burned patients, the newlywed saga, Stratton's injuries, and Milt's confession. He was probably schmoozing some money players in healthcare's high stakes game, besting insurance companies, and finding a way to pay for emergency copter rides. Lawyers, accountants, and financial experts like Todd Delaney circled CEOs like hawks looking for deep pockets while patients paid the price.

Alice had stacked the morning newspapers on my desk, topped with The Buffalo News boldly proclaiming the "$100M wrongful death suit filed by Lebeaus." Even though I wasn't surprised, it riled me to see how much ink they wasted on it. I tossed it in the trash, changed my mind and yanked it out to read the story when my phone rang; it was the Grand Island Police Chief Lance Schuller.

"I have some new information about the Lebeau case. Can you come over to the station?"

"Sure. I need a fresh perspective on a few things. I'll head right out."

The police station was close to Milton on Whitehaven Road, near the town hall. Maple trees along the roadway were turning a golden red against a clear blue sky, so different from the icy chill that spread across the South Bridge just days before, destroying lives in its path. A small road sign pointed the way to a simple, one-floor structure faced in brick with double glass doors. I didn't see bars on the windows or any sign of criminals in residence. A young policewoman greeted me by name and pointed out the chief's office on the right. As I walked through his open door, he stood up, smiled and moved around his sturdy oak desk to greet me. Dark leather chairs, nicked and scratched by fellow officers carrying handcuffs, weapons, and heavy burdens surrounded a large rectangular, Formica-topped table in the center of the room. The dark grey carpet was worn to white in spots from thick-soled shoes and rolling chairs. On the shelf, behind the chief's desk, were photos of his son playing baseball and one of his smiling wife, holding a baby boy.

He extended his hand and thanked me for coming. "It's pretty basic around here, but we get the job done."

"It's just good to get out of the office. I should do it more often."

"Please, have a seat."

He pulled out a chair for me from under the center table then settled into one on the opposite side and placed a case folder between us. When he looked up, I saw the crinkles around his blue eyes and the faintest of smiles. It was good to get out of the office.

"Ann, if you have time, I thought we might have lunch after we chat. I ordered some subs from one of the Island's delis—should be here soon. Of course, if you have to get back, we can pack it up to go."

My normal noon time smoothie was fast and portable when all I cared about was enough calories to get me through the rest of the day. A relaxing lunch with the impressive police chief seemed a solid alternative.

"Thanks. Lunch sounds great."

I almost forgot why I was sitting at the battered table on a beat-up chair. "So, what's the big news?"

He leafed through some paperwork then pulled out a sheaf of yellow sheets from the medical examiner's office. "It's about the capsules we found. Our forensics lab has identified some prints and DNA. The DNA is still processing but we know the prints are not Stratton's. He was in the military briefly, so we have his prints. The ones we found are not in any of our databases. We think someone else filled the capsules. If we had suspects, we might trace them back."

The slim file with its yellow sheets were splattered with forensic acronyms I couldn't decipher until the final page conclusion, "source unknown." Even though the pieces were coming together, it wasn't enough. The chief seemed to notice my disappointment.

"Ann, it's good news. We just need a few more days." I needed to temper my disillusionment and show some gratitude. He'd made our center's crisis his priority and I selfishly wanted more.

"You're right. Guess I'm just anxious. Is there anything I can do?"

"Have you talked to Stratton yet? Do you think we could get in to see him?"

I thought about my awkward conversation with Stratton and if I should reveal anything. "I talked to him this morning. He's in a lot of pain. I think he blames me for his injuries. I guess I am in a way."

"You can't think that. The accident wasn't your fault. Did he say anything else?"

"He said Guy's second surgery … you know, I'm not sure I can tell you yet. We haven't confirmed Guy had this recent surgery. I even told the media I wouldn't reveal patient information. I'm meeting with the legal team tomorrow afternoon. Can I get back to you on that?"

"I understand. We have a right to question Dr. Stratton, since he's the one the Lebeaus think killed Guy."

"Hopefully, he'll get better. I should have an answer on the HIPAA stuff soon."

Lance tucked the paperwork back into the case folder. His assistant knocked on the door, opened it, holding a tray with two boxes and two bottles of water. "Looks like lunch is here." He took the tray from her.

It smelled like meatball subs—warm, messy and so much better than a smoothie on the go. Lance spread some paper napkins on top of the Formica, distributed the boxes and chips and laughed as I broke the sub in half. I loved the grease and the calories and the pleasant company.

We sat back and talked about growing up in the area. He began with a story about his family farm outside Attica, NY, where they raised chickens and a few cows. "I gave them all names and cried when one was slaughtered. I had a horse and lots of dogs. I really miss it and wish my son could have had the same experience." Lance left the farm, graduated from college, played basketball and became a cop.

"I wanted to be one of the good guys. We have a small police force here; only had minor dustups until recently. The Milton Center's arrival changed the island, probably forever. We added more cops and pushed the town to increase its budget. I was grateful the Milton Center paid property taxes even though they're a non-profit."

He raised the blinds and opened a window near his desk. A soft breeze ruffled the edges of our growing pile of napkins soaked in tomato sauce. He seemed content to sit and talk.

"Ann, I know you grew up in the Falls. I'm sure you travelled these roads often across the island."

It was a long time ago. Driving around Grand Island had brought back childhood memories when all I wanted was to be another year older; always in a hurry to move on, take the next step in my journey to somewhere else. "It sometimes feels like I never left—the bridges haven't moved or changed since I was young. I remember coming to the Beaver Island State Park when I was a teenager. We never owned a car. We lived in the city and walked everywhere or took buses. One hot summer day a few friends and I hopped on our one-speed bikes and crossed the island to the park, a good 10 miles."

"I can guess what happened," he said. I smiled at his easy response and was happy to share my recollection.

"The ride over was easy. We baked in the sun, too much, then began our trip back home. I've never been so sore and exhausted, wishing someone would pity us and pick us up. No one did. We pumped our skinny legs up and down in agony. Never did it again. We were so carefree: too young to get jobs, too naïve to think we were in shape. I can almost feel my leg muscles cramping."

Lance laughed. We talked about college, first jobs, my life as a reporter, his life as a beat cop in downtown Buffalo. When we came to the point in our lives when we married, we both hesitated.

"I'm sure by now you know I was married to a guy I met in Boston. Our marriage lasted 25 years, and we have an adopted daughter. She's Asian, graduated from UMass Amherst in May, and took off to see the world. Her name is Julie. I have photos."

"Love to see them," he said.

I pulled out my phone and scrolled through some graduation photos and stopped at the one at the airport as she walked toward the gate, struggling to carry a backpack stuffed with jeans, a laptop, and big dreams.

"She's beautiful. You and her dad must miss her."

"Not so sure she misses her dad. We discovered Todd was living in his own world, cheating. I asked for the divorce just before Julie took off. I left Boston and lots of friends, and started over here, where I grew up. It's only been six months. Scott Marino recruited me. We'd worked together before at a hospital near Boston."

"Sorry about your marriage. Glad you have a daughter. I'm sure you'll have lots of friends here. I don't really know Scott. I hear he's very focused on improving patient care and creating a unique medical center. How is he as a boss?"

I wanted to say he's frustrating, secretive, edgy, controlling, warm, caring and sexy. I was smiling when I answered. "He's a great boss." I paused not sure what to say next. "I know about your wife."

He looked away, shifted in his stiff chair, watching the traffic moving along Whitehaven Road. In the softest voice he talked about Emma. He looked at her photo, said she was beautiful. I thought he was done but I was wrong.

"She was 10 years younger than me. I took my time finding the right woman. We were incredibly happy, even more so when Michael was born. He's 9 now. Three years after he was born, Emma was diagnosed with ovarian cancer. She was only 30. We did everything: treatments, herbals, radiation. She fought so hard and died two years later when Michael was 5. "We miss her so much. It's still hard to talk about her."

I almost cried for a woman I had never met and this man I hardly knew. "Thanks for telling me about her, Lance. She must have been special. I've heard so many sad stories lately. It started with Guy Lebeau, then the accident and the newlyweds. Susan's death was devastating; I can't imagine her young husband going on without her."

"He will. It will take time, lots of time."

We finished our chips and water, scooped up the empty containers and filled one with my uneaten half sub. I wrapped it carefully and packed it in my tote assuring the chief I would enjoy it later. "This was such a great idea. I'll let you know when or if you can visit with Dr. Stratton. Thanks for the yummy lunch and the memories. Does Michael play basketball too?"

He looked at the photo of his smiling, freckle-faced son and nodded. "I used to let him win. Now I struggle, and he loves it."

He walked me out to my car; both of us quiet, not wanting to dig into the rest of our day or hold too tight to sad thoughts. If we could only remember the good times, like surviving a 20-mile bike ride.

CHAPTER 47

Jen clicked a key on the set-up panel in the Smith Conference Room. The blackening shades automatically descended, and the space went dark. Another key click brought up muted lights focused on the wide video screen. Laurie sat next to Jen at the front of the conference room table and motioned for me to close the door. I nodded, moved back to the room entrance, closed, then locked the heavy door just in case the HIPAA police were patrolling the sixth-floor corridors. When I turned around, my HIPAA expert colleagues were shaking their heads, somewhat amused at my paranoia. Laurie and I barely breathed as Jen maneuvered the system's keyboard in front of us. With a few strokes, she opened the medical center's data base, searched James Stratton's patient files and entered the patient number for "John Doe," adding the date of the patient interview with one result.

"OK, Ann, type in the password Dr. Stratton gave you."

They both looked away as I moved closer and typed "angela84." I wasn't sure hiding from the password would make them less complicit in our actions. Any concern they had about moving forward dissipated when the file opened to an image of Guy Lebeau. His face was badly bruised, and he had a deep cut over his left eye. Jen hit "play" and the video began. Dr. Stratton spoke first.

"Guy, as you know, this recording is part of our patient record system. Please say your name, birthdate, and then tell me about your reason for being here."

I could see one of his brothers, Pete or Pierre, pacing in the background. Guy seemed sore and weary; his voice was barely a whisper and his French-Canadian accent pronounced.

"Mais oui. My name is Guy Lebeau, born in Montréal, Canada, 13 November 1982. I was injured playing street hockey with my brothers on our farm. Need to stay in shape, you know." He paused, looking back at his brother. "We play to win, eh Pierre?"

His brother nodded and fidgeted with the change in his pockets.

Guy kept talking. "It gets rough. Hockey sticks all over the place. My face looks bad, eh? I need to keep up appearances," he laughed, then continued.

"Hockey guys always take hits to the face. My knee's the problem. The doc back home told me I blew a ligament, need surgery. You fixed my shoulder. Had no pain. Went right back to skating. Amazing. Need to get in shape for this season. Want no one to know about this, especially coach."

Dr. Stratton said, "We can keep you under your assumed name. No visitors except family."

"I only want Pierre to visit."

"I understand," Stratton said. "I ordered some films. Radiology should be here soon to take you down."

Suddenly Guy's brother blurted out, "It wasn't a friendly game! Guy, tell him. Raymond beat you with a hockey stick; he tried to kill you. If I wasn't there, you'd be dead. Guy, tell someone. He'll only do it again. He could find you here."

"Pierre, enough. This is family stuff ... not ... Doc, can you fix it?"

Stratton agreed to help him as the techs arrived and escorted Guy to radiology. Surprisingly, the video kept running. Dr. Stratton asked Pete to take a seat. "So, Pete, I can see you're upset. Do you think Guy's in danger?"

Pete looked reluctant to say more. "Guy's tough. He's my big brother, always looked out for me. He fought the bullies in our neighborhood. It's Raymond. He's jealous, a good hockey player but never as good as Guy. Then there's Michelle, Guy's wife. Guy's not the best husband."

He stopped, hands still in his pockets, not sure if he should say more, then he began almost choking on the words as they tumbled out.

"Guy treats Michelle like dirt. Raymond ... he's ... he's in love with Michelle. All Guy wants is to get her pregnant, have another boy. His own hockey team. Michelle was pregnant earlier in the year. Guy was happy until he found out she was having a girl; he slapped her around, kicked her in the stomach," he said, gasping for a breath as he brushed away the tears rolling down his cheeks.

"She lost the baby. Ray went crazy, took after Guy with a hockey stick. I dragged Guy away, helped him get here. Raymond doesn't know. Neither does Michelle. They think he's at training camp."

The notoriously crotchety Stratton seemed concerned. "You're a good brother, Pete. I can fix Guy's knee and get him back to the game. We can provide security while he's a patient, even keep him an extra day or so if needed. It will end when he leaves. You'll need to keep an eye on him."

"Merci, doc. Please ... fix him. Don't let him know I shared family business. I will be the one that gets beat up next."

The video ended. It was as if we had just watched a bad TV reality show. No one spoke for a minute, each of us replaying the words of Guy's brother. Jen closed the file and lifted the darkening shade. "Ann, I'm amazed at the content in this video. I doubt Stratton knew the video was still on when Guy left the room. I'm not even sure what we do now."

"I'm not the legal one here," I said, "but it seems less and less like Guy Lebeau's death was accidental. I feel so sorry for Michelle and Pete Lebeau. What do we do?"

"We can't tell the police about the video without violating patient confidentiality rules," Jen said.

"Chief Schuller wants to talk to Dr. Stratton. Not sure Stratton will consent. Even if he does, I'm not even sure he'll discuss any of this."

Laurie suggested we call in Scott and Dr. Milton. I agreed Scott should know but wasn't as sure about Dr. Milton. As I debated my next steps, George called.

"Annie, do you have a few minutes? I need to show you some video."

"Excuse me, did you say video?" I said, thinking he knew about the docudrama we had just watched.

"I had one of my guys going back through some security video and found something you need to see."

"I'll be right down."

CHAPTER 48

George's tiny office was stacked with files and time schedules. He moved a stack off one chair, apologizing for the chaos, and gave me his seat in front of the security monitors. He squeezed in to press a few keys then stepped back so I could see. The date at the bottom of the video was a few days earlier at 5:30 a.m. A thin man in a hoodie, jeans, and sneakers, walked in, looked around the empty lobby, and walked down the hall to my office. The lights were dim. It was dark outside. He bent down, slipped something under the door, stood up, walked back to the entrance and out the door. His Frankenstein mask visible as he exited.

"George, this is the same video we watched before, isn't it?"

"Pay close attention," he said, then uploaded another video on an adjacent monitor.

It was later in the day, on a busy morning. Staff and visitors were entering and leaving the lobby. A thin man, dressed in jeans, sneakers, and sunglasses, walked through the door. George slowed down the video. "Annie, take a close look."

"What am I looking for?"

"Look at his shoes."

They had a blue and gold logo on the side. George magnified the area to reveal a Buffalo with crossed swords or sabers.

"Who is this?"

"I think it's Guy Lebeau's brother, Pete. He was visiting a few months ago. I told you I thought I saw him," he said pointing at the computer screen. "Look at his profile. They look alike, even the broken nose. Now let's go back to the first video and look at his shoes."

He replayed the video showing the hooded visitor. "It's the same guy, same shoes and build, that came in here a few weeks ago and slipped that note under your door."

"Can anybody get these shoes?"

"Only players and their families get this kind of promo stuff."

I realized the hooded visitor, both times, was Pete, and he knew who killed his brother. I grabbed George's meaty hands then stood up and hugged him.

"George, we solved a murder! Well, almost. Stratton didn't kill Guy Lebeau, and the Milton Center is not to blame, and Pete knows who did it and … we need to show this to the chief. He can get a warrant and —"

"Annie, slow down. I'll call Schuller; you might be right," George said with a big grin.

I gushed about his investigative skills and could see tears in his dark brown eyes. "Great work. Tell the chief I need to see him after he views the video."

I felt like skipping on my way to Scott's office. When the elevator door closed, I whispered "Gotcha!" in the empty cab. By the time it reached the sixth floor, I had decided I was being presumptuous and still needed answers. All the video segments and real-life drama were like pieces of a jigsaw puzzle, forming a fractured picture; the bigger pieces were connected, yet gnawing gaps remained. We needed a few more answers and some glue to make them stick.

Milt stood as I walked in. Markers and spreadsheets covered Scott's desk. The lanky doctor seemed even more distraught than the last time we met. Scott, absorbed in thought, hardly noticed my entrance. Neither of them seemed glad to see me. I broke the awkward silence with a weak, "Sorry to interrupt," then turned to Milt. "Dr. Milton, how is Dr. Stratton doing?"

"Not well. He's developed septicemia—that's a blazing infection, in case you don't know. The antibiotics are not working. His blood pressure's dropped but his heart's still working. Time will tell."

I was aware of the medical term but chose to swallow my indignation. Despite the tension in the room, I asked about Chief Schuller's request to talk to Stratton. Milt pushed his slippery spectacles up on his nose, moved his red face so close to me I moved back a step. "What's wrong with you? That's the last thing he needs. I won't allow it."

Milt walked out of the executive suite, shoulders hunched, eyes downcast, on his way to the ICU. Scott's dark eyes followed him, then he turned to me. "Ann, please, come in."

"Scott, what just happened? Is it Stratton or something else? You look as miserable as Milt."

"Hey, you just came in at a bad time. We're all under a lot or pressure. We were working on a board report, financials and then Milt fell apart. So many things have gone wrong," he said in a barely audible voice.

"Maybe I can fix some of it. I have great news."

"I could use some; please sit down." He gestured to a chair across from his desk. "So, what did my hot PR person find out?"

The light came back in his face as he looked to me for the answer to his problems. I wasn't sure I wanted to be a "hot" PR person. I let it pass in my excitement to disclose the content of the Lebeau patient video and the security footage pointing to the note-dropper as Pete Lebeau.

"This whole thing gets more and more bizarre. Now what?" Scott walked to the window and stood still, looking down at the world outside.

"It sounds like Lebeau's death may have been at the hands of a jealous brother," I said. "Sounds like he deserved to die."

Scott turned around. "Sometimes fame and fortune aren't enough. How do we prove this?"

"I asked George to get Lance, Chief Schuller, over here to look at the security video."

"He's Lance, now, huh? Doesn't matter. I'll talk to Jen. She has a close friend that's a HIPAA expert. If the police get a court order, they can see the Stratton video. It should clear him and clear us. Dave and some other board members are getting antsy about too many negative news stories. That's why I brought you here. I'm not blaming you. It's just ..."

I walked over to the window to face him. "I can't believe you even said that. Look Scott, my hands are tied. Stratton knew about Lebeau, but kept it secret. Milt's the anonymous source, and Bob McCarthy makes stuff up. I kept you out of the spotlight. Heard you went golfing yesterday, right after the emergency. Do you think that looked good? Think of the stories Bob hasn't written. That's where I really make my money. Thanks for the support," I said in a huff.

"Hey, don't get so riled," he said without apologizing. "Golf helps me get things off my mind for a few hours. It's been crazy around here: Lebeau, the pickets, that horrible accident. and Stratton's barely alive. Milt and the board are having a meltdown."

The euphoria I felt walking in had evaporated. Scott seemed more focused on Milt's quest for fame and fortune than Lebeau's fate. The board's concern about the center's reputation had him questioning my skills and maybe his own. As I turned to leave, he grabbed my hand.

"Sorry for the outburst. Tell the good police chief Lance we'll do whatever it takes. This is fantastic news, now that I think of it. You're a regular Columbo. Oh, don't forget Saturday night ... still on, right?"

In that moment I wasn't sure I wanted to go anywhere with the brash CEO. "Yeah, it's a date—a first date." I gave up thoughts of skipping out of it and trudged down six flights of stairs.

CHAPTER 49

On the way back, I checked my text messages. Schuller was waiting in my office. Alice was probably drooling. He was such a kind man, soft-spoken, passionate about his work, his son, and his late wife. It was easy to understand why women wanted to take care of him.

He stood up as I entered, so tall I had to look up at his soft blue eyes and big grin. "Hey, Ann, thanks for the heads up. George is a great guy."

We sat down across from each other. I felt giddy and unsure about our discovery. "Great news, right?"

"Ann, we're getting close to solving this Lebeau case. Imagine, the shoes. He tried to disguise himself and forgot about the shoes. George did a super job putting this together."

"What does it mean?"

"We can expand our investigation. If I could talk to Dr. Stratton, he may fill in some gaps."

"He's still critical. How else could you get information about Stratton and the hockey player?" I was leading him on, not sure how much I could tell him about the Stratton patient video.

"There might be something in his patient files we could use. I know HIPAA is tricky."

"So, how can you get around it?" I asked.

"We could get a court order based on this security footage. We're still waiting for more information on the DNA found on the probiotic capsules. Should have that in a day or two. Once I have that, I can get a judge to grant the order. That reporter friend of yours is still asking questions."

"What'd he want?"

"Wants the same thing I do--results."

It felt like we were taking two steps forward and one back. "Thanks, Lance; we all want results."

This hulk of a man, dressed in dark blues, fidgeted with his police cap as he stood up. "It's been a pleasure to work with you, Ann. The PR guy they had in here before you was so plastic. He never seemed to care about people. You seem to have a heart and a mind. Nice combination."

He seemed almost shy after realizing his compliments were overstated, but more than welcome. "Thanks for all the accolades, not sure everyone agrees around here. I love my job, connecting with the people we care for and care about. I'm still learning so much about the medical advances. Some of our staff members, like Meredith, are exceptional. Our lab director is brilliant. Dr. Stratton was a superstar, grumpy but smart; wish I'd known him before the accident. Dr. Milton did a great job in our makeshift ER," I said, pausing briefly, "I've enjoyed working with you, too. Are you up for cup of coffee? Our outdoor cafe is still open."

"Love to join you but another time. I'm anxious to get back to the station, check on that DNA. I'll call you as soon as I hear anything."

I watched him leave, wishing I could give him more information. My thoughts about this gentle man at the center of a neighborhood infatuation were interrupted by a text from George followed by a call from Bob.

"Good morning, Delaney, any update on Dr. Stratton? How was your boss's golf game? I kept it our little secret. Don't worry, I won't print that story."

"I won't tell my friend at Channel 4 about your arrest for trespassing."

"News travels fast."

"Yeah, I just got a text from our security director. Can't say I didn't warn you."

"That was all a misunderstanding. Charges were dropped anyway."

"I know, I dropped them—this time. About Dr. Stratton: the good doctor is still in critical condition—no visitors allowed in case you're thinking of faking a long-lost relative story."

"Nah. I'm just doing an update on the Lebeau murder. The family's still waiting for someone to admit responsibility for the goalie's death. The DNA results on those probiotic killers should be in soon."

"What are you talking about?"

"Seems the Grand Island police found evidence at the scene. I bet Stratton's prints are on his deadly concoctions."

"Really? I think you should wait for the police to decide who is responsible for Lebeau's death. Find another story to write. Weather updates are always a reporter's favorite topic. Or you could interview people about the changing leaves, the charm of fall, and their hopes for snow."

"He's guilty."

I hung up. I couldn't imagine how he knew about the capsules but then a lot of people were working on this case: two police forces and forensic teams. The only prints they should find were Lebeau's. Lukas King had explained the process when I first visited the research lab. The capsules are sterilized and filled with the probiotic ingredients using the latest equipment that counts out the number per bottle, fills the bottles, and seals the screw top.

I cancelled my afternoon meeting with the road race committee. The annual fundraising event was still months away. I was sure the rest of the team would be glad to get out a few hours early on a warm October day. We had too many meetings, even had meetings to discuss what meetings to eliminate. Our track record was not good.

The curser pulsed on the next item in my calendar, my Saturday date with Scott. In my paranoia, I had labeled it "event"—not wanting to signal my relationship with the boss in any permanent sense. The more I thought about it, even event was suspect, so I deleted the date from my calendar. It was the reason for the date that had me edgy. Scott seemed so cavalier about the whole thing. When I was with him, I could feel his pull on my emotions, his warm hands, those probing eyes. When we parted, I thought about Todd, not so much missing him but becoming him.

CHAPTER 50

My date with the CEO was only hours away. Why had I agreed to this? I scrubbed and polished the meager furniture I had to a glossy sheen, remembering Scott's gleaming home. I stashed the stack of unopened boxes into the guest closet and closed the door, sure Scott would not be wearing an overcoat that needed hanging. I primped my bedroom as if House Beautiful was coming to inspect, not even sure Scott would ever cross its threshold. Gossamer curtains, pale blue silk bedding and soft ivory carpets blended beautifully against my white-washed furniture. Bouquets of chrysanthemums filled vases in every room, even the bathroom.

I was equally nervous and excited. I showered, wiping the water spots off the glass shower doors, polishing the faucets, the sink drain, and the mirror. My reflection was a blur of wet, stringy hair, blotchy skin and overall panic. I wrapped myself in thick white towels, sat on the side of the tub and considered calling Scott with some excuse to skip the date. I was a terrible liar, couldn't fake a cold or conjure up an outbreak of influenza he might believe; even a headache seemed lame.

I slipped on my guilty purchases from Victoria's Secret, black lace with tiny sections of black silk. I wasn't sure anyone but me would see them, then covered it all with a simple black, sleeveless sheath with a jewel neck. Not too short, not too long, it covered my knobby knees. Iridescent black heels added just the right amount of zing for a 48-year-old mom, ex-wife, or new girlfriend. What was I doing? Why did I agree to this take-it easy-and-slow date? I couldn't decide what to do with my hair. I put it up, then down, then half up, half down. Finally, let it fall loosely around my neck.

My mom's pearl necklace was waiting in a small drawer in my dresser for this event. As I removed it from its purple velvet case, I thought of Susan—dear, sweet Susan, such a beautiful young bride, dreaming of children, a long life. Their marriage ended too soon. Perhaps mine did, too.

Scott was picking me up at 7 for dinner at the Park Casino's top-floor restaurant, overlooking the Falls on the Canadian side. It seemed so distant, in another country, yet it was only a few miles away. I was ready for the suave CEO well before the appointed time; spent it tripping around my small apartment in stiff new shoes.

The doorbell rang at exactly 7 p.m. I opened the door to a stranger. Scott seemed taller, tanner, leaner, more than I could handle. He exuded elegance in grey linen slacks, navy blazer and a collarless white shirt unbuttoned just enough for a second look. My hands trembled as he passed me a stunning bouquet of white roses.

"Something beautiful for someone even more beautiful," he said.

"Oh, Scott, they're lovely. Thanks ... come in, please," I said, my heels teetering on the tile floor.

As I arranged the flowers, he walked over to the window. The sun was slipping in the sky, glowing gold and red. I poured each of us a glass of wine, and placed a narrow plate of bruschetta and olives on my shining, glass coffee table.

"This is the best view. No wonder you love it here," he said, as I handed him a long-stemmed crystal goblet.

"It's a Torresella Pinot Grigio from Veneto, Italy."

"Ah, my grandparents' home was in the Veneto region, in Padua, before they moved here. Salute—to a night to remember," he toasted. We clinked glasses, tasted the smooth, dry vintage. His musky fragrance filtered through the air as we sat next to each other on my pure, white sofa.

He leaned back and crossed his right foot over his left thigh revealing a film of black hair above tan ankles and no socks. The soft leather loafers enclosing his nude feet were probably handcrafted in an Italian village on the Amalfi coast where the sun warmed bare skin and romance simmered until ... What was wrong with me? I swallowed to get control of my emotions and reminded myself: this was just a date and Scott was being the perfect gentleman.

"Ann, before we go, I want to apologize for my comments about the board and the news stories. I know you're the best; they're just having a hard time with all this attention. I react too quickly at times, as I'm sure you've noticed. I can tell by the way you look at me."

"Apology accepted," I said as we sat quietly, sipping our wine. Neither of us touched the appetizers.

He broke the silence. "We should get going. Our reservations are for 8. Traffic on a Saturday night across the Rainbow Bridge can get backed up; it's still tourist season."

"I know; remember, I lived here. My sister and I used to walk over the bridge to hang out with people from all over the world, listening for foreign languages, never worried about too much traffic. We counted license plates from the different states and provinces on cars parked along the river road, always looking for the one from farthest away. We walked around the gardens, bought ice cream cones from cart vendors, leaned against the fence rails, watched the Maid of the Mist go under the foaming falls … I still love it."

"Yeah, it is special. Let's go."

My nervous rant about cars and fences probably made him wonder why he'd asked me on this awkward date. I took a deep breath trying to slow my heart rate. "Oh, can you fasten my necklace? It's tricky."

"Sure, I'll try. If I can throw a football, I should be able to do that."

He picked up the necklace, holding it like fragile glass, slipped it around my neck as I pushed my hair away. He took his time opening the clasp, connecting the ends, then moved his hands across my shoulders, down my arms. I turned to see his face searching mine, looking for something in return.

"Scott, remember—slow and easy. This is our first real date. Let's have fun."

He grabbed my hands, then let go. "Lead the way."

The United States Border Patrol was busy. We declared our citizenship and showed our passports. The agent looked at us to confirm we were the same people as in the photos, then looked around to the back seat; seeing nothing, he asked why we were visiting Canada. "Business or pleasure?" We both blurted out, "Pleasure!" He laughed.

"Go ahead, enjoy your evening," he said as we pulled out onto the parkway. The park casino jutted high above the trinket shops, amusements, and lush gardens. Its contemporary design, with sleek, tall windows, sparkled against the rose-colored sky. The elevator to the top floor opened to a majestic view of the American, Horseshoe and Canadian Falls, doused in early evening white lights. No matter how often I looked at the roaring falls and churning basin, it took my breath away. For a moment I was that same teenager leaning on the rickety railings, letting the mist swirl around me. Our table for two was tucked inside a windowed niche, dangling close to the river's precipice. A little unsettling at first, I realized this was the only niche in the restaurant; it must have cost a fortune to reserve. Scott was aiming to impress. It was working.

The menus were slim, made of black leather. We chose lobster bisque as our first course and wild Alaskan salmon for our entrees. Scott ordered his favorite scotch. I opted for a sauvignon blanc from Vancouver. We talked about our week as if it were historical fiction, trying to avoid the tension that was churning inside us. As our first course arrived, the white lights on the Falls turned to colored lights, filling our extended space with warmth and a touch of Disney.

Scott reached for my hands. "Is hand-holding okay?"

I had to smile. "Yeah, it's okay."

He ordered a bottle of the Vancouver wine as he reminisced about his youth and sports, growing up in Rochester where his parents still lived. He left home and drove 90 miles to attend the University of Buffalo on a scholarship, majored in business. His dream of being an electrical engineer evaporated when the reality of the hard work needed to succeed met with his first D grade.

"I wasn't nerdy enough, I guess, and the feel of a football in my hands kept me focused in another direction. Then I met Milt. He was a music major, babied his hands, never did anything too risky. He wouldn't touch a football. All of sudden, he switched majors. Pressure from his dad, an orthopedic surgeon, who'd determined his son should follow in his footsteps. Milt didn't have many friends. I might have been the only one close to him. He was brilliant. I guess you know that."

"Go on. I'm fascinated," I said, smiling at his openness.

"Milt's father was a wealthy man, but Milt was intent on separating himself from the family. He invested in stocks, started gambling. After we graduated, I never heard from him again until he called me about this job. And, here I am."

"We've all come a long way," I said. "Milt's a real puzzle, seems so distraught about Stratton. I can understand some of it, the jealousy. I sense there's something else that's got him so upset."

Scott turned away, looking at the colored lights, silent for a few moments. "I think you're just super sensitive. He regrets what he did. We should accept it and move on."

"We all regret things. I guess his jealousy didn't stop him from recruiting Stratton."

"Above all, Stratton is the best in his field, his research, probiotics ... all amazing. Milton needed him and his reputation."

"You mean Milton the medical center?"

"Yeah, why?"

"That reminds me of something Dr. Stratton said when I visited him the other day. He told me Milton had secrets. I thought he meant Dr. Milton. Now, I'm not so sure."

"Ann, Stratton's hardly alert or making sense, I'm sure he was talking about the doctor not the medical center."

"You're probably right. I'm always reading between the lines."

The dashing CEO was clearly not concerned. He filled my wine glass took my hand again. Scott seemed eager to leave Milt and his specialty hospital back on Grand Island. Maybe it was the wine, the mystical surroundings, or the good-looking man across from me that pushed my concerns far away from the top floor of the casino. We finished the bottle of wine, ordered tiramisu to share, our forks clashing in the sweet confection, giddy like children at a party, enjoying every moment.

The ride back across the international bridge was quiet. The traffic congestion had dissipated. The border patrol agent waived us through to the U.S. without stopping. Scott parked in my building's underground lot. Our elevator ride was oddly silent. His hands were in his pockets. Mine held onto my clutch purse like it was a vessel filled with stolen diamonds. Scott stopped at the solid wood door to my apartment waiting for an invitation. I almost said goodnight, then reconsidered.

"Would you like to come in for ... coffee?"

His face lit up; his eyes sparkled. "Ann, I'd love coffee—do you have any Amaretto to spice it up?"

I laughed, "I do. Not sure you need any more spicing up."

I kept the lights low, so we could see the Falls in the distance, sprinkled in white again. Scott took off his blazer as he settled into the cushiony couch, looking at home, comfortable. His eyes followed me around the kitchen as I clumsily made the coffee, kicking off my high heels. I reached up to get the liqueur glasses, when I felt him next to me, close, too close.

"Ann, would you like me to undo those pearls?"

"Oh ... uh ... thanks, please."

His hands were warm, hesitant. He brushed my hair aside in slow motion. Undid the clasp. I caught the pearls before they fell to the floor. His hands paused on my shoulders; his thumbs massaged my neck. I could feel my heart beating. He picked up the tiny metal pull on my dress's zipper, moved it down an inch, another inch. He stopped when he heard me gasp.

He brushed my ear with his lips and whispered, "Ann, I've wanted to do this all night ... from the moment I touched those pearls and saw this really long zipper."

I turned to face him, his hands still on my shoulders, eyes burning into me. I looked at the pearls, the floor, my shoes. "Scott, you're my boss. I know what you want. I want it too, every time you touch me, I tremble. I want more. It's been a long time since ... can we talk about this?"

"Talk? Ann, we've talked about everything tonight—license plates, football, bad grades."

"We haven't talked about this."

"This ... this is us, coming together. We both want this. Ann, say 'yes'."
He stroked my face with his hand, lifted my chin, his lips touched mine, soft and tender. His kiss grew deeper. I could feel the edges of his tongue, probing. His body enveloped me. I didn't resist. I wanted everything he wanted. His arms tightened around me, reaching for the zipper pull, inching it down further until it no longer held me together. As my dress collapsed on the floor, he asked one more time, "Ann?"

With all control evaporated, I nodded. He picked me up as if I weighed nothing, slipped off the thin black lace, placed me on my lush silk bed. The only lights came from the pulsing Falls beyond. His eyes never left mine as he slipped out of his loafers, unbuttoned his shirt, undid his slacks and let his clothes fall on the plush carpet. He slowly slid in next to me, olive skin glistening in the dim light against the pale sheets. His touch was explosive as his fingers explored, caressed. His mouth was hot, wet, open. I was consumed by his need and my own—nothing else mattered.

CHAPTER 51

The sun was streaming through my bedroom window. I could hear dishes clinking, smell the coffee I never finished the night before. Scott continued to amaze me. He could be gentle and fierce at just the right times, knew what to say and when not to say anything at all. His muskiness was embedded in the wrinkled sheets, in a bed too warm to leave. My Victoria Secrets lay on the floor next to his grey slacks and white shirt. Was he cooking in the nude? I pulled the covers up to my neck trying to blot out a growing sense of guilt. I could feel my stomach tighten. Was this a one-night stand, a fling, or something more? How do I work for this guy when he and I both know the textures of our skin, the outline of our bodies, the sensitive places?

Not quite nude, he strutted in, hard muscles and hard places on full view, wearing tight knit boxers, black with tiny red hearts. I laughed. "Guessed I missed the hearts last night—too dark, huh?"

"Didn't miss much else, though, did you?"

"Hmm … I think we covered everything."

"Maybe not everything," he said, brushing my hair back, kissing my neck, shoulders, arms, tossing the black and red underwear on the floor. My phone pinged.

"It's from Lance, says 'DNA results, call.'"

"Ann, forget Lance. Let's mix up some DNA of our own."

I left him sated, headed for the shower and lotion to salve the brush burns from his bristly beard. Fully dressed and smiling, his eyes followed me around the room as I cautiously opened drawers, wishing I had invested more heavily in sultry lingerie. Scott then took over the wardrobe search. He chose the flimsiest pieces and began dressing me, adjusting straps, connecting hooks, sliding his steamy hands beneath elastic trim. It was as breathtaking as undressing me. He leaned down, kissed my cheek, then my neck and whispered. "Good morning. So, how are you today?"

"Happy, guilty … sexy."

"Oh, I like that last part. Ready for more … uh … talk?"

I stepped back to break the tension, swallow and remember my name. I tugged on jeans and a jersey, turned toward the kitchen, and found my spokesperson's voice. "Right now, that coffee smells seductive, and yes, I am ready for more talk, and I mean actual talk before I see the chief."

He sank back into the mussed sheets. "It's Sunday, Ann, a day for rest and talk. Can't he wait?"

I jabbed a finger at his chest. "I still have a job and my boss is tough. I should find out what he has. Bob's waiting for the results too. We need to get them first, plan a response."

"Fine. Go ahead, call Lance, the cop. I hope he's one of those fat, sloppy guys. I don't want a competitor." I giggled at the thought of these eligible bachelors dueling for my affection.

"He's good looking and available. Not to worry, I can barely handle you," I said, resisting the urge to give in.

"Ann, I'll let go for now, but not for long."

Scott slipped his sockless feet into his Italian loafers and draped his blazer over his shoulder, waiting for me to close the door to my apartment. If only I could close the door on my feelings. Scott was whistling an inane tune that made me giddy. Who was this guy? What was I thinking, sleeping with the CEO? Bob would burst blood vessels if he knew about our decadent liaison. The thought made me shiver on this warmer-than-usual fall morning as we walked to our cars, and I looked around for the reporter's furtive shadow. Scott pulled out of the parking space next to mine, rolled down the window and bid his farewell. "See you tomorrow, Ann. Get some sleep tonight. We'll talk soon."

CHAPTER 52

Lance had asked me to meet him at the police station on the Island. As I pulled in, I noticed an older model Ford pickup truck parked next to the dull, grey cop cars. Sunshine reflected off its chrome bumpers and bright blue exterior. I was sure it was Lance's ride; it looked freshly washed and something he prized. The neighbor women surely watched the comings and goings of this carefully tended truck, but I suspected his only passenger was a 9-year-old named Michael.

"Good morning, Ann, thanks for coming. I know it's Sunday, but things get hectic around here on Monday, so I thought you wouldn't mind seeing me."

He wore khakis and a white polo shirt with the Grand Island Elementary School logo above the words "Football Coach." His usually slicked-back hair under a rigid cop hat was blowing in his eyes, resisting his attempts to placate the stubborn strands and reminding reminded me of Todd, the man I fell in love with so many years ago. Could I ever love another man?

"So, Lance, what's the verdict?"

We moved into his office, sat on the old leather chairs. The DNA results were on top of the table. "I wouldn't call it a verdict, exactly, but it may help us get there. The DNA on the capsule was not in our database, but we learned something important. It was a woman's DNA. Now, my first thought was Guy Lebeau's wife—Michelle. It might make sense that she sorted his pills or somehow handled them. To the best of my knowledge, they lived together. But someone tampered with the capsules, laced them with fentanyl. There were no other prints, not even Guy's. I think the pills we found fell into that crevice in the bed and were just missed. If he was trying to commit suicide, I doubt he would tamper with his own pills; he would just take the lethal drug. And, if Stratton was guilty, he wouldn't have to tamper with the pills at all, he would have made them with his own system."

After viewing the patient video, I knew Lance was on the right track. "So, what about the note left under my door?"

"That's another piece of the mystery. Thanks to George and his surveillance systems, we can identify the note-stuffer as Pete Lebeau. We haven't run tests on the paper yet, but I believe Pete will talk to us, since he was so eager to send this message."

"I think you're right. When he wrote, 'Stratton didn't kill Lebeau,' it implied he knew who did. I doubt he did it himself."

I could see the hint of a smile as he shifted in his seat. "You have good instincts. If Pete caused his brother's death, he would have written a confession. He wanted us to find the killer. My guess is it's someone in his family, but we don't have a motive yet. All we have is circumstantial evidence; it'll still be hard to pin this on anyone other than Guy himself. When we talked to his team members, we learned he was close to being a drug addict years ago ... maybe he went back to his old behaviors. I think Dr. Stratton knows more about this."

Sometimes not talking was the hardest thing a spokesperson had to do, I thought. "He's in tough shape. Do you think you have enough information to get that court order? I understand Stratton was a stickler for keeping thorough patient records."

"Ann, can you look at the records?" He noticed my hesitation. "You already have, right?"

I left his question hanging in the air between us, trying to avoid his steely blue eyes and boyish charm. "Lance, I think you should get the court order ..."

"Ah. Seems like a great idea."

"I'll check on your request about Stratton. Not sure he'll be with us much longer."

Lance was quiet, looking over his notes, trying to fill in the blanks from my unspoken words. He got up from his squeaky desk chair, picked up the folders and dropped them on his desk. "Ann, I suspect you're probably torn about having information and not being able to share it. Don't worry. We're close to solving a murder and getting the Milton Center out of the headlines."

"No more front-page drama, huh?" I said, trying to get him to smile, and it worked.

We left through the main entrance into a sunny morning and shook hands. He coaxed windblown hair under his coach's cap and climbed into his pickup. A streak of blue faded onto the highway as he drove off, presumably to the ball field.

It was a perfect day to walk along the river and hold hands with a new lover, but an invisible thread tying me to the Milton Center pulled at my sense of duty, so I drove in that direction. I could shift through some emails and think about my new life as Scott's ... what? That tension in my stomach came back. Do we pretend we don't have carnal knowledge of each other in the next exec team meeting? Will he look at me with those deep, black, knowing eyes and get me flustered? Will I see those tiny red hearts stretched over his curves and valleys? How do cheats and mistresses do this stuff? Todd did it for years without me noticing. I was just having an affair ... with my boss. As I parked my car, my phone rang.

"Ann, it's Meredith. Dr. Stratton's asking to see you. Can you come in soon?"

"Meredith, I am in. I stopped in to do some paperwork. Do you know what he wants?"

"I don't know. He's failing fast, refused intubation, knows he doesn't have long. Just come up."

"I'll be right there."

Machines blipped and beeped, conversation was hushed, the lights were low, and tensions high. Death was a frequent visitor in an ICU, where sliding glass doors blocked out moans and gasps from patients and family; it was the final stop on the way to other worlds for some, or a respite from injury on the way to recovery for others. There was a faint smell of fresh coffee near the nurses' station in the otherwise antiseptic environment. The interior curtains were drawn behind the glass doors on Room 4. Dr. Milton walked out, passing by without seeing me. Dr. Stratton's nurse opened the sliding door.

"Dr. Stratton. Ms. Delaney is here. You asked to see her, Dr. Stratton?"

He spat out some expletives and opened his watery, red eyes and asked in a raspy voice, "God-damned bitch … what?"

"Dr. Stratton," I said. "It's Ann Delaney; you wanted to see me?"

He struggled to get words out. His eyes wandered around the room. I was not sure he could see me. "Yes … Ann, I need to … please … closer."

I wasn't sure I wanted to be so close to this dying man. I had watched my father die an agonizing death; he too swore loudly. In my last visit he spewed bile from his mouth, let go of life with my hand in his. It broke my heart. Here was another man, too young to die; a man who had lost his will to live long before the tragic accident that was taking his life away. Part of him had died years ago with angela84.

"Ann … I need to know." He took a deep breath. Talking was so difficult. "It's Milt—he's …" Jealous? Should I finish his sentence?

"He's crook."

"A crook?"

"Milton … sham."

"What?"

"Milton … this place … wrong …"

Maybe he was delirious or just bitter. I couldn't tell. I needed more. "Does Scott know?"

"Scott … he's … he's in it."

None of this made sense. I hesitated, unsure if I wanted to know. "Scott's in what?"

He choked on the words, "Wrong … fucking rehab … Ann … you …. need to …"

His crackling cough sent shivers through me. I turned away, dropped my head in my hands and sobbed. Stratton caught his breath, closed his eyes, the hissing of the morphine pump the only sound in the room. His nurse came in, checked his failing vitals, and hovered nearby. I stood up and touched the cool hand of this dying man, a pale hologram of the amazing surgeon he once was.

"I think we're done," I said, Stratton's revelations erupting emotions, strangling previous thoughts. Only minutes earlier, I was worried about being the boss's lover. Could any of this be true? I had moved back home to be free of a philandering husband. Now was I sleeping with a criminal co-conspirator, or was Stratton running a deception to the end?

CHAPTER 53

The anxiety I felt earlier in the day was mild compared to my now hyperventilating state after leaving the ICU. The words scam and rehab bounced around my brain with images of Scott and Milt, conspiring in his office only days earlier. If it was just Milt in some absurd scheme I wouldn't be as surprised, but Scott? I trusted him, believed in him, followed him, shared my bed with him, left my old job, left my friends, and Todd. I came here to change, learn, grow and love. Maybe it wasn't true. But Stratton was dying and delirious. Why would he lie?

I found Meredith outside the ICU, looking tired but smiling. We walked into an empty waiting room across the hall and sank into overstuffed chairs meant to sooth worried visitors.

"How was your visit, Ann?"

"Dr. Stratton's barely holding on. He's angry with Dr. Milton ... kept talking about rehab, then started choking and stopped talking. I couldn't understand what he was trying to tell me. What could Stratton's issue be with rehab?" I avoided the remark about a scam, wasn't sure I even heard it myself.

"Are you sure that's what he said? He's been in and out of consciousness. From what I know, our rehab unit is a powerful component in recovery; many patients gain complete functionality and joint mobility. They have a deep-water pool, the Lily Pool, named after one of generous donors; it's almost a spa—maybe better."

I'm sure I looked confused. "Who's in charge of rehab?"

"Dr. Milton," Meredith said. "It's one of his special interests. Some joint and spine patients only get rehab; it's often better than surgery, although it may take a little longer to heal. Why don't you talk to Dr. Milton, maybe he can help resolve the confusion? You should get out of here while you can. I'm leaving soon. We all need days off. See you tomorrow."

We eased out of our upholstered comfort; Meredith headed toward the elevator. She was right; I needed time off. My brain and emotions were supercharged. Maybe Milt wasn't jealous, perhaps he was more concerned about Stratton's erratic rantings and revelations. I understood why a medical center like Milton had a rehab unit on campus: it would ensure comprehensive medical care and support the bottom line; maybe it made too much economic sense. Milt had a successful career investing in the market, generating grants, and influencing donors who gave him mega funds to build this orthopedic wonder. What was he up to? I texted Milt, asking to meet. He responded within minutes, inviting me to his depressing office in the bio lab.

"Ann, please come in. I suppose you want an update on Jim Stratton?"

"I just left him, passed you in the hall, but you were checking something on your phone and didn't see me."

"Sorry, it's been crazy around here. Please, sit down," he said, looking at his computer screen, scrolling past Innovation is standard… patient care is exceptional.

"Thanks. Dr. Stratton was very agitated. I'm not sure why he wanted to meet me… he swore a lot—not unusual, I know. Guess I'd be swearing, too."

"We're trying to control his pain. I doubt he'll make it through the night; so hard to see him this way."

"I'm sure it is, especially for someone who has known him as long as you have," I was struggling to open up about my concern. "He also yelled out something about rehab—secrets and a scam, something wrong. He asked me to find out."

Milt shifted away, collapsed in his chair, silent. After a long minute, he turned, his eyes focused on his inert hands and whispered, "My God … he knows."

The only sounds were the hum of the overhead lights, my twitching knees and the breaths of two people wondering what to say next. "Knows what, Dr. Milton?"

He lifted his head, then spoke. "Ann, Stratton's smart, maybe too smart. It's complicated. We have the best equipment and best docs research money can buy. I've made a lot, invested a lot. I built this center but gambled some invested funds. I needed some way to pay them back."

He pushed his slippery glasses back up on his nose as I fiddled with my notebook and Milton Center pen, unsure how to capture this new confession. Milt broke the silence, his voice growing more forceful as he spoke.

"When the bills came in and the government changed the rules about how we were paid, we adapted. Medicare bundled payments to save money, then we created combined services, but the dollars weren't enough. We talked about cutting back, getting rid of the helicopters, closing the restaurant, the inn—all the attractions, the reasons patients come here."

"Who's we?"

"Scott and me. Scott was worried about our future viability, asked me to think of ways to increase volume, reduce costs, make it all work. He's been working with your ex, by the way."

His rant about Scott and Todd made no sense. "Working on what?"

"I tried to re-engineer a grant we already had to make it sound like new research worth an additional $1 million. It almost worked. The NIH team reviewed the application, sent a few reps in to talk to Scott, warned him about fraud and abuse. Scott was livid, told me to cancel the request. Reamed me out good."

"Milt, how could you do this?"

His act of contrition continued. "Money. We needed more, so I took another path. Started small at first, discovered a way to create fake patients and bill insurance, Medicare, collect for surgery and rehab—just a few, here and there. It worked. Doesn't matter anymore, does it?"

It mattered to me. I hoped it mattered to Scott. "Dr. Milton, when did you do this?"

The gangly surgeon twisted in his chair like a child, ignoring the world around him. "It took months," he said in a voice so soft again, I had to lean in to hear him. "I created patient files, ordered rehab … only on paper. Scott thought I just had more patients, then he called me in a few weeks ago to explain the numbers. It was awkward; after all, I'm his boss."

"What did Scott do?" I asked.

Milt straightened in his chair, grasping the arms with his bony knuckles. "Scott couldn't believe I would destroy my career and his. I convinced him it was the only way to get extra revenue around here and the only way to keep his job. That's when he and Todd came up with a plan to keep the lights on, as they say."

Todd's in this too? I felt so naïve, touting the high standards and values of the Milton Center when its founder and my two lovers were, in fact, backstage directing an illegal money-making scheme to save their jobs and reputations.

"Please, go on," I said, not sure I wanted to know more.

Milt shrugged, moving away in the small space before he continued. "Everything stopped for a while. We got caught up in this Lebeau mystery until a few days ago. Scott hauled me in, told me it had to stop, or he'd let the board know before Stratton called another ethics committee meeting. The things that were once important didn't seem to matter. We talked about options and how to get through this."

Milt's revelations were overwhelming. My knowledge of bundled payments and new regulations, from the Centers for Medicare and Medicaid Services, was limited, although I knew government watchdogs would eventually uncover the scheming doctor and his CEO accomplice.

"Dr. Milton, I don't understand. There are too many safeguards, too many checks and balances. How can you create patients? It's like Frankenstein's lab—building bodies," I shook my head, "I can't believe this. Why did you think you could dupe finance people, the government, and the employees who work here caring for actual patients?"

In a contorted version of righteousness, Milt explained what he called "the game." ID info was captured from legitimate patients who had previous surgery or some other treatment but did not need or declined rehab. He ordered a series of rehab services, covered by CMS and payable to the Milton Center. CMS paid the hospital lump sums monthly for all patients from a list of patient numbers already in the system. Volume varied month to month, so no one raised a concern. It almost sounded ethical. He admitted Scott was nervous and had asked him to stop.

"Scott had convinced me, so I shut down the system. I almost thought we were under the radar. You know Ann, I think I've already said too much. I know you value your job and I'm sure Scott values his. And, if I'm right, Scott has a deeper interest in you; perhaps you already know. I hope you keep this to yourself."

Words escaped me. I got up and left. "Jesus H. Christ" was all I could think to say to myself. If my liaison with the CEO had me ruffled, this news was an electric jolt. None of it made sense. It was like living in a Wall Street movie where manipulators spent their days concocting new schemes and almost getting away with it. None of those films ended happily. If I said nothing, even to Scott, somehow, I'd be complicit. If I went to Scott, and he asked me to keep quiet, could I? If I was once worried about being his spokesperson, now I was worried about being his jail mate.

I grabbed my keys, left the Medical Center and drove and drove, until I ended up at the state park, mist from the Falls coating my windshield. Clouds were moving in from Canada, mixing a light rain with the mist. I sat in my car listening to the thump of the wipers. I threw on a windbreaker, took out my umbrella, walked down the leaf-covered path to get closer to the river. Watching the crazy water always soothed the edges of most problems and helped me sort out my next steps.

CHAPTER 54

I ignored the dampness and chose a bench close to the river's edge. The ebb and flow of the crackling water only heightened my anguish, swirling memories of the seductive CEO, his touch, his kiss, and his evasiveness. Did he want to save me from walking through the mire with him, acquiescing to his boss's inflamed ego, or was he keeping more secrets? Was there a heart inside his sensuous body or a soul in those searching eyes?

My phone vibrated. It was Scott. "Hi, Ann. Can we talk?"

"Scott, now you want to talk. Talk was the last thing you wanted last night."

"Milt and I just met. Where are you?"

"I'm on a bench next to the Falls."

"Stay put, I'll come to you."

The warm fall day had turned chilly. The maple trees at the park's entrance were dropping leaves on the slick tarmac, and piling up on my wooden bench and me, reds and golds and greens concealing the Milton Center spokesperson. Would Scott be coming to test my allegiance and try to get me involved in his coverup? I wasn't sure I could even be his friend.

Puddles formed around me. The river bashed stalwart boulders and pushed rocks out of its way; nothing could stop its tortured journey. I thought of testing its edges when I heard footsteps behind me. Scott slipped in next to me, stealing a corner of my umbrella. His heavy, dark hair was drooping onto his forehead.

"Ann, let's go back to your place—where it's warm and ..."

Part of me wanted to lean into his strong shoulder, let him guide me back to the warmth of his car, the heat of his body. I thought I could trust

239

him. Would he tell me the truth? Would I even know if he did? I slid back on the bench and turned to face him.

"Scott, tell me about the fake patients, the false billing … everything."

He was about to speak then halted as two squirrels escaped the shelter of a nearby shrub and chased each other up an old oak tree, knocking an avalanche of acorns at our feet.

"I wish a few of these acorns could solve our problems," he said, shaking his head. "It's not what you think. I'm not sure what Milt told you. Sometimes we, I, did things that were … uncomfortable."

"Uncomfortable?"

Scott pulled out a neatly folded handkerchief from his pants pocket to wipe his forehead. Who used handkerchiefs anymore? After all this time together, I really knew so little about this dripping man next to me. He continued his uncomfortable revelations.

"Milt was manipulating grants, padding the budget. I thought it was over until, one day, when I was looking at a revenue report, I saw an unexplained spike in the practice numbers. It took a while to track it back to Milt. He had ordered rehab services for patients—paper patients as it turned out. We billed CMS and they paid, no questions, no concerns."

He pocketed the damp handkerchief, moved closer, covering my hand with his. "Milt seemed proud of what he was doing: a new money-making scheme. Then the Lebeau thing hit us, then the accident happened. I told him to end his game. He was so upset about Stratton's accident, he finally agreed."

"It's not a game, Scott," I said, struggling to be heard above the roaring water. He thrust his hands into his pockets, leaned back on the wet bench.

"It is a game … to Milt. He's addicted to gambling and risk-taking. He made a lot of money in his life. I hate to think of how he did it. Can't we get out of the rain?"

Even though I was shivering, I resisted the urge to leave with this chameleon so adept at changing roles to suit his surroundings. "Scott, this is illegal. The government paid these fake bills. Our taxes pay the government. Someone will find out. You need to report this and pay it back."

His arm reached around my shoulder, his eyes dark, pleading. "Ann, I can't. Not yet. I'm the CEO. I could be implicated, and others could get hurt. You need to understand. I went to see Stratton and apologized. The man was dying. He called me a bastard, then closed his eyes. Guess I deserved that."

He was quiet for a moment, caressed my cheek, then he said something I didn't expect. "He said, 'Take care of Ann.'"

"Another piece of fiction?"

"No, he really said that."

The rain was pelting my umbrella, the river was surging over its banks and the path was strewn with wet leave and acorns. We were both soaked as Scott continued his defense.

"Ann, I need your help. Milt's falling apart. I'm bringing Todd in. He did this for another client. This happens more than you know."

"Are you serious? Todd's blarney could get you into more trouble. How long will this take?"

"Weeks … months. I don't know. I need you."

I could feel his warm breath, smell his musky fragrance. I wanted those eyes, those hands, his arms around me. I wanted to be warm again in rumpled sheets.

He picked up my moist hands and inched closer on the bench.

"Ann, you've already done a great job. This Lebeau thing is going away. If you have any feelings for me, you will—"

"Scott, stop. When I woke up this morning, I was in such a good place. Now, I'm so confused. I need time. You're right about the Lebeau case. I was worried I'd have to violate HIPAA to help the police. The new DNA evidence should be enough proof. At least that's one violation we don't have to worry about. Good news for Milton, both Dr. Milton and the Medical Center. I'll talk to you tomorrow."

He hesitated, then let go of my hands, stood up, pulled his collar up around his neck and left me alone. As his luxury car pulled out of the parking lot, my phone beeped.

"Ann, it's Milt, I wanted you to know Jim passed away a few minutes ago. Thanks for being his friend. I know he was grateful … so am I."

"I'm so sorry," I said, crying for a complex man I knew too well and for one I barely knew at all. I slogged back to my car, drove home and rode the elevator solo clutching a collapsed umbrella. My pearl necklace rested on the kitchen counter. I closed my eyes and felt Scott's hands on my neck, his lips on mine. He was everywhere I turned. My cell pinged. Bob had texted, "Call Me."

I wasn't sure if I had the emotional strength to battle the reporter. He needed to know the Milton Center for Advanced Orthopedic Medicine was not guilty of murder, not guilty of harboring a murderer, or growing monsters, or hurting hockey stars. I called him back.

"Hey, Delaney, I heard Dr. Stratton died. Do you have a statement?"

"I have a few words—my words: 'Dr. James Stratton passed away today. He was a passionate surgeon who gave his patients extraordinary care. I only knew him for a short time. I wish it could have been longer. We will miss him.'"

"Looks like he escaped murder charges."

I was furious. "Listen Bob, I've had it with your snide remarks and screwed up stories. Dr. Stratton only cared for Guy Lebeau, he had nothing to do with his death. You will soon get a call from Chief Schuller that will exonerate the Milton Center and Dr. Stratton from any wrongdoing—too bad he died trying to prove it. The only reason he was on the bridge that day was to meet with me to straighten out the mess you created. Your news stories have ruined lives. Raymond and Michelle Lebeau will be implicated in the Guy's murder. I hope you cover that story with a dose of reality."

"What the hell are you talking about? I'm just doing my job. Don't blame me."

"Then who do I blame? Your stories are unbalanced, trying to be sensational just like some of those crappy reporters from the big shot newspapers and the biased news stations with their secret insider sources and background distortions. Just tell the stories of real people, the lives of men and women who struggle. You might even begin with a proper eulogy for Dr. Stratton. His life was full of meaning, anger, love, and passion."

He was silent for a few moments. "I'm sorry, Del. I still need to cover this story."

"I'm sorry too, Bob, for going on this rant. It's been an emotional time lately. It's hard watching such a talented man in midlife suffer so much and pass away."

CHAPTER 55

It was still raining the next morning. I had listened to it all night, unable to sleep. I changed into some sweats and turned on my laptop. The Buffalo News broke the story. Bob's byline ran under the headline, "Police find new evidence in Lebeau murder, vindicates Milton Center." My remarks were simple, "Throughout this investigation, the Milton Center has consistently rebuked any suggestion of the Center's or Dr. Stratton's involvement in the death of Guy Lebeau. We are grateful to be exonerated and appreciate the efforts of Chief Lance Schuller, the Grand Island Police, and the Williamsville team involved in this investigation."

A sidebar carried a simple header, "James Stratton, MD succumbs to injuries." A much older photo of the good doctor ran with the story. He looked confident and close to happy. At my request, Bob inserted, "According to Milton Center spokesperson Ann Delaney, Dr. James Stratton passed away late Sunday from injuries sustained in the recent South Bridge explosion. Delaney said, "Dr. James Stratton passed away today. He was a passionate surgeon who gave his patients extraordinary care. I only knew him for a brief time, I wish it could have been longer. We will miss him.""

As I finished reading, the cursor on my laptop kept pulsing, my heart beating in unison. I looked at the calendar; it was my birthday tomorrow. Another year had passed. What a year. I looked out at the mist rising in the distance, imagined Scott's outline as he admired the same sight. I could almost feel his touch, feel the slim zipper release. He was waiting for me to call. Would he put words in my mouth or take them away, ask me to be quiet, avoid the topic, stand by Dr. Milton without question? Then I thought of Meredith and the newlyweds; she'd never left their side. I thought about Jen, Laurie, Ian Rogers, Alice, Matt, even Lukas and George; they were all good friends and exceptional caretakers. If Scott was true to his word, they would soon hear the sad news of Dr. Stratton's death and Dr. Milton's deceptions.

Milt should have stayed with a career in music and ignored his father's push into surgery. He was such a lonely man, too focused on money, not focused enough on integrity. The Milton Center for Advanced Orthopedic Medicine would survive somehow. The name might change; yet its mission would continue if Scott stayed on to repair the financial mess and the false reporting. I poured a cup of coffee, not eager to get into the office too early, and still questioning my role as spokesperson. If I thought Lebeau's murder was a PR problem, how could I handle federal charges of fraud and abuse. Maybe I should resign, leave the tainted CEO to find another eager PR hotshot. What was it Lance had said, "a plastic PR person?" I was not plastic. I was flesh and blood and full of stories of love and worry and hope. I was a news junkie, a reporter. I could do it again. Maybe The Buffalo News needed a stringer. I could get my medical reporter job back again, be on the other side of the media stage with April and friends, asking probing questions, investigating wrongdoing, and telling the truth.

My doorbell rang. I spit out a mouthful of coffee and looked at the time on my monitor: 6 a.m., then I heard a quiet voice in the hall, "Ann, it's Scott. Can we talk?"

If I asked him to leave, it would be my last day as spokesperson, the end of a deepening friendship, an unrequited love. If I opened the door, would I forget thoughts of resigning, be ready to take on the next challenge with a man I wasn't sure I could trust?

I opened the door. Scott held me for the longest time. Even though he had on his CEO trappings, white shirt, stripped tie and dark suit, I could still feel his heart pressed against mine, feel his breaths grazing my ear. We didn't speak or move. I was enveloped by a man I wanted to hate, a man I wanted to love. I hardly knew him, yet I knew him so well. I wanted to hear him say he was sorry for Stratton's death, for Milt's crimes, and for all the things I didn't know.

He let go, taking my hand in his. "Ann, where do I begin?"

"Let's sit down. I made coffee." We sunk into the sofa cushions, not touching but close and quiet.

Scott broke the silence, stuttering, "I … I don't have excuses. I knew Milt was up to something. I thought it was something to do with the grant; I was right about that. Told him to stop. He did and I let it go."

I handed him a Milton Center mug filled with coffee.

"Thanks," he said. As he spoke, his finger ran across the name on the mug. He looked at me, questions in his eyes.

"What happens next?" I asked.

He moved closer, picked up my hands and smiled. "Oh, I think we have more work to do on us."

I pulled back, not sure how I felt. "We have a lot more work, if you ask me, and a job to do. Have you called Todd?"

"Todd? How did he get in this?"

"Have you?"

"We've had a few phone calls, haven't met yet."

"His specialty is risky deals and circling the truth."

"Don't worry, I'll keep him in line and away from you." I could see desperation and longing in those black eyes. It was time to get to work.

CHAPTER 56

Scott had set up an afternoon meeting with Jen, Dr. Rogers and me. The air in the conference room was thick with sadness and confusion. Scott walked in a few minutes after I had settled in my rolling chair, waiting for his direction. He greeted everyone by name then stopped to look at me longer than necessary, I thought. Milt was mysteriously missing.

"Thanks for coming in. We've all been through a tough couple of weeks … Jim Stratton left us yesterday. He was probably the best orthopedic surgeon in the country and maybe the saddest. We found his sister last night vacationing in Montana. She's coming into Buffalo this morning and asked to have her brother cremated so she can take his ashes back to Colorado where he will be buried next to his fiancée. She's grateful to the nurses, the techs, Dr. Milton, and everyone who took care of him."

He sighed, as if the weight of the cantankerous surgeon, physical and emotional, had dropped on him. The room was quiet. I stayed a conference table length away admiring but questioning the CEO's leadership and intentions.

"I have some good news and some tough news." Scott said. "The good first: The Buffalo News got this right this morning. The police have found enough evidence to turn their investigation into Guy Lebeau's death away from the Milton Center. It's focusing on his wife Michelle and brother Raymond. They even traced the letter to the editor back to Raymond and the note under Ann's door to the younger brother, Pete."

There were sighs of relief. Dr. Rogers looked impatient and blurted: "So what's the bad news, Scott?"

"Ian," he said, looked at me, then turned to some words he had written on a yellow pad. "I met with Milt yesterday. As you know, he was Stratton's partner. He had noticed an unusual uptick in some of their practice numbers; it seems Dr. Stratton may have created some fake patient records, mostly for rehab, to counter a loss of revenue and to make sure he could continue at Milton."

Did I hear that right? Was he blaming Dr. Stratton for the scam?

Scott paused, looked around the room. His charcoal eyes seemed fixated on me. He knew I was shocked at the distorted revelation and seemed to be waiting for my response when Ian Rogers spoke up.

"Are you serious? How long has this been going on?" Rogers asked.

Scott turned to look at the rest of the team. "From what I know, not long."

He glanced back at his notes and continued his response.

"I noticed discrepancies in the monthly rehab numbers, thought it was an accounting error at first, and I asked Milt to check it out several weeks ago. He discovered Stratton was manipulating patient data, creating bogus records filled with billings for non-existent rehab. We were still trying to unravel the mystery when the Lebeau stories hit, and the pickets arrived. It's all been overwhelming. We planned to meet with Stratton, then the accident happened. Milt's been so upset. We should have come to you, Ian. I can't believe any of this happened."

Dr. Rogers looked right through Scott as if he'd find Stratton hiding behind him.

"Jesus, Scott. I'm the chief around here. I noticed an uptick in volume but thought it was real. I can't believe I missed this," he said. His bristly hair seemed to collapse on his scalp as he tried to fathom his colleague's transgressions.

"You know we have to report this, Scott," Rogers said, "we'll need to make amends, pay back the amount we overcharged. We could be fined a lot, even though Stratton's gone. How much did he bill?"

"I don't know, Ian," Scott said, digging deeper into the lie. "Milt will trace it back. I'm calling Todd Delaney in to sort this out. He's dealt with similar cases. Jen, I need you to check out our rights in all of this; our jobs depend on what we do next."

All I could do was watch in amazement as this play-by-play unfolded. It was surreal. I thought someone would yell "foul" any minute. Surely, Jen could detect the sham, challenge her boss, ask for the truth. I watched her and waited.

"If we pay it back, it might not be a big story," Jen said, looking at me. "If the DOJ considers this a civil case, a violation of the False Claims Act, paying it back may be all that's needed since Dr. Stratton cannot be charged."

"I agree, Jen," Scott said. "We'll get through this unscathed, especially since we've been vindicated in the Lebeau death."

"What do you think, Ann?" asked Jen.

My throat was dry. I wasn't sure I had a voice. I thought of screaming that Scott and Milt were liars, cheats, and adding a litany of other shameful names. I was still swallowing the farcical story of two men so intent on surviving they would destroy the reputation of the man who made their careers. Whatever happiness I felt earlier in the morning had evaporated. I was guilty of loving someone who loved himself more, his job, his golf habit, and his home on the hill. I had never been so unsure of what to say. I was quiet for a moment, then pushed back my chair on the top floor of this center dedicated to innovation. I stood up and headed for the door.

"Jen," I said, "a few weeks ago, I met with the board and exec team and convinced them I needed to be the spokesperson for the Milton Center to handle the false accusations of the Lebeau family. I was comfortable about handling that crisis, even boastful—right or wrong—"

"Ann?" Scott tried to interrupt.

I moved closer to the door. "Let me finish. Scott clarified that he wanted to speak on behalf of this center, but he acquiesced to my request. These past few days weeks have been difficult for all of us. Based on the information we have all received this morning, I am turning the role of spokesperson over to our CEO to manage the reputation of this incredible medical center."

"Ann, there's no need for that," Scott pleaded.

"Let me continue. Regarding Dr. Stratton's alleged malfeasance: Even though I had never met him before his accident, my brief and tortuous conversations with Dr. Stratton convinced me he was a rare and genuine man with extraordinary talents and a broken heart. I will mourn his loss."

I opened the door and left the conference room, rushing into the adjacent ladies' room. I felt nauseous. I took some deep breaths, soaked towels in cold water, and pressed them on my eyes. It was several minutes before I felt steady enough to walk out. I wasn't even sure where to go. As I passed by Scott's office door, his assistant Mary motioned me in. She picked up a document from her desk and handed it to me.

"Ann, I wasn't sure how long that meeting would last, but I thought you might want to read this. Dr. Stratton's sister dropped it off. She'll be heading to Colorado with her brother's ashes and couldn't wait to meet with Scott."

I sat down in a chair near her desk with a copy of the "Last Will & Testament of James D. Stratton."

I read through the legalese intro until I came to the "I bequeath" segments. In the first section, he left a significant amount of his estate and the family home in Colorado to his sister. The next section described a special request to create a healing garden at the Milton Center to be named, Angela's Place. He even specified the plants and flowers to make sure they would bloom from spring through fall. In the last section, he bequeathed the remainder of his estate to the Milton Center for a surgical wing to be built in his name.

I smiled as I read it, then laughed. Mary looked up startled, "Ann, are you all right?"

"Sorry for laughing. Dr. Stratton was an amazing man. I wish I had known him longer. I'm sure Scott will be surprised at Stratton's generosity."

I picked up the document. "I'll wait for Scott in his office. He shouldn't be much longer."

"Would you like coffee?"

"No thanks. I've had enough caffeine today."

I placed the will on Scott's desk and took a seat in one of his leather guest chairs. I unclipped my ID badge from my lapel and thought about the pride I felt when HR had handed it to me six months earlier. It gave me access to every corner of the medical center: the doctors' lounge, security, back hallways, and the surgical suite. The only place I could not penetrate was the CEO's secret hideaway. I had found his front door and some inside places. I had watched him comfort patients and laugh with colleagues, yet I'd missed the man deep inside. How could he think I would concede to his deceptions?

Milt and Scott had figured out how to salvage their careers. Todd would work his miracles, manipulating the business side of healthcare. No one would notice. These con men had no idea that the solution to their financial peril, outlined in this Last Will & Testament, was the very doc they had just disparaged.

I flipped to a blank page in the notebook I carried as my daily sidekick to record the words of others and filled it, instead, with question marks, over and over, when Scott walked in. "Ann, I'm glad you're here. I wasn't sure —"

"Scott, don't say anything. Read that document on your desk, then we can talk."

I watched his eyes travel back and forth; his hands turned pages as the dilemma set in.

"How much is the remainder of his estate?"

"I'm guessing millions of dollars."

"It's unbelievable, after all we've been through. I knew he inherited his dad's fortune; never thought he'd share any of it with us. Looks like he put lots of time designing this garden. That unfinished spa might be the right place for this garden. Imagine."

"Scott what about the last request? How are you going to put his name on a building when you've just accused him of scamming this institution? You were willing to blame him for Milt's crime, and you didn't have the guts to admit —"

He got up from his chair. "Ann, I can make this right. We have time. There were only three people in that meeting. No one else heard ... except you."

I felt his hand on my shoulder. I turned slowly; not sure I should let him in on my thoughts. "I've been thinking about my future. I spent the last hour writing question marks in my notebook and kept coming up with one answer. I need to leave."

"Leave?! Ann, I need you. What are you talking about?" he said, pulling me closer.

I pushed back. "Scott, I can't lie or massage the truth like you and Milt and Todd. I've been a spokesperson a long time, reached a pinnacle in my career, an amazing career. I'm so grateful for all the opportunities I've had.

I'm ready for another challenge, something else ... not sure where right now, but I'll find it."

"Ann, don't do this. I need you here ... in my life," he said, reaching out for me.

"Scott, did you really think I could keep this quiet?"

I tore the sheets of question marks from my notebook and handed them to Scott without speaking, then turned away to look at the world outside. That two-bedroom bungalow was out there somewhere waiting for me to find it. All I needed was room for my carefree daughter, some unpacked boxes, a few bottles of Italian wine, a commemorative cork-screw, a new notebook, and a place to keep my stilettos.

A helicopter landed, cars filled the parking lot, and employees walked along cobblestones that would one day be part of Angela's Place. A black lab puppy escaped the confines of a scruffy path chased by a man in baggy jeans. He picked up the little guy, ruffled his ears, and carried him home.

About the Author

Noreen A. Biehl received a Bachelor of Arts degree in English/Journalism from the University of New Hampshire and a Master of Science degree in Communication Management/Health Care Administration from Simmons College, Boston. She worked as a reporter for *Foster's Daily Democrat* before beginning a 30-year career at Wentworth-Douglass Hospital, retiring as Vice President of Community Relations.

She is the author of *A Place of Healing: A History of Wentworth-Douglass Hospital.* Noreen lives in Dover, NH, where she continues to write, travel, garden, and enjoy her family.

Made in United States
North Haven, CT
14 March 2022